THE YOCHNI'S EYE

ABIGAIL MORRISON

ATTENTION TYPO HUNTERS

Find a typo? Let me know at amorrisonbooks.com/typo-hunters. I'll send you a free gift as a thank you and add you to the typo hunters wall of fame.

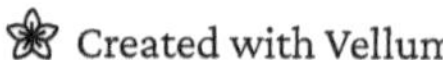 Created with Vellum

To the Creator, Mom, Dad, and, as promised, Lanny Wong.

PROLOGUE

Atlan Qierce, third-place prince of the Bogey Empire, sat at the massive feet of his father, Ethran, on the hearth rug of his playroom. His cousin Crucius, the fourth-place prince, sat beside him. Together, they gazed up into Ethran's wise red eyes, the elder bogey leaning down from his considerable height to meet them face to face.

"Well now, boys, what story would you like to hear?" Ethran asked.

Crucius hopped up on his back paws, gray and brown tail wagging as he set his hands on Ethran's knee. He was only four at the time, Atlan six.

"Bogeys!" he shouted.

"Not again. Something new," Atlan begged.

"You picked last time," Crucius said.

"No, I didn't."

"Yes, you did!" Crucius bit his cousin.

Atlan shoved him down.

Reaching a clawed hand down to each of their scruffs, Ethran pulled them apart, setting them back on the rug with a warning and a few feet of space between them. Like most bogeys, he was tall, a little over eight feet with broad shoulders and a sloping snout. Atlan licked blood from his arm. Crucius nursed a scratch on his knee.

"I won't have you fighting or there'll be no story at all, eh?" Ethran scolded.

The two cubs nodded, each glaring daggers at the other. Ethran folded his arms, trying to hide a smile. He could still remember when he and his brothers had fought just like the two princes. Sometimes he still felt the temptation to pick up the habit again. He rubbed his chin as the two cubs made truce, feigning making a decision. In truth, Crucius had had the pick of the last three stories, despite his protestations to the contrary, and had chosen the rise of the bogeys each time. It was only fair to give Atlan his turn, and the high prince already had the perfect story in mind.

"Have I ever told you the story of the Age of Dwarves?" he asked.

Crucius let out a moan, rolling flat on his back as he realized he had lost. Atlan lit up, forgetting the bite on his arm as his yellow eyes grew wide.

"Is that the story?" he asked, black ears peaked.

"Yes."

"When did it happen?"

Ethran smiled down at his son, the young cub always eager to learn about the ages. The stories of the yochni's incredible ability to grant wishes enthralled the young bogey: rises and falls in and out of power, daring adventures, unlikely champions. The high prince had spent a great deal of time studying the ages himself, the only of his family to do so since his own father had, fifty years back. He had nearly exhausted his knowledge of stories for Atlan already, this last tale one of the few left untold besides those from the wicked ages. Those he would keep to himself until the prince was older. Greed and fear had made the world a very dark place for several millennia. He did not wish Atlan to know just how dark things had become. Not yet. Ethran leaned back in his chair.

"This was many, many ages ago. Dwarves are one of the oldest races," he said.

"Then why are they slaves?" Crucius pouted.

"Hush," said Atlan.

"They work for us because they like to work, and we need what they can provide," Ethran said. "They are not slaves. In any case, the world did not always contain dwarves. They are a wish-crafted race, like us."

Crucius moaned again, rolling onto his stomach. Atlan nudged him with his foot, which was met with a weak-willed swipe. Ethran ignored them and continued his story.

"They began as a wish in the heart of a constant named Eleata. Now, she was barren, an uncommon problem in elves, and she wished for nothing more than to be a mother herself. All around her beautiful elven children played, elves borne of her friends, her sisters, cousins, but none would come to her, no matter how hard she tried."

Crucius picked up a toy horse from the floor, trotting it over the rug. Atlan barely breathed as his father spoke, listening in rapt attention.

"As you know, elves are by nature creatures of hope. Beauty, craftsmanship, art. And while her hope faded in her heart, so did her beauty and charm. She grew listless, gray, and weepy, waning to the point that the other elves thought she would surely die, her broken heart ceasing to beat. She haunted their library on a regular basis, researching magic, spells, potions, anything to help her conceive. Her mate Syden tried to cheer her, but not even he could assuage her sorrow. For many years, she diminished, until one day, she burst from their library, a new determination hard in her eyes.

"Her friends asked her what she had found, some new trick she could try or something to help. She told them it was not that but that she had made a decision. Though it would not blink for another century, she had decided she was going to see the yochni.

"'You?' they scoffed. 'You? Look at yourself, your eyes, your muscles, your teeth. You are fragile as a fluted glass. You would not survive outside for a week.' Her friends did not think her worthy, thought it a foolish dream and fatal. They urged her not to go, begged her to stay, but Eleata would not listen. She started eating, sleeping, and exercising, each in ever healthier portions. She trained in swordsmanship, archery, and hunting, studied maps, saved her money. She did everything she could to prepare herself, and when at last the time came and her people, still convinced it was an ill-fated plan, denied her the title of champion, she decided to go on her own, outside of her people's blessing."

"What does this have to do with dwarves?" Crucius interrupted, bored with his horse.

"Be quiet," Atlan snapped.

Crucius stuck out his tongue. Atlan raised a clawed hand. Crucius flinched, but Ethran interceded, catching his son's arm. "What did I say about fighting?"

"Sorry, Father."

"As for dwarves, that part is coming."

"I'm bored," Crucius said.

"Then leave," Atlan suggested.

"Don't be rude," said Crucius.

"Then don't interrupt."

Ethran let out a low sigh, and the two cubs fell silent. The high prince continued. "Eleata left her home and all of her friends and family behind, taking a secret route so as not to be stopped. Syden followed, hoping he might overtake her, but he was ambushed and killed by other champions along the way, and he did not see her again. Eleata, unaware of his death and driven by her desire to reach her dream, continued her pilgrimage, using all the skills she'd learned in the previous century to outwit, outfight, and out-hide any and all that stood in her way.

"By the time she reached the yochni's mountain, she was battered, dirty, and tired. She had spent weeks on the road, and after so many fights, long nights, and beasts, she could hardly believe she'd almost made it. Climbing up the side of the yochni's mountain, she found a cave leading down to its heart, past twisting tunnels, a raging river, and down through the Chamber of Sorrows into the darkness, the last, thin veins of the mountain. Rocks scraped at her palms, deathly quiet bit at her ears. Still, she knew her dream was near, and nothing would stop her. By that point, nothing could, so long as she chose to keep going."

Crucius was asleep on the rug. Atlan struggled against the heat of the fire, eyes drooping as his father's sonorous voice rumbled through the tale.

"Finally, she reached the yochni, an eye five feet high crouched on four clawed feet. Collapsing, Eleata wept for joy at her success. She closed her eyes, imagining her children around her, a family held close to her chest. Happy tears streamed down her cheeks. Holding the picture in mind, Eleata made her wish, and, finally, the yochni blinked.

"When she opened her eyes, two short creatures walked out of the darkness. A male and female dwarf—the very first of their kind—they came and hugged their mother. They guided her out of the yochni's cave, then down the mountain to a field where several more dwarves played in the grass. It is with them she stayed for the rest of her days, guiding them as a mother should. No dwarf borne of her wish ever grew larger than the size of a child no matter how long it lived, and it is said that none of them ever will. Thus, were the dwarves created."

Atlan had collapsed on the rug, straining to hear the end

of the story through a sleep-fogged mind. He felt the strong arms of his father lift him, fought the darkness of rest, then surrendered.

It was little more than a decade before the yochni would blink again, reshaping the world into a new age.

Atlan dreamt of being a champion, and of what it was he might wish.

CHAPTER

ONE

Mira Goldfist, champion of the dwarves of Haufin Mountain, fingered the four long scars along her back as she washed in the stream. Her miniature hart, Batcha, grazed at the edge of the water, his broad scoop-like antlers gently spotted by the dappled light. She'd looped his reins over a low branch. Her axe lay ready to hand on the bank, just out of range of the water.

As her fingers followed the old, bumpy ridges, she closed her eyes, flashes of bogey fur, teeth, and claws leaping through her mind. She had gotten the scars when she was six. When the bogeys had taken her mother.

Her father had told her not to go on her pilgrimage, that reaching the yochni was too dangerous, a fool's errand. But she was just as much her mother's daughter as she was her father's, and where her mother had gone down trying, she would succeed. Had to succeed. Her people would die if she didn't.

Shutting her mind against the memories as she had done so many times before, Mira resumed her washing, scooping sand from the streambed to scrub her sun-freckled skin. The water, flashing brown as she scrubbed away layers of dirt and

7

grime, washed clean as she did. Unknotting the twin thongs on her braids, she combed the tangles out of her crinkly blond hair with her fingers before ducking her head in the water.

That was when she heard the first rumble. Mira whipped her head up. The sound had come from upstream, around the bend from what she could see. The pebbles under her knees started to twitch. A splash rang through the trees.

Mira didn't wait to hear more. Springing for the shore, she scrambled for her clothes, throwing her vest over her flat, child-like chest and knotting her belt around her waist. She heard shouting in a language she didn't recognize. Then, as she hauled her pants up to her waist, the source of the noise thundered into view. Mira gasped.

A bright blue, twelve-foot-tall dragon was hurtling down the stream, barreling towards her with a young man in blue and green silks clinging to its shoulders.

Mira grabbed her axe and boots and sprinted for Batcha. The mini hart was in a panic, shrilling and rearing. She reached for his reins, and he reared again, this time striking her in the chest with his hooves.

Mira slammed back into the water, catching the boy's attention at last. She was right in the dragon's path.

He shouted, "Drake!"

The dragon reared.

Floundering, Mira threw her arms up over her head. The dragon's massive, bird-like front feet loomed, the creature unable to stay upright for long, and she bunched her legs, trying to make herself smaller still. She curled tighter. The feet fell. Water washed out her vision.

The dragon missed. Nervous whistles and clicks poured out of its chest as it pawed and stomped, its massive feet churning up a storm of sand and pebbles. She could hear the boy from closer now, splashes where he must have fallen.

Shielding her head, she scrabbled to her feet, dashing out from under the dragon's legs to the bank.

"Drake? Drake, *c'est bon. Tout va bien. La fille, où est-elle?*" The boy's frantic voice came from the dragon's opposite side, his form just visible between the creature's scaly legs. Sloshing his way to the dragon's front, he ran his hands through the shallows, arms flapping like some broken fledging bird's. No doubt he was looking for her corpse, her own hands still feverishly checking to make sure she was still all there. He appeared to be around her age, perhaps fifteen or sixteen. His hair was brown and choppy with a short ponytail drawn in at the base of his neck. He wore dark gloves, some pattern stitched onto the backs that she couldn't discern, and silken clothes now several shades darker for the wet. The shirt was done in overlapping blue and green scales, the extravagance marking him clearly as a noble. If he were a fellow champion, he didn't appear to be a good one.

Still, there was always something to be said for caution.

Turning his search farther afield, he at last caught sight of her on the sand. His face went slack with relief, but his expression quickly soured back into worry, almost irritation. As if he hadn't just nearly killed her. He glanced back upstream, features going even more grim, then rushed forward, grabbing her shoulders and twisting her from side to side.

"Oi, oi, oi," she snapped, jerking out of his grasp. He looked confused for a moment, then, perhaps realizing his mistake, held up his hands, shaking his head.

"*C'est bon, c'est bon. Je ne vais pas te faire de mal. Est-ce que ça va? Es-tu blessé?*"

"What? What are you saying? Who are you? What's happening?"

"*Euh? Euh, désolé.* Sorry," he said, his accent thick, voice impatient. He glanced once more upstream. "You are...okay?"

Mira scowled. "No, I am not okay. That thing could have killed me. Who are you and what are you doing charging down the stream like a lunatic? And where did you even get a dragon?"

But the boy was hardly listening, attention already drifting back the way he had come. A shout came from the same direction, and he flinched. Jogging towards his dragon, he waved his hands at her in the classic gesture for "Shoo."

"Sorry," he said again. He turned back for just a moment, expression landing somewhere along the broad spectrum of distress before settling into urgent severity. "*Vous devez partir. Go. Now.*"

The dragon lowered its head as he approached, and he took one of the proffered horns with a gloved hand, swinging himself back up onto the creature's neck.

"Wait, what? Where are you going?" said Mira. "What's going on?"

"Sorry," he said a third time, then ordered his dragon, "*Allons-y.*"

He gave a swift kick to his dragon's chest with his heels and they were off, the dragon sending up a spray of water, sand, and pebbles as they left.

"Wait!" cried Mira, splashing into the shallows. "What—who—?"

But the boy was already gone. Splashes joined the sounds of the shouting coming from upriver, distinguishing themselves first as the thundering of hooves, then the clatter of several distinct horses, all coming at a gallop.

"Forge's tongs," Mira hissed. The boy was being chased. And that could only mean one thing for her.

Trouble.

Turning on her heel, Mira ran for Batcha. He was still in a panic, antlers flailing. Lucky for her, her fear of getting hit by him again was nothing compared to her fear of facing whoever was around the bend.

Mira grabbed her axe and pack and shoved her feet into her boots. Batcha swung his antlers to the left, trying to smack her, but she ducked under the blow with ease. Throwing a leg over the mini hart's back, she sliced through the ends of the reins. He tried to buck, but she'd been working with him since he was a calf, his tricks as well known to her as her own. Wrenching the reins to the side, she curled him in on himself instead, spinning his momentum into a tight circle. She searched her surroundings. He was too wild to lead up the track she'd taken to get down to the stream, his antlers threatening to tangle in every nearby bush and tree. With the horses blocking the path upstream and the opposite bank dense with bushes, there was only one way left to go.

Mira swore. Hauling Batcha into line, she kicked his sides, sending him after the boy.

It didn't take long for the horses to catch up. After a few initial turns, the stream steadied out into a more even line between the trees. The dragon—boy low over his shoulders—came into view, but then, coming fast from behind as they turned the final bend, so did the riders.

Mira swore again. With their saddles covered in jangling ropes, bolas, hooks, and stakes, there was no doubt who the riders were now.

Bounty hunters.

Two humans and an elf, all three rode with their knees, their arms dedicated to their bows. The stream ticked to the left, momentarily hiding them from sight. As they made the bend, the tip of the elf's arrow started to glow orange and hot.

With a sharp, clucking cry, he set the arrow aflame and released it, the shaft arcing high above Mira before slamming into the stream with a violent hiss, inches from the dragon's tail. The humans fired their arrows as well, one pinging off a tree, the other zipping into the woods.

Leaning low over Batcha's back, Mira urged the mini hart on. No doubt if the hunters didn't catch the dragon, Mira would make an appealing second.

Rogue dwarves always sold well.

Thankfully, for the moment, the hunters' attentions were focused on the larger prize. The stream was shallow, no higher than her knees at deepest. If she could find a break in the tangled brush on the banks, she might still have a chance.

The elf nocked another arrow, the humans releasing their second shots. Mira drew her head in close to Batcha's antlers. Heat rose from his body in heaving waves. She could hear the air growing hoarse in his chest, a wheezing sound threading into the thundering of his hooves.

Over his ears she saw the boy, staring at her from the back of his dragon, face twisted in disbelief. The elf's second arrow zinged past his ear, and he shouted at her in his strange language, waving to either side of the woods as if that could help.

Behind them, the elf nocked a third time, this time aiming for her.

"Stop, no. I'm not with him," cried Mira. "He's the one you want!"

Their pursuers were not convinced. The elf fired, and a quick shift of her axe was all that saved Batcha's rear from bursting into arrow-sparked flame. The dragon slowed, as if stopping to help her, but the boy gave a shout, speeding it on once more.

Mira growled. If she ever caught up with the boy, she'd kill him herself.

But the boy was no longer paying her any attention. Letting out another cry, he urged his dragon forward, pushing him hard into a final sprint. He leaned in close to the dragon's back as its thick muscles coiled under its skin then momentarily disappeared as the creature released the tension in a single, powerful leap. The dragon's long body soared through the air, sending up a shower of dirt and leaves as it landed, its thick, shark-like tail cracking branches as easily as twigs. Rolling off the beast's shoulders with a gasp, the boy vanished into a tangle of brush.

That was when Mira noticed there was no river where they had landed nor, far worse, any land in the ten or so feet directly behind them. The boy and his dragon had jumped across a ravine, and she was heading straight for its edge.

Mira searched for options—a thin trail, a hole, a gap. The others she'd passed had been too narrow to navigate safely, too tangled for her to get through. But even smashing her leg on a tree would be better than falling off a cliff, capture better than death. She had to reach the yochni. If she didn't make it, her people would die.

There was no path but forward. No gap in the trees, no respite from the hunters. If she stopped now, she would be trampled.

"Go, Batcha, go," she said. "You need to jump. You can make it!"

Kicking her heels hard into the sides of her mount, she felt a single, weak pulse through his ribs, the desire to reach greater speeds where there was no energy remaining to do so. The boy's face popped out of the leaves on the other side of the ravine, head shaking out the pain of his impact. He turned at the splashes of Batcha and the horses, and his blue eyes went wide, any last cobwebs withering away as he realized her plan.

They both knew the mini hart wouldn't make it. The jump would have been a stretch for a horse from dry land. For Batcha, only half their size, it was impossible.

Still, the mini hart tried.

Mira saw the boy reach for her, the swiping claws of the dragon trying to catch them just a little too late. Batcha squealed beside her as she fell. A strange roar filled her ears. Time slowed for a moment, and then she felt something she feared almost more than the slam of stone.

Water. They'd fallen into water.

Mira, like most dwarves, couldn't swim.

CHAPTER

TWO

Kraven Monteyeaux, second son of the house of Monteyeaux and apprentice physician of the Guard, watched the dwarf fall, her fingers slipping past his, past Drake's, and out of sight.

He had expected he might die on his journey.

He hadn't expected to be the cause of death for somebody else.

With the hunters still firing arrows, however, he wasn't given long to consider the girl's demise. Snapping his hand back as three arrows pinged against a rock only inches from his exposed face, he let the thought drop, another grasping to take its place as Drake yanked him deeper into the undergrowth.

The sea dragon plowed his way through the trees, and the pair half-crawled, half-stumbled their way to safety, Drake not letting Kraven so much as get to his feet before they were well out of arrow range. Though Drake, like all dragons, possessed little more intelligence than that of an unusually keen pack animal, he still gave a derisive snort in the direction from which they had come when they finally stopped.

15

Loyal to a fault, had Kraven not insisted they flee, the dragon might well have torn the hunters in two.

Leaning back against a tree, Kraven wiped the sweat from his face, Ines' gloves sticking against his skin. The second thought was still there, trying to form. It was...something he had seen...no, thought...heard? It had been right before Drake had pushed him. They had been running from the hunters, Drake had jumped, the dwarf had jumped, and then...

Kraven closed his eyes, sucking in a deep breath as the thought snapped into focus.

A splash. He'd heard a splash.

Kraven smacked his forehead with a palm, letting out a stream of self-deprecating comments in Fransec. If the girl and her mount had fallen into a river, there was a chance they were still alive. If they were, it was his duty to help them. Or at least, it was what Ines would have done.

Kraven stared at the gloves on his hands, the white shields embroidered on the backs. They had been hers, his best friend's, before she had died. She had belonged to the Guard, a loosely organized group of do-gooders determined to help others in whatever way they could. She had been a physician until one day she decided to help the wrong people.

Kraven clenched and unclenched his fingers. The gloves were already getting tight on his growing hands, stretching to the point where soon they wouldn't stretch anymore. In theory, if he continued on his current path, he would get a pair of his own someday, a position in the Guard himself. Not, in particular, that he wanted it. At least, not yet. Ines had believed that would change. Maybe someday it would.

Drake butted him in the shoulder, letting out a huff. Looking up, Kraven met the dragon's shiny black eyes, their expression as innocent as it was accusing.

"*On a pas le temps*," Kraven chided. They were already running behind.

Drake let out another huff.

"*Non*, Drake."

The dragon whined, a high-pitched sort of twitter.

Kraven frowned, looking back to the gloves. Assuming the dwarf had survived, the odds of him running into her again were slim, her chances of accusing him of being a false Guard member even less so. And, to be fair, he wasn't a false Guard member, ulterior motives for joining or no.

All the same, as much as he wanted to complain about the time—their encounter with the hunters had set them back a day already—it wouldn't cost him much to go find her, certainly not more than Drake could make up in a morning's progress. And, of course, it was what Ines would have done. He sighed.

"*D'accord, d'accord,*" he said, reaching for one of the dragon's horns. "*Allons-y.*"

Swinging a leg up and over the sea dragon's neck with the horn's assistance, Kraven settled himself into position. Wheeling the dragon with a knee, he set their course on what he hoped was a long diagonal to the dwarf's location.

Assuming of course that he and Drake were heading downriver. And that the stream at the base of the cliffs hadn't been too shallow or full of rocks. And that the dwarf hadn't already drowned or sped past.

Kraven urged Drake into a trot.

With the sea dragon's water-tuned senses in charge of navigation, it didn't take long for them to loop back to the ravine. Kraven had been right at his guess, and there was indeed a river at its bottom. Deep enough to support a dwarf and her hart if they fell, it was also, unfortunately, fast enough to drown them, especially if she was hurt.

Kraven dismounted, then leaned over the edge to scan the waters. He couldn't hear any sound of her or their pursuers.

He couldn't see any sign of her either, though whether that was a bad thing or not, he wasn't sure.

He glanced at the other side of the cliff, trying to gauge their odds as Drake shuffled up to the edge beside him. It would be faster to simply drop down into the ravine, and better for Drake, but if the hunters found them again....

Drake screamed.

The soft stone of the ravine walls had crumbled under the dragon's weight. Tumbling in a cascade of rocks, grass, and sapphire scales, limbs thrashing for purchase, the sea dragon hit the water with a loud slap.

Kraven rushed to the edge, hoping what was left of the cliff would keep under his weight. "Drake," he cried. "Drake!"

The dragon, tangled in his own legs and up to his chin in water, gave an embarrassed whistle. Straightening with some effort—Kraven's heart settling as he did—he set his massive feet against the walls of the ravine. His claws raked across the stone as he attempted to climb back out. Scraping off a decent chunk of the wall and nearly collapsing the portion on which Kraven was standing on his first attempt, the sea dragon subsided, letting out an unhappy chirrup.

Kraven frowned. At least he didn't have to decide if he should get down into the ravine anymore. He looked up the river a final time to check for dwarves and hunters, then sat on the edge of the cliff, grabbing onto Drake's horns and twisting down onto the dragon's slim shoulders. Sliding into a seated position around the dragon's neck, he winced as the cool river rose up his legs, past his thighs, then groin. He could tell Drake's front legs weren't touching the bottom. If he slipped off now, he could drown. Assuming Drake didn't rescue him first, which, of course, Kraven knew he would.

In any case, it was too late to turn back now. Settling into a more comfortable position, he gave the order to go. Drake, diving under the water, shot forward, back legs springing off the river floor. With the river rising almost up to his chest as the dragon wove his way under the water, Kraven clamped his knees hard on his dragon's neck, doing his best to keep an eye out for hunters in the brief up-and-down snatches when he could see above the cliff tops.

The river threaded through the ravine for perhaps a half a mile, the walls rising and falling with its course though never fully dropping their guard. The water, swift and cool, raced along the narrower portions, never quite rapids, but always close. Drake, with his webbed back feet and strong, thick tail, raced through the canyon like a thread through a needle, the slight twists as he navigated always alarming, but never dangerous enough to make Kraven slip off. They didn't see any sign of the dwarf or her creature as they went. Perhaps it was already too late.

Then, just as the ravine walls started to widen, he heard the voice. Slapping lightly at his dragon's neck, he pulled Drake to a stop. Placing all four feet on the river's floor, the sea dragon tossed his head, huffing pleased clouds of spray from his slotted nostrils. Kraven rubbed his friend's neck, quieting the creature further still, then closed his eyes to listen.

"Help!"

Kraven nodded. It was the dwarf's voice. He gave another order and Drake's head slid back under the surface to speed them forward.

As if in response to the dwarf's call, the cliffs at last surrendered their ground, crumbling down and out into a broad expanse of shallow rapids. Drake trotted out of the last vestiges of the ravine, the river now no higher than the dragon's shins. Kraven took in the landscape. They had come out on what appeared to be the ruins of an old mining operation, long since washed away by a broken dam. Dense woods banked the river on either side, and circular mine shafts of varying sizes dotted the river's breadth, some still guzzling water through their ravenous mouths, others long since flooded so that they lay only as deep and treacherous pools beneath the rapids' roiling surface. Rusted mine cart tracks snaked their way under the water, and a cart lay upended on the far bank, not far from a rotting pulley.

Kraven pulled Drake to a stop, closing his eyes to listen. The calls were coming every minute or so, the dwarf's location hard to pinpoint over the splashing of the river. When the next one came, however, he managed to home in on its source. Nudging his dragon with a heel, Kraven directed him towards one of the smaller branches the fracturing river had taken, this one running close to the water's edge. The river was shallower there, barely up to Kraven's ankles, though he knew it could still have a dangerous pull. Careful of his footing on the slippery stone, Kraven dismounted, then leaned over the edge of one of the shafts.

The dwarf was on a shelf of rock near the bottom, blinking against the spray from the waterfall that had dropped her there. Her shoulder was twisted at a terrible angle. The mini hart she'd been riding limped a few feet below her at the mine shaft's bottom. The water that fell on them from the rapids flowed past the animal's feet and out of sight down an adjoining tunnel, running over cart tracks and rotten elevator pieces into the dark.

Kraven glanced to the woods on either side, searching for any signs of the hunters. He didn't see any, though that didn't mean they weren't close. The dwarf, shielding her face as the waterfall took a new course around his feet, called up to him in Itsrec, the common language of the Central Lands. He'd only been learning the language for a couple of weeks, the vast majority of the language far beyond him.

Kraven sighed. With her wounded shoulder, there was no way the dwarf would be able to climb up on her own, let alone secure the mini hart. If he was going to help her, he was going to have to climb down himself. He crossed his arms, receiving a reproachful look from Drake for his reluctance, then, relenting, uncrossed them and called down to the dwarf, parroting one of the few phrases in Itsrec he knew. "I am here to help."

The dwarf called up to him again, repeating the words "help" and "please." The mini hart, limping along on three hooves, let out an unhappy moan.

Kraven did not know enough Itsrec to decipher most of the rest of her complaint, nor enough to give a decent reply. "I am here to help," he repeated instead.

Slinging his pack off his shoulders, his gloves clammy and unpleasant in the wet, Kraven dug around for his rope. Crammed in under his flint and tinder, food, his knife, his medical kit, and a spare shirt, it was coiled up in the bottom like a cushion. When he'd been packing, he'd been certain he wouldn't need it. Now, starting to shiver in the water, he wished he'd kept it closer to the top. At length, between brief snatches of checking for the hunters, he managed to pull the rope loose, barely catching his flint before it could go over the edge as he did.

The hole the dwarf had fallen down was not much wider across than she was tall. If he fell or the rope broke, Drake would not be able to rescue them.

Kraven chose not to think about what would happen if that were the case.

Handing one end of the rope to the sea dragon—Drake's grip more certain than that of any of the nearby stones—Kraven threw the other end down to the dwarf, giving the rope a few gentle practice swings and pointing between it and the dwarf to broadcast his intentions first. Ordering Drake to stay, he grabbed the rope and set his feet on the edge of the hole.

As he descended, he tried to assure the dwarf that everything was okay, that he meant her no harm, but she never responded, only watching him as he descended. She was filthy, her crinkled blond hair mussed with mud and waterfall mist. Her shirt was little more than a vest across her chest, a dirty scrap she'd torn or cut from the bottom cinching the waist. Her pants were equally tattered, worn thin and lined with stitches. The mini hart looked to be in better shape. Where her axe had gone, he couldn't tell. Kraven had never met a dwarf before. They were primarily absent from the Coast, though a few stories had managed to trickle down through Ines and the travelers that passed through the inn. They were not a popular topic for discussion, both too distant and too reclusive to provide much interest or gossip. Mostly he knew that they were miners who worked for the bogey empire to the South. What she was doing out in the woods by herself, he had no idea.

When he was only a few feet from the dwarf's ledge, Kraven let himself drop, flexing the cramps out of his fingers and rubbing his burning palms through his gloves. The dwarf said nothing, eyes to the ground. Kraven opened his mouth to speak, ready to ask what was wrong.

Then he saw the hunters hiding in the shadows behind her mount, the thinner man and the elf with arrows nocked. They stood shadowed in the tunnel that led from the shaft, straddling the ruined mine cart rails. The tip of the elf's arrow glowed a deep and smoldering orange, ready to ignite. Their leader, a fat, pouchy man, had a knife, hand pulled back in a lazy arc that Kraven knew could snap tight as a whip in a second's time. No doubt in his line of work, his aim was sharp.

"Hello, boy," the man with the knife said. "How nice of you to join us."

The words were just simple enough for Kraven to catch

the gist, the man's greasy manner more than enough to fill in any gaps. Reaching out, he yanked Kraven from the shelf, his knife finding a new home just under Kraven's ribs.

"That's a good boy. Nice and easy. Now keep him calm or we roast him," the man with the knife warned, indicating Drake. The hunter's breath was hot on Kraven's neck, his grip hard as a vice. The man repeated his instructions in Fransec as the elf stepped out of the shadows, aiming at Drake, and Kraven gave a tight-lipped nod. When the inevitable nervous whistles and clicks fell down the shaft from Drake, he called up soothing comforts and steadying orders. He thought of sending the dragon away, shouting for him to run, but he knew Drake would never leave him for long. The elf was ready to draw at the drop of a bean. His best friend would burn long before he scraped his way down. The best Kraven could hope for was to get out of the hole unharmed and escape later, before the hunters could kill his dragon.

Kraven glared at the dwarf, anger burning deep in his gut, but when she finally met his gaze, her own eyes were just as reproachful, her round lips set in a frown.

The thinner man started to climb up the narrow shaft, his fingers sure even on the slick stone.

Kraven looked up to the silhouetted circle of sky, Drake's shadow a hostage above.

He never should have come back.

THREE

The hunters had made her do it.

After she had fallen into the water, the hunters had followed Mira all the way down to the rapids, where Batcha had run both himself and her right over the edge of the abandoned mine shaft. She'd hit the stone shelf hard, her shoulder wrenching out of place when Batcha's tangled reins followed him down the extra few feet to the bottom.

It hadn't been long after that the hunters had caught up with her, the thinner of the two human hunters, Johann, climbing down the side to collect her while the elf Havar and his flaming arrows kept watch from above. Then they'd heard the dragon's cry, and the fat, lead hunter Spider had given the order to hide the horses and climb down to join them.

With several pointies directed right at her back, she'd had little choice but to play the bait.

Mira doubted the boy would reason that far in his own interpretation of events. Based on the way he glared at her, when he deigned to look at her at all, she suspected he hadn't tried. That was fair, she supposed. Had their positions been swapped, she'd have chopped him in half.

It had taken nearly two hours to get everyone back out of

the shaft, a careful rationing of prisoners, ropes, and the hands to hold them. Batcha, still limping, had been slung up on a harness on the dragon's side in that same time, the dragon itself anchored between the horses. Mira's shoulder, still burning, had been popped back into its socket and her hands tied behind her. The boy, Kraven as she had since learned, had fared less well, a large bruise blossoming under his right eye from his singular attempt at fighting. He'd struck out when Spider had stolen a thin silver chain from off the boy's neck. Spider had put a swift end to that.

Now, with all their prey secured, it was time for the group to leave. Havar slung Mira over Johann's saddle—the boy hoisted up to sit pretty in front of Spider with a knife to his ribs—and the party turned north. According to Spider, they were going to a village a day's ride off where he claimed to have friends.

Mira doubted a man like Spider had friends, but she supposed money did have its appeal. In any case, assuming she didn't do anything stupid enough to get herself killed before then, that was where she and the dragon would be sold. What would happen to the boy, she couldn't be sure.

Not that she cared.

Except...he did still have that dragon.

The more Mira ran her various plans through her head in fact, most involving not a few number of knives in eyeballs, the more clear it became she was going to need the boy's help. For all their lesser qualities, the hunters were experienced, and without greater numbers, weaponry, or the dragon, getting free would be nearly impossible, to say nothing of making up the time she had lost. The boy could, through his sea dragon and cooperation, supply all three, if she could only convince him that it hadn't been her fault. Stealing a glance at him when they finally dismounted for the night, Mira realized that might be easier said than done.

The boy, gaze set permanently on some vague, distant point, wouldn't even look at her. Shoulders hunched as if he'd never known of a worse fate than his, he stood next to Spider with his lips drawn tight in a grim, angry line, the perfect image of a moody teenager. When Johann tied them together for the night, securing them to a nearby tree, the boy squirmed at the touch of her shoulder.

Mira did not have time for him to be stubborn.

Digging through his saddlebags, Spider drew out their supper, a crust of bread and half a canteen. He tossed them, both bouncing a few inches shy of the boy's feet. At first, Kraven didn't even respond. Mira nudged him, and he stirred from his sulking enough to at last do something useful. With effort, he managed to wriggle down against the trunk and hook both items with the tip of his boot. She assumed he would keep it all for himself, but after a long look at his gloves, he reluctantly ripped the crust in two, handing her an equal half.

"Thank you," she said, but he didn't turn to face her. Heartened by his sharing and pressed by time, she pushed forward.

"Kraven," she said softly.

"*Arrête.*"

"Kraven, I'm sorry."

The boy's jaw tightened. "*Arrête.*"

Johann glanced over from his position leaning against a tree. Spider followed his gaze to the two prisoners, and Mira's cheeks grew hot with anger.

"I don't think he much wants to talk to you," Spider sneered, spreading fat fingers over the fire. "'*Arrête*' means stop."

Johann, unamused, turned back to the fire. Havar fiddled with the dragon's restraints.

"Look, I'm sorry, alright?" Mira continued, trying to keep

her voice low. She felt loud in the silence, the fire popping as if laughing in response. She was embarrassed, but if getting on the boy's good side meant getting free, she wasn't above begging. "I shouldn't have tricked you into coming down. I should have warned you."

Kraven stared at his sea dragon, his expression mulish.

Mira paused, then added, "Thank you, for coming to get me."

She put her hand on his arm, trying to turn him, but he shook her off. He looked away, and the dark swallowed the last thin slivers of his face that she'd been able to see from the fire.

Spider was still smirking when Mira looked back, his tightly packed teeth lining his mouth like a crooked fence. Havar had moved on to dinner, a thin soup of greens and rabbit. Johann watched the dragon.

A familiar anger boiled in Mira's gut. She was on her own.

It took most of the next day to reach the buyer's village. Denied breakfast and lunch, by the time the small party pulled off into a modest clearing on the village's outskirts, Mira's vision was starting to twist from hunger. She'd tried several times throughout the day to make progress with the boy, but he seemed determined to leave her to her own fate, or rather, to abandon them both to his, which looked even less positive for the fact he wouldn't fetch a price. She'd spent the vast majority of the day slung over Johann's lap like some kind of blanket, his knees, saddle horn, and belt buckle biting into her in turns. Given the boy's stubbornness and the hunter's cruelty, she was starting to find hope in short supply. The travelers they'd met on the road, most of them champions or the merchants and thieves such crowds attracted, had ignored her, each too busy attending their own business or marveling at Drake—that was the name the boy used for the dragon—to pay anything so mundane as a captured dwarf any mind.

Still, she thought, at least there still are champions.

It was common fact that most of the villages along the Confluence—the main network of roads to reach the yochni —would flood with champions at one point or another along the pilgrimage, each inundation shrinking as champions died off or quit. If Mira could just keep up with them, escape before they left, she still had a chance. She could still reach the yochni in time.

She was desperate enough to try to run when Johann finally dropped her from his saddle. She ducked towards the woods as soon as her feet found the ground, but he had her by the collar before she'd gone more than a few steps.

It wouldn't have mattered anyway. So close to the village, she wouldn't have gotten far, at least not without a mount. Batcha still hung from his harness on Drake's side. Even had he been released, his bad leg meant he had neither the strength nor speed to help her.

Havar left to contact their buyer. If Mira didn't do something soon, she'd be sold before the sun rose.

They waited for over an hour. An early moon lit the night, bright enough they made no fire. The horses grazed at the edges of the clearing. Drake moaned and whined in his ropes. Mira watched and waited, alert for some final, desperate exit, some gap in the hunter's attentions, but none came. Spider and Johann remained as sharp as tacks and Kraven did not depart from his resentment, his gaze shifting from her like water from oil whenever she tried to catch his eye.

Had Mira been free, she might well have strangled him for his obstinance, but she was not presented with even that opportunity.

Finally, just as Mira's fear was starting to fade to boredom, a rustling came from the trees. Johann's bow flashed up in an instant, his hands free with Mira's ropes safely looped around his saddle horn, but it was only Havar, who raised his hands and called to identify himself as he emerged from the woods. Johann waited until Havar was fully in sight before lowering his bow, but the elf was alone.

Havar lowered his hands, and his shaking fingers quickly found their homes at his sides, fluttering like nervous birds. His anxious manner brought Mira to attention. A spark of hope flickered in her chest.

Spider glared, eyes narrowing. "Where's the buyer?"

Havar wrung his thin hands. He offered a placating smile, but it quickly fell. "She's not coming," he mumbled.

"What?" Spider stormed over to the elf, dragging Kraven behind him. If he hadn't been holding the boy, Mira thought he'd have had the elf's neck. "What do you mean she's not coming?"

"She won't take it."

"Why?"

"She said it's too busy. Too many people in town. Prying eyes."

"This is a dragon. A *real* dragon."

"I know what it is, and I told her the same, but she doesn't care," whined the elf. "She doesn't want it."

Spider opened his fat-lipped mouth to argue, then, slowly, closed it, a dangerous canniness marking his features. Kraven looked to Mira. His stare, confused at first, turned urgent, and she realized he was looking for a translation. She gave the hunters a brief tip of her head, then gave him an encouraging nod. If the hunters' deal fell through, perhaps they still had time. Perhaps they could still escape.

Spider shoved Kraven to Havar, clearing space to pace by the fire as he drummed his fingers against his lips. Even with her limited knowledge, Mira knew dragon skins were tough, their teeth and claws the perfect size and sharpness for tools and knives, to say nothing of their rarity. If the hunters could find a buyer, they'd make a fortune. But if they couldn't, the longer they waited....

Spider glanced at the dragon, his free hand fiddling with the hilt of his knife.

"We can't kill it," said Johann. "Not on our own."

"I know," the man growled, though his fingers stopped tapping. He looked at Mira and frowned, her entire body practically buzzing from excitement. Then, recognition sparked, and a broad smile split his features.

"Havar," he said. "Did you see any bogeys there?"

Mira's body went cold, even the other hunters stiffening. Kraven looked between them, no doubt sensing a conversational shift.

The elf exchanged a wary look with Johann, then nodded. "Yeah. One."

Mira shuddered, the scars along her back tightening at the words.

"Good," said Spider. "That witch doesn't want our business, we'll take them to someone who does."

"Spider," Johann started, but the lead hunter put up a hand, cutting him off.

"No. No arguments. We need to sell it and her. It's perfect."

The thinner man frowned but didn't argue.

Mira did her best not to choke on her tongue. If anyone would have the means to tame or kill a dragon, it would be the bogeys. And for a runaway dwarf, there was no better buyer. Or, from her perspective, worse.

"We'll take them to the back of the inn. Bring the bogey outside to us," Spider said. Mounting his horse, he held his hands out for Kraven. Havar hoisted the boy up to sit in front of him as before, but for once Kraven looked back to Mira as he was lifted, expression urgent. He was finally ready to deal, but Mira, too numb to think, didn't even respond. Havar hefted her back over Johann's saddle and her view of him was soon obscured by the hunter's knee and his jangling stirrup.

The hunters nudged their horses back onto the wide, well-beaten road leading into the village, keeping Drake sandwiched between them as they'd done before. The stream of travelers the elf had joined on his first foray into the village had died down to a trickle, the few champions and merchants remaining on the road giving the bright blue dragon a wide berth, some whistling in admiration, others exchanging excited or nervous whispers.

Mira, face down over Johann's lap, ignored them, mind unable to think beyond the current danger. She knew she had to plan, to act, but it was like trying to pull her mind through sap. Every time she managed to wrangle her thoughts in a new direction, her dread of the bogey snapped them back. How could she escape? What would happen if she couldn't? Would the bogey ask how she had gotten there? Kill her on sight? Maybe it would just send her back to the mines. If so, perhaps she could still fight.

Yes, yes. Fight. That was what she had to do. Mira doubted the bogey would let her live, but even the thought was enough to galvanize her, to break her free from her cyclical terror. She looked up, hunting anew for ways to get free. She looked to Kraven, hoping his change of heart had endured.

He was still looking back at her, his head twisted to look over his shoulder. His expression was no longer mopey or despairing, but bright and alert. He was still ready to help.

Good, thought Mira. *Finally*. It was likely too late already, but if they worked together, maybe, just maybe, they still had a chance. They had to try.

Following the outer edge of the village, it didn't take them more than ten minutes to reach the inn's stables. Turning her head to avoid Johann's saddle horn when she felt the tell-tale nudge from the man's left knee, Mira spread her feet, catching her weight as the hunter bumped her off of his lap. Landing half a step outside a pool of horse urine, she turned just in time to see Kraven's humiliated cringe as he fell into another, his much more violent fling from Spider's lap darkening his odds at controlling his fall. A flash of pain sparked over the boy's face as he hit the ground—Spider cursing as splash-back hit his boots—but his sour expression was quickly replaced by surprise. When Kraven stood, he didn't shake out his dripping gloves, but kept his fingers clenched, something wrapped inside that he wouldn't let go of even when Spider grabbed him by the neck.

The lead hunter dragged Kraven over to Johann, the smell of urine slamming into Mira's nostrils as Spider shoved the boy into his lieutenant's arms. Not nearly so wide as his boss, it took the full length of both of Johann's arms to hold both captives together. If not for the man's hand wound into her shirt, Mira could almost have wiggled free. Kraven pressed the tip of what he had found against her skin. For a moment, she froze. Then she gave his arm a small, acknowledging nudge in return.

Maybe he wasn't as stupid as he looked after all.

"Take the boy with you into the stables," said Spider. He'd gathered all of the horses. Back turned to the trio, he looped their reins to a post at the stable's entrance. Havar tied triple knots on Drake's anchors. "I don't want any trouble while I talk to the bogey. The dwarf comes with me."

Before he had a chance to turn around, Mira nudged Kraven hard. Slamming her foot down, she hit Johann's toes with enough force to feel the bones crack. He howled in pain, and his arms released like a spring. He sprang to recapture them, reflexes lightning quick even with his injury, but Kraven was ready, swinging the nail he'd found deep into the man's thigh. Johann dropped his knife, clutching at the wound. Kraven grabbed the weapon, shouting for Drake.

The dragon's response was instantaneous, a thin mewl the only whimper Havar managed before the dragon's tail slammed him into a wall.

Chaos erupted around the stable. Horses reared. Batcha squealed. Spider dove for Kraven, but Mira shoved the boy out of the way, her face skidding into the mud as the hunter's heavy weight landed on her instead. Footsteps slapped and squelched through the muck as Kraven darted for Drake. The sea dragon roared, his blue scales flashing, and Johann screamed, the crunch of bone ripping the air. Spider scrabbled to his feet, lifting Mira with one arm locked around her neck. He spun towards his men, but Havar was no longer moving, Johann leaning heavily against the stable. He was missing an arm, his remaining hand clutching his bleeding stump. Drake hissed and growled, his snout shiny and wet with red.

Kraven mounted the dragon. "*Naine,*" he called, looking back. His gaze flitted over the carnage. Mira kicked, heels bouncing off the hunter's stomach, but he flicked out his knife, the blade finding perch on her throat. Kraven's gaze settled on them both, and anger seized the boy's features, his mouth snapping into a line.

Spider shook Mira. Hard. "Good. I've got your attention. Now, get down before I kill her. *Descendez, ou je la tue,*" he threatened.

Mira didn't need the man's knife tickling at her throat to know the hunter was serious. Dragons were worth a fortune, far more than any single dwarf's life. If Kraven didn't dismount, the man would kill her. He repeated his demand, moving his knife just long enough to gesture for the boy to dismount, and his voice rumbled through the back of her vest.

Mira closed her eyes, waiting for the boy to leave, to abandon her. It's what she would have done. At least he'd taken down two of the hunters for her. Maybe with only Spider left, she could still launch an escape.

Soft boots thumped on the earth. Mira opened her eyes. Kraven had dismounted. Drake crouched ready behind him, blood still dripping from his teeth. A low hiss leaked out with his breath. Resolution bent deep into the boy's face, and his round eyes shone like a cat's in the light of the moon. *"Laissez-la partir."*

"No," snarled Spider.

"Laissez-la partir," Kraven repeated, stepping forward.

Spider, watching Drake, took a step back. One of the horses, still stamping, whinnied.

"Arrête. C'est assez.," Kraven said, arm flashing out to the side.

The creature fell instantly silent. Mira blinked. The boy was in the shadow of the stable now, but his eyes still shone. It wasn't reflected light. Kraven's eyes were glowing, pale blue light gleaming from deep within. Mira felt Spider swallow behind her, the hunter's body stiffening as he reached the same conclusion.

"Donnez-moi le dragon et je la laisse partir," Spider bargained.

"Non. Laissez-la partir."

"Mais—"

"Maintenent." Kraven continued his advance. Drake loomed behind him, his growl rumbling through the earth.

Spider took three steps back for each one of Kraven's, his grip on Mira's neck loosening almost enough for her to break free. He threatened her again, practically babbling in Kraven's tongue, but his voice was high and pinched, terrified. His knife trembled against her skin, nearly breaking the surface.

Kraven stopped. The glow had grown brighter, the pale

blue light now shining out of his face like twin lanterns. Splashing down on his cheeks and the ground before him, it lit his every feature with an alien glow.

The boy spoke again, giving some kind of order or ultimatum. Spider trembled. Drake, now standing on his hind legs like a giant bear, rose higher even than the stable roof, horns and sapphire scales glinting in the silvery moonlight. Batcha, still hanging from the dragon's side, moaned and brayed. The horses stamped and whinnied.

Mira felt Spider's grip on her neck falter and fail. He dropped his knife, then her. She fell coughing into the mud and sucked in precious air.

"*Ne me tuez pas, s'il vous plaît, ne me tuez pas.* Don't kill me. Don't kill me. Please," Spider pleaded. He collapsed to his knees, pants soaking in the foul liquid he had spurned mere minutes before.

Mira got to her feet, waiting for the death chomp to come, the order from Kraven to kill. The bandits deserved nothing less. If Drake didn't kill him, she hoped for the right.

The boy gave no such order. For a long moment, his face twisted as if fighting to keep the command inside, but then he closed his eyes, drawing in a deep breath. When he opened them again, he was no longer divided, but calm. He looked at her. "*Naine. Ici.* Come."

Pointing first to the horses, gloved hands black as night, he then pointed to the mud beside him.

Mira tried to move, but her knees locked. The dragon had dropped back to all fours, but he was still hissing a low, terrible growl at the assembled group. She could feel it up through her boots, the sound freezing her to the spot.

Kraven scowled.

He gave a command to Spider, and the hunter grabbed her, hefting her up onto one of the horses. On further orders, he gave her a lantern, the other two horses' reins, and finally, the silver necklace he'd stolen. Giving her horse's backside a slap when she still didn't move, the hunter sent her to Kraven's side, the horses giving the dragon as wide a berth as possible even as they obeyed. Kraven ordered her to stop when she reached Drake, and, despite herself, she did.

Kraven stood for a moment longer, fists slowly opening and closing as he watched the hunters. Mira wondered if he would give the killing order now, but he shook his head, retreating to Drake and remounting. He pointed to Johann and Havar, then spoke to Spider again.

"Help men. I, you," he said, pointing a couple of times between Spider and his own eyes. "*Drake va vous tuer.*" Mira recognized the word *tuer*, the same one Spider had used when threatening her.

Johann slumped against the wall, one hand loosely grasping his bleeding stump. Havar struggled to gain his feet. Spider looked to them, then, with a final venomous glare to Kraven, moved to help them. His legs shook as he walked, face pale as the moon, but Mira could already see the desire for revenge bubbling underneath, the resentment held below the surface.

Nudging his dragon, Kraven pointed his mount towards the forest, the light in his eyes beginning to fade.

"Wait, what?" said Mira. "You're not going to kill them?"

The boy looked at her, confused.

"*Tuer,*" she guessed, pointing at the men.

Kraven's fingers clenched, jaw tightening, but then he forced his muscles loose, shaking his head. "*Non,*" he said.

"Fine, if you're not going to, then let me." She reached for her axe, retrieved from one of the saddles, but Kraven held out a hand.

"*Non,*" he said. He pointed to the woods "*Vas-y.*"

Mira scowled, trying to turn her horse around, but Kraven stopped her again, light flickering back to life at the backs of his eyes. Suddenly, Mira knew if he wanted to stop her, it would be well within his power to do so.

In any case, he still had Batcha, the mini hart moaning in his harness, and with her size, three ratty horses wouldn't do her much good, even if she had their supplies. She could not kill the men on her own, nor continue her journey without his help.

With no other alternative, Mira nudged her horse after the dragon, leaving the three bandits to follow the boy.

FOUR

Kraven urged Drake into a loping trot as soon as their small party left the stable yard. Covered in sweat and shaking, he locked his fingers tightly around his sea dragon's horns to stay upright, consciousness swimming up and away from him with frightening vigor. Dragging it back down like a fish to the depths, sagging with Drake's every step, he closed his eyes, trying to conserve enough strength to make it to the trees.

He made it, barely, his hands falling from Drake's horns as soon as he felt leaves brush his hair. Drake slowed, letting out a nervous coo, but Kraven urged him on with a gasped order, his mind holding onto reality just long enough for them to move on. Vague pain throbbed in his stomach, darkness pressed in on his vision. Time warped as his consciousness wavered, and for strange minutes or hours details became his world. Smooth scales. Cool air. A lantern in the dark. He smelled wet earth, heard the gentle, whoomfing footfalls of Drake. If he slept, he didn't know it.

He focused on his breath. With time, vision returned.

With it came a slow mental sharpness, like waking from a dream, like catching a bird in his hand. One minute, he was fading, falling, the next he was awake, reality's edges sharpening so that everything that came before it seemed false. Drake's scales cooled his skin, and the light night breeze tickled his cheek. Sleep called him from somewhere deep, but introspection was the louder voice, calling him up from rest.

So that had been arbitration. His stomach ached.

In truth, Kraven was not unfamiliar with the fact of his magic. His father and even his elder brother Arnaud possessed it, arbiters all. But with the rest of his family more obsessed with the noble fashion of not having magic and he never in any position to put it to use, he had never tried to use his magic before. He hadn't even known how to until now. One minute he had been angry at the bandits for bullying the dwarf and threatening him and Drake, the next he had felt authority, real authority. When he had given Spider his terms, he'd felt certain of what the hunter would choose, and once the man had agreed to them, he'd been even more certain they would be followed.

That's what arbiters did. Negotiated and sealed agreements. Once Spider surrendered, cut the deal, it was over, magically over, and Kraven and the dwarf were free.

At least for the moment. Once Spider's men were tended as agreed, he'd be free to chase them again. Kraven knew Spider would know it, too. The man would feel it, just as Kraven had.

Kraven wished he had put Spider to stronger terms. He wondered if he even could have.

Horse tack and a small oil lantern jangled to Kraven's left, interrupting his thoughts. The mini hart, still harnessed to Drake's side, groaned in alarm at the sound. Kraven looked down from his perch to see the dwarf holding her lantern high.

"So, you aren't dead after all," she said.

Mud smeared her freckled face, her vest and pants

painted in a thin, drying coat of the same. Brown flecks spotted her hair, too, but her eyes were keen and wary even amidst the grime. Kraven propped himself a little higher on Drake's neck.

"*Euh, est-ce que ça va?*" he asked, unsure of what she had said.

"What happened back there? Who are you? What was that?" she demanded.

With her axe in hand, she seemed far less nervous than when they had left the village. That hardly improved his understanding of Itsrec, though, his vague expression growing genuinely blank in response.

She glared at him, axe haft wiggling in her hand.

"Are you a wizard? A champion? What did you do?" she insisted.

Kraven raised a hand to stop her, his mind unready for so many questions even if he had understood them. Gathering his limited senses, he forced himself to sit up, suffering a surge of lightheadedness for his effort. He shot her a disapproving look as he grabbed at his temple, hoping to dissuade her from her inquiries, but the look she returned was just as stubborn as his own.

For a moment, he regretted saving her at all, but he knew that was ungenerous, to say nothing of his current role in the Guard and his goal to live like Ines. He had joined to better understand his friend, to learn why she had lived the way she did—died the way she did. That meant, at least to start, parroting her choices, whether or not he agreed with them. That, in turn, meant being kind to the dwarf, at least for now. And, in any case, she had rescued him when Spider had tried to tackle him. Perhaps there could be further benefit to keeping her around. He sighed, then straightened, forcing the fog from his mind.

"My name is Kraven. Kraven Monteyeaux," he said,

pressing a hand to his chest. He put a hand on Drake's neck. "Drake."

The dwarf scowled. "I thought you didn't speak Itsrec," she said. "So, what are you then, some kind of wizard? Magician? Sorcerer? Mage?"

Kraven shook his head. He grabbed it a second later, temples pounding. He took an educated guess. "*Non. Je suis arbitre.*"

"What?"

"*Arbitre,*" he said. He pointed to his eyes, then wiggled his fingers with an *ooing* sound.

Her eyes narrowed as suspicion crawled back onto her features.

Kraven sighed. "*Je ne suis pas dangereux. Je ne vais pas te faire de mal.*"

"Speak Itsrec," she said. "You can, right?"

Kraven scowled. He opened his palms like the pages of a book, trying to get the gesture right, then, remembering, dug in his pack, retrieving his Itsrec phrase book. He tossed it down to her. "I speak...Itsrec book."

She flipped briefly through the pages then let out a huff. "Great," she muttered, and threw the book back at him.

Kraven barely caught the precious pages. For someone who had nearly gotten him and his dragon killed, her ingratitude was astonishing.

"So, are we your prisoners?" she asked, pointing between herself and her mini hart. "Why didn't you do that earlier? What did it even do?"

Trusting their languages were more similar than he'd originally thought, Kraven took a guess, shaking his head. "*Vous n'êtes pas prisonniers. C'est...*" He stopped, her eyes already shifting to blank. He rolled his eyes and tried again. "I am...new doctor. Guard." He pointed to his gloves, the white shields on the backs. "I am here to help."

He hadn't understood the latter half of her questions, assuming his guesses about the first half were correct, so he stopped where he was, hoping it had been enough.

She paused, though whether she was considering his answer or trying to understand it was difficult to tell. She pointed to the mini hart. "Are you going to give me Batcha back?"

He nodded.

"*Oui.* Yes, *mais sa jambe...*" He slapped at his own leg, then pointed to the mini hart. "I help. *Je l'aide.*"

Her expression fell to suspicion again. "Why?"

"*Quoi?*"

"Why are you helping me?"

With effort and a great deal of assistance from the phrase book, he managed to puzzle out her question. With a bit more consideration, he puzzled out his answer.

"I am a doctor. New doctor." He flipped through the pages. "Apprentice. It is...job." He flipped through more pages. "*Non,* duty." He paused, considering further. There was, of course, more to his story, but to try to explain Ines, the pain he had felt when she'd died, the gap she had left...he felt certain such a thing went far beyond his current capabilities in translation, assuming he even wanted to explain in the first place, which he did not.

It didn't seem that she needed any further explanation, however, and she let the subject drop. He was glad she did, though he found it did raise a rather pressing question in its place: What, exactly, was he going to do with her now that they had escaped? They were still quite close to the village, easily within catching distance if Spider was quick. Or, he thought grimly, if either Johann or Havar didn't make it.

Regardless, to leave her behind would be an invitation to capture, the mini hart in too poor of shape to carry her alone and too slow to keep up if she took the horses. He bit back another sigh, knowing there was only one real option if he were going to remain true to his current quest of copying Ines. The limitation was annoying, especially given the dwarf's clearly ungrateful attitude, but he knew his chosen path was only going to get worse from here. Pilgrimages to the yochni were unpleasant affairs full of foul wishes, foul people, and fouler actions. If he was truly going to help people like Ines had, he had to get used to that fact. And help them anyway.

Still, just because he was beholden to give his aid did not mean he had to be uneducated, and there was little harm in at least knowing who he was helping, even if he was going to wind up with her axe in his back. The word for champion was, mercifully, the same in both their languages. After a little grammatical consultation with his book, he asked her if that was what she was.

Her eyes slammed down to slits. "What's it to you?"

Her rebuke did not need translation. It was also more than enough for him to confirm she was, indeed, a champion. He resisted the urge to roll his eyes. She could at least have tried to lie. On the other hand, surely it was better to travel with someone he could read than someone skilled in the art of deceit. If, or more likely when, she decided to turn against him, at least he would see it coming.

Kraven sucked in a deep breath, knowing the time of his procrastination was near an end. Whether she had been a champion or not, it would not have changed what he had to do next, and any other protestations he could raise would only delay the inevitable. He turned to face her.

"*Euh....*" He paused, realizing he did not know her name. He waited, but she did not give one. He continued the best he could. "You, me, go...." He made a walking motion with his fingers before lacing them together. "I help Batcha. We go?"

It was a sloppy attempt at building a sentence, but the

dwarf seemed to understand his meaning. For a moment, the now familiar distrust settled on her features. She looked to the mini hart, then Drake, and let out a small, thoughtful hum.

She asked a question about direction, or at least what he thought was a question of direction, and he pointed north, towards the yochni. She pinned him with a long, hard stare, then gave a supercilious toss of her head. "Fine, but you better not slow us down. And we're done if you try anything fishy." She put a hand on her chest. "Mira. Batcha."

Kraven nodded. With the matter settled, the exhaustion he had been holding back poured in like a rushing tide. It would still be hours before he felt they were far enough from the village to be safe. He knew he would not be able to stay awake that long.

Luckily, in all his time traveling with Drake, he'd mastered the art of sleeping while on the move. Sliding farther down on Drake's spine, he leaned forward to lay on his stomach.

"*Deux heures*," he said. Holding two fingers high, he made the walking motion again before pointing forward in the direction they were traveling. He repeated the order to Drake, whose uncanny ability for keeping time had saved Kraven from his mother's berating on several occasions, then closed his eyes, breathing deep.

He was gone before Mira could ask him for a better translation.

When he woke again, it was to the smell of roasting apples. Hunger snagged at his gut, and his arms and legs felt stiff and restless. His stomach still bit at his sides, his head muffled and vague as if it had been stuffed with sea down.

For a moment, he squeezed his eyes shut, fighting the discomfort to go back to sleep. But the scents were insistent, and when the aroma of warming bread added itself to the mix, the last of his will vanished. Opening his eyes at last, he turned to face the fire. Mira was crouched on its opposite side with a small loaf held out over the flames. She'd nestled two small, early apples in a bed of stone and dirt just outside the embers. Kraven himself lay ensconced between Drake's legs like an egg in a nest. The dragon's head was lying across his leg, cutting off the circulation from mid-thigh down. Pulling himself up, he slapped at the offended limb as it started to prickle. Drake lifted his head to release him, then nuzzled him in the chest.

"About time," said Mira. She drew back the bread, feeling the sides for heat. "How are you feeling?"

Kraven pushed Drake's nose aside, giving it a rub for the dragon's trouble. He didn't understand what the dwarf had said, but he smiled at her anyway, nodding at the fire. "*Merci.* Thank you."

Mira nodded at the apples with a grunt, nudging one out of place with her boot. Kraven let it cool before handing it to Drake. He split his bread in half to do the same before tucking in himself.

The dwarf watched him while he ate. Her meal lasted much longer though he was sure she was just as hungry. He gave her a plaintive look when he was finished, hoping she would dole out more for his sharing with Drake, but she pretended not to notice. Kraven pretended not to have wanted anything in the first place.

She had released the horses while he slept and unhitched the mini hart from Drake's side. The contents of all the saddlebags—and Kraven's pack—had been spread out around the camp, and she had sorted everything into piles of food, medicine, clothes, and weapons. There were also small stacks of miscellaneous tools, several chains, ropes, and a skillet. Her own pack sat stuffed and closed a few feet away.

When Kraven drew her attention to his emptied pack, she only shrugged.

"So," she said, eyeing him over the fire. "You a champion?" She sat in a crouch, ready to spring into action at any moment, axe ready to hand beside her.

Kraven paused, momentarily surprised by the question. It was not an unreasonable one—in fact he was sure he'd have faced it eventually. He just hadn't expected it so soon.

"*Non*," he said slowly. She raised a brow, clearly expecting a faster answer for such a simple question, and he tried to explain. "Guard...I am new." He reached for his book, then realized he didn't know where it was in their reorganized supplies. She tossed it to him, the pages skimming dangerously close to the flames. He flipped through the pages for several minutes, painfully piecing together an approximation of what he wanted to say. "I am learning," he said at last. "Will make...job."

It was not, again, a full answer, but it was the easiest one he could give, and the only one he was willing to offer.

She studied him for a long moment, perhaps trying to gauge his honesty. He had no idea if dwarves had the Guard or an equivalent or if she would believe him if they did. She looked to her mini hart, one of his legs still painfully lifted as he grazed. Then, she got up. Tossing her apple core into the flames, she brushed the last of its juice onto her pantlegs. Selecting a few small sticks for the fire, she fed them in, then moved off towards her mount.

"Fine," she said. "But if you're lying, you're going to be sorry. We're far enough for tonight. I'll—"

A terrible cry drifted into their camp.

All of them, including the animals, froze.

The call was distant, coming from deeper in the woods. A high, whining moan slithered in in its wake. The first cry had almost sounded like a voice, but then a third sound came, a noise Kraven knew no human or elf could create.

Mira grabbed her axe. Drake let out a low, warning growl, sides twitching with other sounds Kraven knew he couldn't hear. He kept his hands on Johann's knife.

"Mira…"

"Shut up."

"*Qu'est—*"

"*Shut up,*" she hissed.

Kraven did.

Except, while at first it seemed like the sounds were getting closer, soon, they stopped moving. Certain he was mistaken, Kraven waited, hushing Drake to silence as well. He strained his ears, searching for thundering feet, slashing leaves, but the only sounds were the moans, each iteration no closer than the one before.

After several minutes, Mira lowered her axe, eyes narrowed.

"*Qu'est-ce que c'est?*" Kraven whispered.

She shook her head. Wandering over to Batcha, she muttered something in Itsrec. Kraven couldn't make any of it out. Except, he realized, for one word. Champion. His heart sank.

"*C'est un champion?*" he asked.

"Yes," she said, returning to her supplies.

Kraven did his best to keep the despair from his face. Mira picked up her bedroll and, picking a spot where she could have a trunk to her back, unfurled it on the ground. She laid down, pulling one edge over her shoulder, and curled up, axe in hand.

"*Q-qu'est-ce que tu fais?*" he asked. She opened one eye, and he pointed to the woods, towards the noise. Kraven had little desire to get closer to the whatever-it-was, but surely leaving it alone without even knowing its identity was more foolish, to say nothing of what he had to do if it was in trouble.

Mira shook her head. "No way. Whatever that thing is, it's either dying or dangerous, which is worse. We barely got away from those hunters. I'm not about to go hunt down something else."

The next call came, and Kraven flinched. It had been a terrible, pleading cry. Whatever it was, it sounded hurt. Frightened.

He looked at Mira, who had closed her eyes again, then down at his gloves. He frowned. Surely it had to be a trap, some way to lure foolish champions into their doom. To try to investigate would only land him in the same situation he had been in before, if not worse. He couldn't go.

Another howl came, desperate, moaning.

He gritted his teeth, closing his eyes. A picture of Ines skated across the backs of his eyelids. She was riding off into the woods on the journey that would end her life. He squeezed his fists, her gloves tight around his hands.

He got to his feet. *"S'il est blessé, nous devons l'aider,"* he said, trying to keep the bitterness out of his voice. "Help."

Mira opened her eyes. She laughed, a short, quiet bark. "No way."

"I am a doctor. I am here to help."

The look Mira gave him landed somewhere between disbelief, condescension, and disgust, as if it were the stupidest thing he could have said.

"If you want to help, help Batcha," she said, sitting up and pointing to the mini hart. "Help me."

He shook his head, moving with reluctant steps to repack his things.

"You're going to get yourself killed," said Mira. "Champions *tuer* Kraven."

As if he didn't already know. But there was little point in

explaining. Ines' logic had never been that of the world's, after all.

Kraven rifled through their packs, gathering his belongings as well as extra medicine and gauze from the hunters' bounty. Mira watched him like a hawk. Perhaps she was hoping he would change his mind. Except, when he was nearly finished, she started packing, too.

"*Qu'est-ce que tu fais?*" he asked.

She glared at him.

"Mira...help?" he tried again.

Her glower only deepened. "No, Mira is not going to help. Mira is going to follow the fool boy who promised to help her and his exceedingly helpful dragon in the hopes that neither one of them dies before she can make full use of their aid."

Kraven could only assume from her tone that she was being sarcastic. Regardless, it seemed she had decided to come. With her ferocity, he had to admit he was glad of her aid. They would have Drake, too, and there was little the dragon couldn't handle. Perhaps he wouldn't be killed after all.

The sounds dwindled further while they packed, the time between each howl soon measured in handfuls of minutes rather than seconds. Homing in on them the best they could, they followed a mostly northward path, the sparse moonlight poking through the trees painting the world in muddled grays and darks. Undergrowth snagged at Kraven's muddy silks, no doubt scratching Mira's exposed skin. They were hardly ideal conditions for treating a wound, though he supposed he could always light another fire if needed.

They walked for nearly half an hour before the sounds finally stopped. At first, they didn't even notice, the time between each having stretched so far, but when no new sounds came after first five minutes, then ten, they started exchanging looks. After fifteen, they started to give up hope.

"Guess it died," said Mira. "Too bad."

Kraven shushed her, trying to listen. He knew they'd been getting close. He'd even thought he'd heard snapping twigs, though with Drake's large feet crushing sticks of his own, it had been hard to tell.

"Let's go," whispered Mira.

He shushed her again, but he still heard nothing. Maybe she was right. Maybe whoever it was really had died or, if it were a trap, given up. It was almost dawn, their surroundings already graying in the morning's first attempts towards color. But he could hardly give up now, could he? Not when they'd come so far.

Ines would not have given up. Not until she had found a body, proof she was no longer needed. Stepping forward, Kraven told himself that was the only reason. He kept walking, Mira reluctantly following behind him.

And then, finally, they found something.

Mira saw it first. Kraven, unable to see as well from his position, only saw it as a flash of red, a thin line along a collar. It was a shirt, just poking out from a massive backpack. A dark shape lay beside it. The shirt was silk, which could only mean one thing: it belonged to a noble.

If Mira knew, she didn't care. Raising her axe with a sudden, furious scream, the dwarven champion started to run.

CHAPTER
FIVE

The bogey's fur was all black save a dark red stripe running from between his ears to the tip of his nose. Shattered twigs surrounded his outstretched fists, evidence of his cries for help. He was perhaps a couple of inches over seven feet, his weakly rising back broad enough for Mira to sleep on, arms just a little too long, ankles a little too high. Deep gouges and rashes covered his skin, his face swollen beyond almost all function. Based on the severity of his condition, Mira guessed he had hours to live.

Hours wasn't fast enough.

She twisted her axe, ready to swing.

Kraven got to her first. Tackling her with a flying leap, he took her down hard. Her wounded shoulder ground into the dirt. Swinging an elbow back into the noble boy's face with a snarl of rage, she was rewarded with a small, sharp crack. Kraven cried out, still tangled in her legs. Kicking at his stomach and arms, Mira forced her way free, reaching for her axe.

Something roared behind her.

She'd forgotten Drake.

Slamming his head into her back, the sea dragon sent

Mira flying, her axe shooting out of her hand. She rolled as she landed, her back and shoulders screaming with pain. Gasping for breath, she forced herself back up, thankful he hadn't hit her spine. She staggered for her axe.

Kraven grabbed it first, snatching it out of her reach. Drake screeched at her, ready to strike, but Kraven held him back.

Mira ran for the bogey. Kraven got in her way. She lifted her fists, ready to force him aside, but he grabbed her wrist. He shouted at her, had been shouting since she'd started to run, but she only shouted back, pounding wherever her free fist could strike. Behind Kraven, the slaver moaned. Mira froze. They turned to the bogey.

Stiff, clawed hands flexing in the dirt like maggots, he twitched like something coming alive, pained whimpers crawling out of his throat. His legs shifted, and he let out an agonized groan. Even injured, Mira knew bogeys could be dangerous.

She leapt for her axe. Kraven jerked it out of her reach. She pointed between the axe and the bogey, making fierce claws and fangs with her hands and face as she rattled off her explanation, but he only pointed to the creature's pack and the fancy silks spilling out of the top. Mira hadn't even seen them.

The bogey whimpered beside them, his initial questions quickly blossoming into panic with the noise. He tried to slide back, but his arms and legs were too weak to support his weight. Blisters split all along his black-furred flanks. Kraven, looking over his shoulder, shifted his voice to calming tones. Mira punched him in the gut, trying to duck past when his grip released.

"You're going to die, slaving scum!" she shouted. "I hope it hurts!"

The bogey yelped as if he'd been struck, following up with

a warning growl. He tried to lift his swollen head, fat lips curling, but without sight or smell, his head swiveling in uncertainty, there was more of fear to him than anger.

Mira poured on more insults, threatening him with every unkind thing she could muster. The bogey bared his teeth.

Kraven changed tactics. He still had her axe and was, somehow, managing to hold her back. Calling to Drake, he pointed to the bogey before moving his hand in a flat, downward motion.

"It won't work. Whatever he tries, you're going to die," jeered Mira.

The bogey snarled. Kraven pushed her back and urged his dragon again. Drake lowered one large foot onto the slaver's waspish waist.

The bogey screamed.

Snapping back with a strength and speed Mira would have thought impossible, the bogey turned on the dragon, wounds splitting like sausages all the way down his neck and sides. He tried to roll, then pull and push his way free. When that didn't work, he sank his claws deep into the dragon's flesh, jaws snapping blindly at the air. Drake shrieked, squeezing the bogey's narrow waist, but the bogey only dug in more.

Mira stopped fighting, insults dying in her throat. He'd been nearly dead. Should have died from his first attack. And here he was, fighting and, no, not just fighting, nearly winning. Kraven was screaming, gesturing wildly for the combatants to release, but with little effect. Even bleeding to death, blind, the bogey was nearly cutting his way free, would cut his way free.

Mira couldn't move, couldn't speak.

Luckily, Kraven was not so similarly affected.

Dashing forward, Kraven slammed the flat of the axe head hard against the monster's temple. With a final high-pitched yipe, the bogey dropped like a stone. Drake shrilled in victory, bringing forth his other front foot to wrap around the bogey's waist. He started to squeeze.

Kraven intervened, waving his arms for the dragon to stop. Drake ignored him, hissing and sputtering like an angry kettle, but the boy didn't give up, grabbing his dragon's front feet to try to peel back the giant, bird-like toes.

Mira fell back on the earth, shaking harder than a scatter snake's tail. Her body felt numb, her mind unsteady. Even in the worst of the bogey raids, she had not seen such ferocity, hadn't seen the full strength of what they could do. The enormity of her pilgrimage seemed suddenly larger than she ever could have imagined.

But making a wish didn't require a fight. Things would be different at the yochni's cave. Assuming she made it that far. Warnings from her father, her brother, rang through her mind. They had warned her not to go on her quest. Told her it was too dangerous. Risky.

Mira shook her head. She couldn't give up now, not when her failure would end her people. First things first, she decided. She forced herself to her feet.

Kraven had managed to calm Drake. Though the dragon was clearly unhappy, huffing and tossing his head, he was not, it seemed, unhappy enough to resume his revenge, his protestations subsiding further with his master's every gentle word. When the dragon at last gave up the fight, Kraven patted the creature's leg, pressing his forehead against the ever-cool scales. The dragon accepted the gesture only reluctantly, letting out a resentful snort.

Kraven laughed, a weak, unsteady sort of chuckle. Mira's axe lay unattended at his feet. He brought himself up to his full height, his hands shaking from adrenaline, and then, finally, turned to her. His expression lay somewhere between suspicious, angry, and worried. A large purple bruise was already blossoming on his cheek where she had hit him. He pointed to the mark with one gloved hand.

"*Hurts*," he said, reproach clear in his tone.

Mira looked away.

He didn't say anything for a long moment, then more gently asked, "You are okay?"

"No," she said. "Give me my axe."

"*Quoi?*"

She pointed to make herself clear. "My axe."

He scowled, shaking his head.

"It's a bogey, Kraven. You have to kill it. *Tuer.*"

"*Mais—*"

"Kraven, if you don't *tuer* the bogey, bogey *tuer* Kraven. *Tuer* Mira. Is that what you want?"

Her words seemed to strike a nerve, at least at first. Drake was still bleeding, long, deep scratches hashing his skin. Mira pointed them out, and Drake let out a mournful coo. Kraven flinched at the sound. He looked to the bogey, then down at his gloves. The black leather kept his attention for a long time. Then he shook his head.

"I am here to help," he said, and moved off towards his pack.

Their supplies had been scattered along the long, weaving trail Drake had cut on his way to strike her. Digging through his bag, Kraven brought forth his canteen, gauze, and several dark bottles. Though Mira feared he was going to tend the bogey, he went to Drake instead, setting down his supplies before at last removing his gloves. Given his dedication to keeping them on, Mira had assumed they were to cover some kind of deformity or scar, perhaps even a burn, but his hands seemed healthy and clear, only paler and softer for their constant casings.

Tucking the gloves into his back pocket, Kraven set about the task of stitching his dragon's skin. It wasn't easy, dragon skin being of a particularly hearty make, but even so, he worked with quick, even stitches, his demeanor as businesslike as if he were tending some unexpected irritation rather than grievous wounds.

When he was finished, he wrapped as much as he could with gauze before bringing his hands up on either side of his head in an antler-like pose. Mira heard him ask the dragon a question, just catching "Batcha" in the jumble. Though the sea dragon gave both her and the bogey a dirty look, he did as he was asked, limping off into the woods in search of her mount.

Kraven turned to the bogey.

"Don't," she warned as he knelt. He didn't listen, reaching out a hand. "You're going to get a rash."

The boy frowned, but if he understood her, it didn't seem to make any difference. He didn't even put on his gloves. Mira huffed as he started his examination. The slaver's wounds were from skin fang, a particularly potent bush of the rash-giving variety. Her clan had tried using it to keep the bogeys out of their caves on several occasions, though the bogeys had always burned it down. The plant's oils were highly transferrable, the boy's fingers almost certainly headed towards painful swelling and blisters. She'd tried to warn him. Too bad.

Briefly, despite his refusal to wear his gloves, Mira wondered if he was a good enough medic to save the slaver. It was a disconcerting thought, the bogey having already proved his ferocity even while gravely wounded, but she reminded herself the slaver was still unconscious. Even if he survived the rash, she could always kill him later. Kraven would not be able to guard the monster forever.

As the boy got to work addressing the bogey's wounds, Mira set about examining herself. Her shoulder still ached and no doubt her back would have a terrible bruise, but other than that and a few scrapes, she seemed unharmed. She took a moment to dust herself off, then began the process of pulling their various packs and bags back into a single, large pile. With a great deal of promising not to attack, she convinced Kraven to relent and allow her to keep her axe. Then, at last armed and well supplied, she went for the bogey's pack.

Kraven, fingers already turning an angry fuchsia, scowled at her as she dragged it away. Mira didn't care.

The pack was huge, nearly as heavy as she was and just about large enough to fit her inside it. With a little ingenuity and not a small number of pangs in her bad shoulder, however, she managed to tip it over, dumping its contents across the forest floor. She kicked and shoved the various items into a pile, then settled into the nest of their belongings to start sorting.

She found a jangling bag of coins first. That, she tucked into her bag. When she got to his whip, she threw it into the woods, giving Kraven her most innocent look when he shot her a suspicious glare at the sound. Mundane items like rope, food, or tools she placed in their respective piles. A large map case and assorted documents she set aside for later snooping.

Which brought her at last to the most interesting and largest of the bogey's possessions. His satchel. Dyed a beautiful eggy yellow, it had a well-worn handle and a golden latch on the front, leaves and vines stamped onto the surface. Inside, she found a large wooden case, smooth and black as mud with similar, golden shapes even finer and more intricate than the ones on the leather twining across its surface. Two more golden latches shared the top with the handle. She tried to open them, but they were locked, not even a whiff of a key to be found amongst his belongings. She tried smashing one with a rock, but after a second try left two thin scratches across the finish, she set the tool aside.

She couldn't sell it later if it were damaged after all, and bogey belonging or no, the craftsmanship was exquisite. She slipped the case back into the satchel, then propped the satchel against the packs. If the bogey survived, perhaps she would ask him about it before he tasted her axe.

Probably not.

Items sorted, she dug through the bogey's food for a snack, drawing out an early apple. Drake was just returning with Batcha, the mini hart wobblier than she remembered but otherwise unharmed. Kraven, fingers now puffed up to twice their size, scraped his pestle furiously against his mortar. As soon as he noticed his dragon's return, he put in another request.

Drake's reluctance was even greater than the last time, but when the boy's tone turned pleading, the dragon acquiesced, returning several minutes later with teeth and claws overflowing with minty stems and leaves.

As great of an imposition as Kraven's requests might have been, however, it seemed they were worth the dragon's effort. Soon the medic had whipped up a pungent green paste. Spreading the salve up to his own elbows first, he then smeared it over his dragon's feet and legs, soothing the swelling pink lines that pressed up between the creature's scales. When both he and his dragon were tended, Kraven returned to the slaver. An hour later, he let out a victorious cry.

The bogey was awake.

Mira rushed over, axe at the ready. Kraven put out a hand to stop her, shooting her a stern look. She mimed teeth and claws at him, gesturing to the bogey, and, with a look to Drake's bandaged foot, he relented, letting her draw near. She stayed well out of the bogey's range of sight all the same. There was no telling what the slaver would do once he fully regained his senses.

With less chaotic surroundings, the bogey's return to the world of the living was easier than it had been the first time. Moaning like a dying dog, he let out more of the garbled whines they had first heard in the woods. Kraven cooed at him as soon as they started, trying to calm the bogey down. As the whines grew louder, the medic raised his voice to match, never ceasing even when the bogey's body started to seize and shake. He put a hand on the monster's chest. The slaver's face twitched in pain, arm jerking weakly as if to swat the boy away, and a bubble of vomit burst from his mouth. Kraven wiped him down.

Whatever the boy was saying, it seemed to help. With time, the bogey's seizing slowed, his breaths evening out as his long fingers eased out along his sides. He still shivered, but less often. His whines ran themselves down to hisses. Mira's fingers tapped on her axe as the slaver's pained tears ceased their flow.

Kraven stopped talking.

The bogey, breathing deeper than Mira liked, tilted his head in the boy's direction. "*Merci.*"

Mira's fingers twitched. Kraven's jaw went slack. They spoke the same language.

Kraven recovered quickly. Shaking his head clear, he rattled off a response.

The bogey gave the tiniest attempt at a nod, then spoke again. His voice was deep and coarse as stone, half-strangled by his own tongue. He had to stop every few words to gather his breath, but it was enough to communicate, and that, she knew, was enough to get her killed.

The boy and the slaver exchanged introductions from what she could tell and a couple of questions. As difficult as it seemed for the bogey to speak, he seemed eager to talk, and Kraven, idiot that he was, just as eager to engage him. As he answered the bogey's final question, he turned towards her.

Mira could have strangled him.

Too late.

The bogey, with effort, opened a single, bright yellow eye. Crouched in its socket like a jewel in a ring, it searched for Kraven first, then in a larger arc around its head for her. Mira took half a step back. Kraven waved her forward. She shook her head.

The bogey swallowed, gathering breath. Then he spoke. "My name is Atlan. W-who are you?"

Mira's eyes bobbled, jaw dropping open. Half lifting her axe, half responding, her mouth worked with unformed sound, lips twisting in fury. "Like I'd ever tell you," she finally managed. "You're supposed to be dead, you *gojan* monster."

The bogey winced. "Are, are you from the village?" he asked.

"Go die."

"Your people have committed treaso—"

"Good."

The bogey stopped, swollen black ears twitching. "I apologize, if I frightened you. The boy says you are angry. Why?"

"That's rich."

"Please"—Mira almost laughed at that—"I haven't done any harm to you."

"No harm? No *harm?* I ought to kill you right now, you *gojan* slaving monster. No harm," she snarled.

"Slaving?" the bogey asked. "What are you talking about?"

"How dare you. Lying, murdering..."

"I don't under—"

"Lying scum!"

The bogey didn't respond this time, fragile skin cracking on his green-stained forehead as his brow furrowed in thought. Then, with a sharp hiss, the wrinkles eased, his nails digging through the soil. Realization.

Mira felt her muscles tighten all the way up her spine. She folded her arms, but kept a strong grip on her axe, fingers tapping the haft.

"What clan are you from?" he growled.

"Wouldn't you like to know?"

"Are there more of you?" the bogey pressed. "Where are you from?"

"I'd rather die," she said.

The bogey fell silent. His fingers twitched, fattened lips twisting. Then he spoke to Kraven.

The medic's eyes widened in surprise, his gaze going curious as he looked to Mira.

"Stop it. What are you saying? Leave him alone," she shouted, lunging at the bogey.

Kraven dove over the slaver, stretching his arms out to keep her back. Drake let out a warning snort. The bogey kept talking, voice soft but urgent, and Kraven's features pinched with growing suspicion.

She shifted tactics, changing her target from the bogey to Kraven. "Please, whatever he's saying, it's a lie. He's dangerous. Listen. Please." Miming teeth and fangs, she pointed to the bogey. She put on her most innocent, pleading face, trying to convince the medic.

She heard Atlan say *"dangereuse"* and Kraven's focus switched to her axe.

Face going nearly green, she lowered her weapon, cursing her stupidity. She'd been brandishing it as she yelled. Shaking her head, she pointed to the bogey then waved her free hand, signaling for the boy to disregard the slaver's words. She was close enough now for the bogey to see her. She didn't care.

Doubt flickered in Kraven's eyes, his trust in her, small as it was to begin with, nearly snuffing out like a flame in a lantern. Then, slowly, resolution replaced his concern. Turning to the bogey, he shook his head, saying something in his strange language. The bogey followed up, tone urgent, but Kraven only shook his head, repeating back the same phrase.

The bogey fell silent, fingers tapping. Whatever lie he'd come up with, it had failed. At least for now.

Mira let out a sigh of relief. "Thank you," she said, bobbing her head to Kraven.

The boy gave her a final look, expression doubtful, then shooed her off so he could tend his patient.

Round one, it seemed, was over.

When the bogey was finally stabilized and the last of their belongings loaded onto Drake—including, to Mira's dismay, the bogey's whip, Kraven announced that it was time to find water. He made his point clear when he pointed to several of their now empty canteens, but Atlan translated anyway.

"I don't need your help," Mira snarled.

"Kraven says you do," said the slaver, imperious tone even more annoying for the fact he had to gasp for air every other word.

"Kraven is an idiot," Mira snapped back.

"He saved my life."

"Case in point."

Atlan didn't talk to her much after that.

That didn't stop him from talking to Kraven though, or the boy from responding. They spoke in Fransec, the language Atlan said they shared. It was a habit which, given bogeys' natural penchant for deceit, was as irritating as it was dangerous.

"Alright, fine," said Mira after their third exchange. "Enough. What are you saying?"

"I thought you didn't need my help," said Atlan.

"Don't push it," said Mira.

Atlan only smirked. Or as much as his swollen face would allow. Puffed up fatter than a root worm in a snick patch, it looked as though it had been shoved through a beehive. Or rather, like most of his body had been.

Good, thought Mira.

Kraven, perhaps attempting to cut their sniping short, interrupted. "*Comment as-tu été blesse?*"

They walked in a ragged line. Drake went first, with Batcha harnessed like a saddle bag to his side and Atlan in a makeshift sledge hooked onto his tail. Kraven walked beside the slaver, ready to tend his patient if needed. Mira came last. The slaver, still coated in a drying mix of green salve and blood, readjusted himself on the sledge with an uncomfortable groan, and gave his answer.

"He wanted to know, how I was injured," he said. "It was the village I passed through. When they found out who I was, they attacked, running me out of town. More specifically, through a patch of a, rather aggressive variety of poisonous bush with which I was heretofore previously unacquainted."

"Yeah right," said Mira. "And it's called skin fang, moron."

Atlan scowled. "I'm not lying."

"*Pourquoi vous ont-ils attaqué? Qui es-tu?*" asked Kraven.

The bogey gave her a furtive look this time before answering. When he spoke, the boy nearly missed his next step.

"What did you say?" demanded Mira.

"He asked who I am," said Atlan. "Though, I'm not quite sure, I want to tell you."

"Why not?"

"Because it seems to me, you'd be rather eager, to kill the heir to the empire."

Mira nearly lost more than her next step. Kraven, perhaps expecting a reaction, was there to stop her before she could even lift her axe, his longer legs sliding him neatly into place between axe head and prey.

"I'll kill you," she snarled.

"So you keep saying," said Atlan.

She turned to Kraven. "Get out of my way."

He didn't, only shaking his head and scolding her in Fransec. Atlan smiled at the rebuke but, wisely, didn't translate.

Mira wondered if Drake would still take her to the yochni if she murdered the boy and bogey. She was not optimistic enough to risk it.

Despite Kraven's promises that Drake could sense water, it wasn't until late afternoon that the dragon actually found any. A shallow but swift moving stream, it was perhaps ten feet at its broadest, not even wide enough for Drake to span from tip to tail. It came up to no more than Mira's knees, perhaps mid-thigh at its deepest. Sandbars poked up in places like miniature islands.

It was a poor excuse for a river, but, for the exhausted party, it was more than enough. Advising the rest to stay upstream from the bogey, Kraven helped the slaver into the water. Salve and blood and the honey and herbs the bogey had previously tried to use to treat his wounds washed away in winding golden ribbons and spackled clouds of red and green.

Mira shivered in disgust. Kraven simply removed his gloves, preparing to tend his patient. Atlan, catching the motion, asked the boy a question. Kraven nodded, launching them both into quiet conversation.

"What are you talking about?" asked Mira.

"Guard," said Kraven, who by that point had managed to recognize the question.

"What?"

"The Guard," said Atlan, as if everyone—including those

forced to live underground by their slaving overlords—ought to know the phrase. "It's a group, or guild, of sorts. Though their roles vary within a community, their general goal is to maintain peace and do good."

"And you got all that from him taking his gloves off?"

Atlan, still managing to look smug despite wincing with every motion, nodded. "It's one of their distinguishing features, along with their marks, which only full members wear." He gestured to the silver necklace Spider had returned when she and Kraven had escaped. "I suspect, that's why he's here. To earn one. They only take their gloves off to heal. Clean hands, cleaner heart."

The boy nodded at the phrase, perhaps one he recognized in Itsrec.

Mira scowled. "That's a stupid motto, and a very good way to get a rash."

Kraven, idly scratching at one of his blistering palms, only gave her a blank look. Before Atlan could say any more, Mira retreated back to their supplies. Crouching amidst their things like a rat in its nest, she set to work sharpening her axe.

By the time Kraven finished redressing the bogey's wounds, the sun was starting its descent to the horizon, long, slanting fingers of light disappearing one by one in the denser foliage. Their path to water had taken them predominantly east, costing them precious time towards their northern destination. It was not an insurmountable loss given the speed with which Drake could travel, though if he were to keep dragging the dead weight of the slaver around, the benefit would surely be outweighed by the cost. Yet another reason to have the bogey killed, though that was yet another point on which Mira and Kraven's opinions on the slaver diverged.

She was not the only one considering the future, however.

Though the bogey had made little progress towards turning Kraven against her even with the few snatches of conversation he didn't translate, she knew he wouldn't make himself an easy target.

They had decided to make camp for the evening—or rather, Kraven had insisted they do so, and Mira had had little leverage to argue otherwise—which meant that soon they would be assigning watches. It was the best possible time for Mira to strike, and every one of them knew it.

The bogey brought it up first. He'd spent most of a particularly inhospitable dinner staring at her over the fire through swollen lids, head propped up against a nearby tree. Now, he turned to Kraven. "*Elle va me tuer,*" he muttered.

"What did you say?" asked Mira, catching only the final word.

"That you intend to kill me," said Atlan. "Am I wrong?"

"Rat," sneered Mira.

The bogey's lips twisted in distaste. His speech had grown stronger and swifter throughout the day, though it still required work. His expression grew grim. "Mira, there's something you need to know."

"Not from you."

"Don't be contrary," he said. He paused, gathering strength. "Mira, the truth is, you...you're sick."

Mira's spine went rigid, anger spiking up every bone. "What did you just say?"

"You're sick."

Mira's nails bit into her palms, her knuckles going white. So that had been the lie. The audacity. "I am *not* crazy."

"There is a sickness, from the mines. Gas."

"Gas madness is a lie. You slavers made it up," she snapped.

"No, I didn't."

"Yes, you did."

"Then why did you attack?" he asked.

"Because you're a *gojan*, slaving monster."

"I am not a slaver."

"Yes, you—"

"*Arrêtez-vous*," said Kraven. "*Ça suffit*."

The boy was resting his head in his hands, but there was a new snap to his voice. He paused, taking in a deep breath, then raised his head. "*J'ai pris une décision*."

Atlan's swollen brow lifted, and Mira turned reluctantly to the bogey for a translation.

"He's made a decision," said Atlan.

"About what?"

Kraven looked to Atlan, and the bogey gave an equally reluctant nod, continuing to translate as the medic spoke.

"About us. He says he knows you'll kill me if you get the chance, but that he also can't stay up all night to watch you. If he leaves either of us behind, we'll be at risk, but he doesn't want to restrain you either."

"Damn right," said Mira.

"We're all heading in the same direction, so in order to keep us both safe, he's going to perform...." Atlan stopped translating, yellow eyes widening in their puffy sockets.

"What?" said Mira, gaze flicking nervously between them.

"An arbitration," the bogey said, voice falling somewhere between amused and impressed.

Mira shook her head. "No. No, no, no, no, no, no, no. No way. No deals."

"Why not?" asked Atlan. "If he is an arbiter, the magic would serve as contract. Both of us could be assured safety and neither of us would be harmed."

"*No*," said Mira.

"Why?"

"Because I'm going to kill you as soon as I get the chance."

"Don't be ridiculous. That's absurd. And pointless."

"Not to me."

"*Arrêtez,*" said Kraven. Gesturing for Atlan to translate, he started rattling off what Mira quickly realized was an ultimatum. She turned to the boy, hoping the bogey was lying, but he only swept his hands out towards the woods, backing up the slaver's words.

She could join the contract, or she could leave. Those were her only two options.

Mira snarled, face contorting with rage. "He's a *slaver*, a murderer. We should have kill—"

"*Non,*" said Kraven. "*Arrête. Choisis. Maintenant.*"

Mira trembled with anger, her cheeks flaring red and hot. Her features twitched, arguments rising and dying on her tongue. She glared at the bogey. She looked to Kraven.

"He's going to kill us," she said.

The boy didn't move. Her eyes slid to Drake. Without him...a mount....

"Fine. Blackmailing, *gojan* tyrant..." she muttered.

Atlan passed the translation on, and Kraven gave a relieved nod. Half an hour later, they had the bones of a contract.

The main condition was a mutual one against harm. They wouldn't have to protect each other—a term she had insisted on—but they wouldn't be able to hurt each other directly either. In exchange for not killing each other, Mira would get access to Drake and continued care for Batcha, Atlan would get care and transport for himself, and Kraven would get lessons from Atlan in Itsrec. The last thing left to decide was duration.

Mira's idea of through the morning was immediately shot down. Her next suggestion of a single day was just as unpopular. Atlan suggested going by his health, but that was too difficult to gauge. Kraven shook his head, cutting them both off before they could make any further recommendations.

"J'ai déjà décidé. La grotte de le yochni," he said. *"La Chamber des Douleurs."*

It was enough to make Atlan sit up, even in his poor condition.

"What? What did he say?" asked Mira.

"The yochni's cave," said Atlan. "All the way to the Chamber of Sorrows."

Mira's eyes went wide as teacups. The Chamber of Sorrows was the final room before the yochni itself, practically its doorstep. "You sneaky little liar," she snarled, pointing to the boy. "You are a champion."

"And you're not?" said Atlan.

"I never said that."

"Please. There is no other reason a lone dwarf would leave her clan. Even a madling."

"I'm not crazy. And what about you? I suppose you're going?"

The monster smiled, teeth shining. "Who better to send than the empire's heir?"

Kraven was already there to stop her when she started to lunge. Atlan was both heir and champion. If she could kill him now, it could save her people then and there. Bogeys only sent one champion, after all. Even if she didn't make it the rest of the way, even if Drake or Kraven killed her for destroying the bogey, making sure that somebody—*anybody*—besides the bogeys took the next age would be worth it, could be enough to set her people free.

When Kraven finally forced her back, Atlan was no longer smiling. An expression she couldn't quite read creased his swollen features. Kraven looked ready to shove her into the fire. She could have done the same in return. Stinking, lying noble. He'd been a champion all along. He'd probably been hoping to trick her, to get her help to reach the yochni before having his dragon eat her.

Kraven stared at her for a long moment, clearly frustrated, then took a deep breath. Voice calm, he said something to Atlan.

The bogey considered, then passed it on. "He says he's not a champion. It's to earn his mark," he said, voice quiet. "He had a friend, a mentor in their ranks. She died. He says he hopes, by helping others, to understand her better."

"A likely story," said Mira.

Kraven, perhaps able to catch her meaning by tone, only glared. Atlan continued as if he hadn't seen.

"Maybe, though he's got little reason to lie and no reason to protect either of us or bother when he's got a dragon on hand. I've no doubt even you've caught on to its value, both as defender and for speed." Atlan gestured to his torso, still crisscrossed with scratches from his first encounter with the dragon. "If he truly is a champion, taking us along would only slow him down, put him in further danger when we reach the yochni. If he's willing to give me a ride, if all I have to do is give him some lessons in Itsrec to get it, well, I'm neither too crazy nor proud to refuse it."

"I am *not* crazy," growled Mira.

"*Arrêtez*," said Kraven. "*Avons-nous un accord ou non?*"

Atlan translated in a quiet voice, a final offer to agree or leave. It didn't take the bogey long to answer in the affirmative for himself. Kraven nodded his assent as well.

They turned to Mira. Her teeth ground so hard her jaw ached, but she knew, loathe as she was to admit it, that the bogey was right. Given access to a dragon, the slaver would be nearly unstoppable, and with Kraven likely too stupid to stop the heir once they reached the yochni's cave...if she wanted to free her people, she didn't have a choice.

"Fine," she said. She glared at Atlan. "But you're dead when we reach that cave."

CHAPTER
SEVEN

Kraven began prep work for the arbitration immediately.

So far as Atlan could tell, it did not start well.

In hindsight, that wasn't terribly surprising. Arbiters were almost exclusively Coastals, having retreated to the western coast after their fall in the seventeenth age. As a result, with their once absolute power now restricted solely to willing participants and most of them unwilling to enter contracts themselves, the practice was mostly limited to lesser legal or business agreements, with a select few usually taking on the rather grueling job on behalf of the larger community. Compounded with the noble class' current obsession with normalcy, Atlan doubted the boy had gotten much training in his art, if any, the look of consternation on the medic's face serving as almost absolute confirmation.

Eyes closed, fists trembling, if the boy was attempting the arbitration or simply afraid to try, it was hard to tell. Atlan started to ask what was wrong, but the boy shushed him. Had they been in court, the reproach would have been unthinkable. Atlan decided to let it pass.

Mira glared at him over the fire. She was another mystery, though not nearly so intriguing as the arbitration about to take place. Atlan would consider her further later.

For a moment, nothing else happened, the only sound the muted pops of their fire and the whispered song of the river. Kraven's jaw tightened, his entire body starting to shake.

Then, fragile at first, flickering like a candle, pale blue light began to glow through the boy's eyelids. Electric energy filled the air, and Atlan's patched fur stood on end. Something within him, something ancient and canine, jumped to attention.

Kraven spoke, saying Atlan's name, and the high prince felt a thin thread of power latch onto his chest, squeezing his heart like a rope. His chest jerked on instinct, almost as if to break free, but the feeling didn't leave. Kraven said Mira's name next, and the dwarf rolled her shoulders, no doubt experiencing a similar sensation. Crazy though she was, it seemed even she was not immune to the strange phenomenon.

Kraven began laying out their terms. As he did, loopholes they hadn't even considered sealed themselves off. At first, Atlan translated, but it soon became clear Mira could understand without his assistance, the dwarf frowning or nodding at various stipulations before he had a chance to provide their meaning. Atlan stopped speaking. Heat radiated off the boy, frazzling the cool air around them.

Ten minutes later, he opened his glowing blue eyes and extended the invitation to accept the contract to both his companions.

Atlan, teeth buzzing, went first. Giving his titles in Fransec, he then repeated them in Itsrec for Mira. "I, Atlan Qierce, High Prince and Champion of the bogey empire, accept."

Kraven turned to Mira, who ground her teeth before giving her begrudging response. "I, Mira, accept your terms."

Atlan noted she didn't list a last name or title. Perhaps she didn't have any.

Kraven Monteyeaux, arbiter, physician in training, apprentice Guardsman, and second son of the noble house of Monteyeaux, gave his own name and titles, sealing their contract with a final verbal declaration. The air released like the snap of a bow, and the invisible rope in Atlan's chest soaked through his flesh and was gone.

Kraven's skin went pale as doves, the boy swooning back as a thin sheen of sweat pooled along his forehead. The heat left him too, and instantly Drake was at his side, nestling the boy in his front legs like a mother cat with a kitten.

"First watch," said Mira, and she disappeared into the woods.

Atlan said nothing. He leaned his head forward, running a hand over his chest where the rope-like sensation had been. There was no physical mark or scar, even the memory of the feeling fading. Shifting his fingers down a few inches, he found the gap just under his ribs. Known colloquially as sweet spots, the gaps had garnered their name for being one of the few physical vulnerabilities his species had. He still remembered when his cousin Crucius had punched him there as a cub. The pain had been dizzying, even Crucius' small hand bruising Atlan's organs as easy as rotting fruit. Atlan, painted in vomit and gasping, had been sent to bed for two days to rest. Crucius' hide had been sore for a week.

A single well-aimed arrow or knife to the sweet spot could be enough to kill a full-grown bogey. No doubt when Mira came for him, that was where she would strike.

Letting out a discomfited sigh, the bark of the tree like razors against his delicate skin, Atlan did his best to make himself comfortable. In his current state, there was little he could do to defend against her if the contract failed. He would just have to trust the quality of the boy's work.

He could neither smell nor see Mira, though he knew she had to be close. With his nose still clogged by his own deflating flesh, the mint from the salve, the smoke from the fire, and a small hint of the wet-leaf smell of Drake took up most of what he could sense. He wondered if this was what non-bogeys experienced all the time. To him it felt like being blind.

Atlan tried to rest. Kraven was already asleep or unconscious, Drake settling in to follow suit. Batcha had dozed off while they'd been talking. Soon, he would be alone.

He waited, Drake's breath steadying out at last, and when a twig snapped near the trees, he was not disappointed.

Mira.

She stepped into the light, and the long, bearded edge of her axe shone orange as it arced back behind her hand. The opposite blade, nearer the ground, lacked the long edge, but was also thicker, nearly a maul. Based on her grip, that was the side she would use to hit.

Atlan's fingers moved to his stomach. A blow with a weapon like that wouldn't just cut. It would split his ribs in half.

Catching the motion, Mira smiled. "What's the matter, slaver? You scared?"

Atlan scowled. "I already told you, I'm not a slaver. Bogeys would never—"

"Don't lie to me," she said, drawing closer. "The others are already sleeping. There's no need to pretend."

"I'm not pretending anything. You're sick. You need—"

"Don't tell me what I need," she snapped.

"You're going to hur—" he started, but she was already swinging her axe.

It was like trying to crack stone with a fist.

Halfway through her swing, her muscles seized, her arms crumpling back towards her chest as her axe fell from her hand. It hit the sand a handsbreadth away, not even clipping Atlan's legs. She dropped to her knees. Fingers clenched, she stifled a cry of pain through gritted teeth, tears sparkling in her eyes.

"*Gojan* bogey scum. You knew that was going to happen," she snarled, biting back further and louder curses lest she wake Kraven.

"You're the one who tried to break the agreement. I tried to warn you, but you wouldn't listen."

"Rotten, slaving..."

"I'm *not* a slaver."

Mira looked up from her clenched arms, hugging them both to her chest. "Oh, yeah? I found your whip."

"You went through my things?"

"That a problem?"

Atlan's nostrils pinched in frustration, Mira meeting him scowl for scowl. "Putting aside the fact that's a breach of privacy, to say nothing of general courtesy, Qiersan whips have been the chosen weapon of my family for centuries. It has nothing to do with slavery, and I assure you, it never has."

Mira scoffed. "Sure. Your whole stinking breed uses whips as weapons, and it never occurred to you to use them on people."

"I never said I wouldn't use it," said Atlan, eyes flashing. "But not to own another person."

"Yeah, just make them work in your mines, as if that's any different."

"We don't force you to do anything."

"Right. Stay underground and work or go outside and be slaughtered. Some choice," she spat.

"That's ridiculous. You need help."

"I'm not crazy," she almost shouted.

Drake stirred, almost waking.

She glared at Atlan and he kept his silence. She continued, softer. "That's a lie you all made up so no one would help us, and we both know it."

"You're being ridiculous."

"Oh yeah? Then find me one record of a dwarf going crazy before you showed up, one case of gas madness. We mined for centuries before you shoved us all underground, and not one of us ever got sick. It's a lie."

Atlan opened his mouth, then closed it, his mind paging through veritable volumes of history for any knowledge he held of dwarves. He knew they had been under the reign of the bogeys for hundreds of years, that they had moved almost entirely under the earth in that same span of time, but the idea that it had been against their will had never occurred to him.

He shook his head. Surely if it were true, his father would have told him—or his uncle, the king. "Impossible," he said. "Madling conspiracies."

Mira glared at him. "I'm *not* crazy."

"Say what you want," he said. "You're insane." Rolling onto his side, wincing as the dirt scraped his fragile skin, Atlan closed his eyes. She tried to speak again but he only covered his ears. Despite the muffled effect, he still heard her call him a coward. Mind buzzing, he willed himself to sleep.

The following morning, Atlan woke gray and weary, his skin stiff and fragile. Mira and Kraven were already up and packing, stacking supplies on the sea dragon and working on his sledge. In the light of a new day, the events of the night before felt distant, like he was thinking back on a different version of himself disconnected from who he now was. Certainly, his more logical, current self would never have agreed to such outlandish terms, least of all in partnership with someone so clearly insane.

With the two of them packing their collective supplies and no axe as of yet embedded in his chest, however, he could hardly deny the truth of what had happened, or what they had all agreed to. The deal was already set. He would just have to make the most of it.

When Mira heard him moving, she looked up just long enough to glare before turning aside with a huff. Kraven sidled over carrying a wide, flat stone with wet bread and berries. Finely cubed pieces of fish formed a crescent on the side, already picked free of bones. He asked Atlan if he needed help eating.

Atlan shook his head, clearing his throat. *"Non, c'est bien,"* he managed. "I'm fine."

Dragging himself up against the trunk of his tree to balance the stone on his knee, he took greater stock of his current condition. Though he was still stiff and sore, his skin prone to cracking under his patched fur, the rash had already done its worst. His blisters, once hot and oozing, had already scabbed over, and the swelling, though not gone, had lessened. His fever had faded to a simple heat, and he could smell and hear better as well, if still far from his usual level.

Despite Kraven's age—perhaps fifteen or sixteen at most, he was good at his work. He turned to go, but Atlan stopped him. The medic had mentioned a mentor previously, and the high prince was curious to find out more.

He said as much to Kraven. *"Parlez-moi de ton mentor."*

A look of grief crossed the boy's face, but it was an old wound, and he was quick to recover.

"What are you talking about?" demanded Mira.

"Nothing that concerns *you*," said Atlan, but Kraven raised a hand, shaking his head.

"C'est bien," he said.

Atlan, reluctantly, nodded, translating as the boy spoke. Apparently, the mentor in question had been a girl, Ines, some three or four years older than Kraven. She'd encouraged him to join the Guard with her, but he had refused. Then, while she was away, she had been killed, murdered by the very bandits she had stopped to aid.

The story seemed to strike a chord even with Mira, her normally sour expression gaining a mournful, almost sympathetic tint. Atlan wondered that she could understand such a thing at all in her current condition. The boy hurried on, perhaps eager to finish now that the painful subject had been broached. After Ines' death, he had been uncertain of what to do and how to recover. Then, when he realized the end of the age was coming, he had decided to join the Guard himself, to help the champions in an effort to not only obtain a mark of his own, but also understand Ines better. How she had lived and why she had chosen to help her eventual killers.

Atlan asked what had become of the bandits, then translated the boy's reply. "He says they were caught early, killed for their crimes. He has her mark at home, though it doesn't help."

The boy's expression was somber, but then a tiny, wistful smile graced his lips. His fingers twined in the silver chain when he spoke again.

"What did he say?" asked Mira.

"That he thinks she'd be proud of our deal."

Mira only scoffed. "A poor choice of a mentor, indeed." She turned back to her work assembling their things.

Atlan decided it was better not to translate her remark.

Remembering that she had gone through his things as she tossed another pack into their ready pile, Atlan snared Kraven's attention again, asking the young noble if he would bring him his pack. He was encouraged by the deep trench the bag cut through the sand and asked Kraven to dump out the contents before he left. Then, Atlan began an inventory.

The only items missing were his money and some of his

food, Kraven having rescued his whip from Mira's scheme to toss it at their first camp. Not terrible losses, all things considered, and ones that he felt he could lose. His father's satchel, so far as he could tell, was unharmed.

The last thing to check then, was the satchel's contents. Atlan rinsed his hands off with his canteen and dried them on a scrap of clean gauze. He spread a clean shirt over his lap, then had Kraven help him tip the dark brown box out onto the shirt. Two small scratches etched off from the wood beside the left latch, evidence of Mira's tampering no doubt, but otherwise the case seemed unharmed. It didn't look as though she had gotten inside.

Nor, it seemed, had Kraven, both human and dwarf edging closer as Atlan ran his bandaged hands over the case's top.

Giving Mira a warning look not to get too close, Atlan sank the claws of his thumb and pointer fingers into the small holes on the opposite sides of each latch, pushing in until he heard a click. He opened the box.

Inside, on its bed of thick purple velvet, was his harp.

Kraven shot Atlan a surprised look, even Mira sucking in a breath.

Atlan, careful of the weight in his weakened state, pulled the instrument out of its case. The main body consisted of a large trapezoidal box roughly the height and width of his ribcage with thirteen strings spread over the face. A fine leather strap connected two opposing corners, the sheep skin long since sculpted to the shape of his shoulder from playing. Rounded, leather-lined hinges placed on the top and bottom of the instrument allowed the face and back to bend, creating the half-tones for which the harp was known. A large sound hole graced the middle, allowing air into the body. Fine, olive-green leaves traced the hole and the outer rim of the face, the rest of the body plain but for the natural grain of the yew.

"It's called a chest harp," he said, checking the tuning pegs and the pins that kept the hinges secure. Everything was in its right place. He let out a relieved breath. "They were designed by the elves. They're specifically catered to our anatomy. Not even their makers can play them, only tutor and write the songs."

Kraven asked him if he played.

"One of the best," said Atlan. He flexed his fingers, but the skin was still too tight, fragile. He frowned. "At least, normally. My fingers are too damaged now. Stiff."

He repeated the phrase in Fransec, and Kraven nodded, looking disappointed.

So was Atlan.

Satisfied that the instrument hadn't been damaged, he made a few final adjustments to the tuning pegs before wiping the face clean and putting it back in its case. When the latches clicked, he looked up to find Mira staring at the box, face slack with disbelief. Surprise seemed to have replaced her anger, but when he lifted a brow by way of question, her features snapped back to their usual hatred. Atlan sighed.

They were ready to go within the hour, Drake loaded up with supplies and Atlan tucked back into the sledge. Kraven had rubbed the entire contraption down with the same minty salve from the day before to be safe, and the cool damp herbs sapped the heat from Atlan's skin like water pouring through a sieve. The ride itself was not comfortable, stones and twigs catching at his ankles with what felt like every step Drake took. Still, it was better than walking. And, despite its general discomforts and the pain and itchiness which came with recovery, the day was not an entire loss.

Beginning his lessons in Itsrec with the boy, Atlan was

pleased to see his pupil make rapid progress. He learned more about the boy's past as well, where he was from and how he, Mira, and Drake had come to travel together. Per the boy's titles from the night before, he was a second son, doomed to split his parents' belongings and land with his brother if they both lived long enough to inherit it. From the boy's tone, his parents had been none too sad to see him go on his journey, perhaps even hoping he wouldn't return. He had had the misfortune of bumping into bounty hunters not long after he'd left on his journey. When he had refused their offer to buy the dragon, they had turned to violence, leading him into a subsequent chase. A sadly common story—a fact Atlan hoped to change as future king, though he had to admit the boy's dragon and arbitration certainly added some unique twists, to say nothing of his chance encounter with their resident dwarf.

Mira stayed quiet throughout their conversations, all but ignoring Atlan unless absolutely necessary. When she did speak to him, it was no less cold or insulting than before, though he had to admit he preferred her silence to her previous fountain of venom.

She was nothing less than a mystery to Atlan. Gas madness, as everyone knew, was a sickness of the mind, brought on by continued exposure to the gases found in the tunnels dwarves mined. Known to cause anything from hallucinations to paranoia and confusion, at its worst it could even cause outright madness, outbursts of violence never too far behind. Given the frequency with which Mira threatened to kill him, Atlan was certain she had a more serious case. On the other hand, it was clear her vitriol had a specific target— him—and there was a level of control to it that belied any kind of full insanity. Slanderous claims aside, in fact, she seemed to have great possession of her faculties. The packs she'd helped to tie on to their dragon remained secure, the knots sure and tidy; her care of her mount was studious and tender; and even her general appearance, though dirty and scraped up from her time on the road, seemed of one well in mind, her face often resentful or angry, but never raving. She was keen, bright, and ordered in mind, far from the delirious creature he had long been told to expect in such situations.

Perhaps the effects of the gases were wearing off. Though he'd never heard of a successful rehabilitative case before, perhaps she was starting to heal.

She caught him watching her and sneered.

Maybe not.

Whether or not Mira was on the mend, however, it seemed that he was. Bolstered by the mint and extra meals, Atlan found his health taking several rapid leaps forward. By the first break, he could stand without shaking, by the second, take short walks. In another day, perhaps two, he might even travel without the need for the sledge at all.

He attempted to tell Mira as much on their third break, hoping to both engage and appease her with greater speed, but she wasn't interested.

"Go die," was all she said.

Atlan frowned. If she truly believed her delusions, he supposed he couldn't blame her. Then again, just because she thought she was right didn't mean that she was, and if they were going to be spending their foreseeable future together, they needed to talk.

The stream they'd found flowed in a generally north to south direction. Eager to keep ready access to water, they had followed it for much of the day. Atlan waited until Kraven went down to the river's edge to prepare the fish Drake had caught for lunch, then took his opportunity. "I'd like to speak to you," he said, calling to Mira from the sledge. Kraven glanced over from his place on the bank, but Atlan soothed him.

Mira glared, stoking the fire. "About what?" she asked.

"About what you said yesterday, before your watch."

Mira kept her voice level, resentment buried underneath like a knife under skin. "What do you care?"

Atlan tried to stay mindful of his current task. He pushed forward. "Well, I wanted to offer my assistance. As future king, if there is any truth to your story, if my people are treating you wrongly, it is my duty to stop it."

Mira's eyes darkened. "Arrogant, *gojan*...I don't *need* your help."

"I'm not asking."

"Well, I'm telling. I've got a solution all my own and it doesn't require anything from the likes of you."

"You can't rest your hopes on the yochni, Mira. The next age must go to the bogeys."

"Oh really? And what if I kill you first? What if I wish your entire *race* off the planet?"

Atlan's eyes narrowed, his breath sharp. So that was her wish. "You wouldn't."

"Won't make any difference to you once I get my axe in your chest," she said.

Atlan's hands tightened, claws raking furrows through the sand.

"What's the matter, no whip?" she sneered.

Atlan growled, but before he could answer, a sound came from the woods on the opposite side of the stream. Atlan's head snapped towards the noise, his still-clearing nose and ears quivering. It sounded like thunder, the snapping of foliage, but whatever it was, it was too far for Mira and Kraven to hear.

"What is—" Mira started, but Atlan shushed her.

His eyes went thin as slits, his nose locking in on what was causing the noise. Horses, men, no...something between. He grabbed a tree trunk, starting to stand.

"What are you—" Mira began, but he cut her off again.

Kraven looked up from his work, blood and scales shining on his gloves.

"Kraven, come here," Atlan ordered. "Bring Drake. Hurry."

He looked down to Mira, who must have noticed the fear on his face. Her green eyes were wide, no longer hot.

"What is it?"

"Centaurs are coming."

EIGHT

Mira Goldfist turned to run.

A warning thrum in her chest stopped her before she passed the first tree. She cursed. Of course. She'd promised to travel with the others. Leaving Atlan and Kraven behind now would count as breaching their contract.

She paused, considering hiding, but there was no guarantee the centaurs wouldn't find her.

No, she'd have to play by the numbers. She turned back to join the others. Atlan was already on his feet, Kraven serving as crutch. Drake stood beside them, letting out a nervous whistle.

Kraven asked the slaver a question in Fransec. Atlan gave the boy a sharp look. "You do nothing. *Rien.*" The high prince's eyes snapped to Mira, his voice firmer than she had yet heard. "That goes for you, too. Do not interfere."

"Yeah?" she said, fear making her voice tight. "And what are you going to do? Collapse?"

"No," he said, nostrils pinching in irritation. "I'm going to try diplomacy. I speak Centauri."

"Pucky," said Mira.

"It's not a lie," Atlan snapped. His sloping face soured.

"But it has been a long time. Unfortunately, I don't think we have any other choice. Unless you've got a better idea?"

Mira did have a better idea, but she didn't think either the slaver or Kraven would go for cancelling the contract and leaving Atlan behind, nor for her to waste the time in asking. Which meant, for the time being, Atlan's plan was the best option.

The slaver seemed to know it, too. "Kraven? My shirt. *Chemise,*" he said, not waiting for Mira's response.

Kraven, though he looked a little reproachful for the order, scuttled to grab the shirt. Atlan straightened his pant legs and tightened the red sash that served as his belt, brushing off dirt and dried salve before rising to his full height, just over seven feet. His shirt was black, hundreds of tiny red daggers coating the silken surface in neat, inter-locking rows. Kraven unbuttoned the line of round red buttons down the front, and the prince bent for the boy to throw it over his shoulders.

"*Garde un œil sur Mira. Garde-la en sécurité,*" he said, before turning to Mira.

"What did you tell him?" she demanded, resisting the urge to take a step back as he crouched before her. Memories of raids flashed through her mind at his closeness, but Atlan pushed through them, expression strict.

"To keep an eye on you," he said.

"I don't need his help."

"I didn't say that you did. Now, the centaurs are a proud people, and very strict about trespassing. If we're on their land, I don't know that I'll be able to do anything, but I want to try. In order to do that, I'm going to need your help. Keep your axe down and don't make any sudden movements. Don't do anything unless I tell you, and whatever you do, don't interrupt."

"I'm not your slave."

"Then consider it a personal favor."

Mira bit back a sharp remark, then said, "How do I know you're not going to sell us out?"

"You don't," said Atlan. "But if you don't behave, I doubt either of us will live long enough to find out. I told Kraven to grab Batcha. Keep both of them safe."

Mira scowled, furious he was ordering her around, and even more angry that he was right. There was no time to come up with a better plan, no way forward but to trust. Atlan stood before she could answer, and Kraven returned with a wrangled Batcha a second later.

"I, I don't work for you," she said.

"No, you do not," said Atlan, not even looking back. Stepping in front of his fellow travelers, the bogey turned to face the stream. Kraven drew his knife, placing Batcha between himself and Drake. Mira wondered if he could use his magic, but it sounded like there were too many, the boy trembling too much to try.

She could distinguish individual sets of hooves now, hear the *thwip* of leaves on skin.

"*Ne fais rien,*" said Atlan. "Whatever happens, leave this to me."

Seconds later, the centaurs burst out of the woods, nearly a dozen at once, brandishing their clubs and bows.

The first thing they did was shoot the slaver in the chest.

He fell back with a cry, nearly crushing Mira. He tried to get up as another arrow pinged off his ribs, but the centaurs' leader, a red-coated stallion, followed up with a second attack. Wielding a polished brown branch as thick as Mira's neck, he hit the bogey across the face, sending the slaver reeling.

The next centaur, a dun mare, went for Mira. Striking her with her club, she knocked Mira back far and hard enough to hit a tree. Pain seared through Mira's spine.

Breath gone in a single blow, she bounced off into the bushes.

A staff cracked Kraven on the jaw. Batcha bolted into the woods.

They were going to die before they got started.

Why hadn't Kraven just cancelled their deal?

A pale yellow mare galloped towards Mira, bow already drawn.

A familiar roar tore through the forest. Before the mare could fire, a bright blue tail as thick as the centaur's human waist slammed her out of view. The tail's pronged tip whipped away, and Mira heard another roar, another scream from another victim.

Chaos broke out around the river.

Drake had entered the fight.

Mira slid behind the tree she had hit. Bruises were already blossoming on her ribs, air just leaking back into her lungs. She had to think, come up with a plan. She needed her axe, but it was still on the riverbank somewhere, dropped when she'd been hit.

A sharp yelp split the air, cutting across the whinnies and roars. Leaning forward to peek through the leaves, Mira saw that it was Atlan. The lead stallion was standing over his body, club raised. The bogey was trying to crawl away, not far from where he'd first landed. The arrows, tips only red to the width of a few fingers for his thick protective ribs, had been knocked from his chest when he'd flipped to his stomach. Even with her inclinations, Mira flinched as the branch came down again.

That's when she noticed her axe, not more than a few feet from Atlan on the sand. Two nearly identical centaurs had stayed with their leader. One of them stood over her weapon. There was no way she'd be able to grab it now, no way to sneak past or make an attack. She'd have to wait it out, hope

Drake was strong enough to survive the attack and take her to the yochni when the others were dead. Taking in a deep breath, Mira drew back, crouching down in the bushes.

She felt the twig beneath her palm half a second too late. Then she heard the snap.

So did the centaur pair. Instantly, their focus switched to her. Turning, they raised their weapons. Atlan's gaze followed their path. His eyes met hers, then flashed back to the centaurs approaching her. Determination hardened the slaver's face.

Rolling onto his back with a snarl, the high prince grabbed one of the lead stallion's front legs, nearly yanking it out from underneath him. Grabbing the stallion's branch with his other hand, the bogey ripped it out of the centaur's grip, striking up with both of his feet at the same time. Blood spurted from the stallion's chest as Atlan's claws raked through the skin, but the centaur only reared, slamming his front hooves into the slaver's chest.

Mira heard a loud pop. Atlan howled in pain. The twin centaurs turned back.

Whatever threat Mira had posed, it couldn't compare with a bogey. The twins pinned the bogey's arms, and the lead centaur snatched his branch back. Raising it high, he slammed it into the slaver's face. When he drew it back for another blow, Atlan didn't move. Kraven was under similar duress, the muscled arms of his own centaur drawn tight around his neck.

They were going to be killed, and Mira would be next.

Bird song swept through the woods.

Angry squawks and trills, it came like a wave, rolling in on a crest of half a dozen small yellow birds. A new centaur, a black-coated mare with dark skin and thick black hair leapt from the woods, splashing into the river.

The lead stallion, still poised to strike, froze as if pinned in place. The other centaurs ceased as well. Drake roared, but even those facing him stopped fighting, staving off his attacks by distance rather than attack.

The lead stallion stared at the new mare. The birds didn't stop tweeting, hadn't stopped since their arrival. More came, layering notes sweet and pleading over the harsher calls of the first arrivals. The mare made several huffing noises, which the stallion returned with angrier tones. He pointed to the various members of Mira's group before gesturing to his still bleeding torso. The cuts snaked down the equine parts of his chest and down onto his belly. Blood still dripped in places, and slow-moving rivulets slicked down his legs.

The new mare whickered softly at him, her blue eyes meeting his, which were of a brown so dark as to be nearly black. They were naturally narrow, cut off by the dark hair that fell across his face. He frowned at the mare, clearly still angry, then, letting out a final snort, whipped out his arm, calling off the attack. The birds, at last, stopped chirping.

The stallion stalked off, hooves schlopping through the water, to wait on the opposite bank. The mare gestured for the others to tend his wounds, then stepped forward, reaching down for Atlan. Grabbing him by the collar, she pulled him up towards her chest. His head lolled back, body limp. She slapped lightly at his cheek, and when that didn't work, slapped him harder. She pulled hard on his ear, and at last, he coughed, coming alive with a pitiful groan.

She snorted at him, following up with a whicker and a few harsh huffs. Atlan brought his hand up as if to grab her arm, but she slapped it aside, snorting again.

Head still wobbling on a weak neck, Atlan answered with a soft whicker. He offered a few gentle snufflings so clogged by the blood flowing out of his nose Mira thought he would choke, then a final, coughing whuffle.

The lead mare frowned.

Shoving him back onto the sand, she wiped her bloody hand off on her thigh with a huff. Mira tried to slink back behind the trees while the mare was distracted, but it was no use. Firing off new orders, the lead mare sent a chestnut bay to grab Mira as soon as she rustled the leaves. Another dragged Kraven forward, and their captors threw them down into the shallows next to the injured bogey, who, with effort, managed to sit up beside them. Drake snarled in protest at their treatment, centaur weapons holding him back, but the mare ignored him.

Instead, she spoke to Atlan. Huffing and snorting, she seemed to give him quite the earful, which, for the most part, he took with staid humility, head bowed. At one point, his head jerked up in surprise and he interrupted her with startled whickers, but she was quick to silence him again, raising her hand as if to deliver another slap.

When the full fury of her berating was finished, however, she gave him the chance to speak. After a brief interchange, the bogey spoke to Kraven. The young medic looked none too pleased with the result, but eventually got to his feet, shuffling off with one of the centaurs towards Drake. The lead mare gave Atlan a nod. Atlan bowed his head a final time, letting out a deferential whicker.

The lead mare called the red stallion over then, resting a hand against his cheek when he arrived. They shared a quiet exchange, and she wheeled off, leaving the stallion to stand guard while she and several others tended to the rest of the herd. Mira waited just long enough for the mare to trot out of immediate earshot before speaking.

"What was that?" she asked Atlan. "What did you say?"

The prince smiled at her through bloody teeth, giving her a strangled half-chuckle.

"Told you I spoke Centauri."

"Shut up."

The prince eased himself down to lie on his back, wincing as he explored his damaged ribs.

"We're going to their camp. It seems that for the damage Drake and our medic caused their woods in saving my life, we're to be handed over for some kind of trial. First I've heard of one of those—didn't think they were even capable of anything so advanced anymore, honestly—but then again, it's not like anyone's been on speaking terms with them for the last few hundred years." He prodded what was almost certainly a broken nose, pulling his fingers back red before dropping his head back down to the sand. "Though, if those birds were any indication, they might not be working alone."

"Did you recognize them?" she asked. "Know where they're from?"

He sucked some blood back into his nose, wincing and coughing. When he spoke again, his fatigue was evident.

"I don't know. I tried to ask, but she—Hrrghin, she's called—told me not to interrupt." He took in as deep of a breath as he could manage, eyes closed. "Like as not, we'll be killed regardless, but I'll admit I'm curious either way."

Mira didn't bother to ask him anything else, the prince well on his way towards unconsciousness. The centaurs returned not long after. Kraven had calmed his dragon. With Batcha retrieved and the wounded centaurs tended, the herd was ready to leave.

They traveled in a northeastern direction. The twins carried Atlan between their shoulders, the prince no longer strong enough to carry himself, but the others were forced to walk, centauri spears and bows keeping them moving if they developed any inclinations towards taking a break.

As they walked, trees and dried skins painted with a red, slashing script began to dot the landscape. Though the marks were in a language Mira couldn't read, presumably Centauri, with the gory diagrams of skewered trespassers that graced many of them, it did not take Atlan's fluency to gather their meaning. It was a miracle their group was alive.

Still, when they weren't trying to kill her, Mira had to admit the centaurs were actually quite beautiful. Lean and well-built, their warriors' bodies gleamed in the sun. They came in a wide variety of skin tones and equine coats, each one stunning in their own right. Hrrghin, the lead mare, was the most handsome of them all, a nights' sky of dark brown freckles speckling her hazelnut skin. Another centaur had large spots on his coat, broad pale patches dappling his skin as well. The ring they made around their prisoners adapted its shape to their landscape and speed with an almost thoughtless ease, and they carried their weapons with a care that only came with use. Working with the fluidity of a real herd, their capacity for teamwork was astonishing. Despite their strange anatomy, they had a naturalness to them that made them seem as much a part of the woods as any deer or stream.

Perhaps there was more to the centaurs than she'd initially thought. Maybe she had been wrong about them.

Which was precisely when Atlan's face flashed into her mind, the look in his eyes before he had attacked the stallion. Mira scowled, closing her eyes. That was not a face she wanted to see or thoughts she wanted to think. But she could not escape the fact that he had saved her life. Without his interference, she would have died. She shook her head again, harder this time. Those who bargained with bogeys lost their heads. Even if he had saved her, there had to be another reason for it, some ulterior motive.

She made herself angry he hadn't died.

Forcing her focus outward, Mira studied their surroundings. She counted miles, hoofprints, anything to keep the treacherous thoughts from returning. Thankfully, the forest was rife with distractions, from wildlife to the snares and traps that hid under the undergrowth and even what appeared to be gardens and a small orchard.

The strangest of all however, was not the gardens, or the snares, or the birds.

It was the trees.

She saw her first one some ten minutes into their walk. It was a sapling with several of its branches braided together and tied off with a delicate viny rope. Not long after that, Kraven nudged her, pointing out several older specimens on their opposite side. Several trees had been knotted and grafted into a beautiful lattice, forming a four-pronged arch over a patch of yellow flowers and ferns. They pointed the next ones out to Atlan, the bogey's mind rising once more to the surface as they walked, but if he knew what they were, he lacked either the strength or desire to provide an answer.

The grafts grew more common as they went, and after another twenty minutes of walking, they reached their desti-nation. Mira noticed it first as a change in the ground's texture. Softened with hoof prints, patches of damp earth had been churned into mud, the first of the falling leaves shred-ding into the mix. Then she saw the fence, intermittent flashes of it threading through the trees. A combination of delicate pruning and crude centauri work, it loomed some twelve feet high, half-supported by living trees, half by strung together planks. More of the warnings were painted or pinned along the planks every few yards. The main entrance to the camp was guarded by two centaurs, the pair standing under a beautifully woven arch with their staves crossed. Delicate runes had been etched into the arch, finer and more beautiful than the jagged Centauri hashes they'd seen on the signs and planks.

Atlan, whose recovery had hastened with their growing proximity to the camp, gasped behind her. His gaze was fixed on the arch, but when Mira snagged his attention, he only shook his head.

Hrrghin addressed the guards. The pair seemed reluctant, but then another voice came from inside the camp. Tone soft but firm, she spoke in Centauri first.

Then she spoke in Itsrec. "Please. It's alright. Let them through."

Atlan was off the shoulders of his porters before they could even usher him in. Dropping to a knee, he grabbed Mira and Kraven's arms, forcing them into bows.

"What are you doing?" Mira snapped, jerking free. "Don't touch me."

Atlan kept his head down, avoiding the gaze of the middle-aged-looking elf standing a few feet away. "Show some respect," he growled. "That woman is a constant."

NINE

The elven woman laughed, her voice echoing off the latticed trees like a raven's cackle.

"Please, there is no need for such formality here," she said, extending her arms. Her voice was warm and rasping, like a lathe scraped against wood. "Come, rest."

Stepping forward, she offered her hands to Mira and Kraven. She was just shorter than the boy. Black hair coiled on top of her head, her pointed ears fencing it all in but for a few stray wisps. She wore a long, sage green tunic, dusty tan trousers that may once have been white, and soft leather boots. Her eyes were dark brown and shining, her smile broad and white. She smelled of heady flowers, moss, and earth.

Atlan tried to keep his head down. If the writing above the gate was hers, she was a constant, the language painted on the arch the oldest in the world. Constants were the only creatures unaffected by the yochni's changes, the only creatures to still remember all of the ages. Humans, mortal elves, and even dwarves had all been wished into existence by their kin. With only a few hundred of them left, to stand—or kneel —before her was the opportunity of a lifetime.

Mira, wary as ever, shook the woman's hand as if she

were handling a snake. Kraven offered a short bow. The constant came for Atlan next, but he only snapped his gaze back to the earth, hoping she hadn't noticed him looking.

She chuckled, offering him her hand. "How foolish. Come now, get up. You'll hurt yourself."

Muscles twitching from exhaustion, Atlan did his best to obey. Body failing, he landed back on a knee. Mira laughed. Stifling a growl, he tried again, pain knifing through his ribs, blood throbbing in his nose. His skin, still healing from the rash, stung as it stretched and bowed.

The constant bent to grab his arm, helping him to stand.

He tried to wave her away. "Please, I'm alright."

"Of course you are," she said, and tightened her grip. "Welcome to camp. My name is Naveen. I—we, are honored to have you with us. Now, I suppose it would not be too much of an imposition to ask for your names?"

She looked to Mira first. The dwarf gave the woman a mutinous look, then, perhaps in light of the centaurs' continued presence, muttered, "Mira."

Kraven offered a short bow. "*Je m'appelle Kraven Monteyeaux. Je suis apprenti médecin et membre de la Garde.*"

"*Fransec, euh? Très bien,*" said Naveen. She was still holding Atlan's arm. She looked up at him, his tall form stretching nearly two feet higher than her own.

He bowed his head. "You honor us with your hospitality. I am Atlan Qierce, high prince of the bogey empire." He attempted a deeper bow, but Naveen propped him mostly upright, preventing the full motion. His head swam even still, blood pooling in his mangled face. She patted his arm, fingers already sticky with red.

Gesturing to a building on the far side of the camp, she indicated they should move. She matched Atlan's slower pace as they walked, and while a few of the centaurs trailed them and the animals, they no longer seemed to be acting as guard.

Naveen called Hrrghin, the mare who had rescued them, from their ranks, and sent the mare for medicine.

Like most of the buildings in camp, the one the constant had indicated consisted of an open-air platform on stilts with a high thatched roof for cover. Several thatched or wooden wall panels sat in a stack along one side, and a low table and pillows lay near its center with paper and jars for ink and quills. A stout metal kettle sat on a tray on the table. A fire smoked in a gap in the middle of the floor, and several strings of herbs and kitchen instruments hung in garlands from the ceiling, several heavier tools hanging from pegs nailed into the roof's support posts. Naveen gestured for them to wait on the steps, then went up to retrieve the kettle, replacing the liquid within with fresh water from a rain barrel before adding a few handfuls of herbs and hanging it over the flames to steep.

"I apologize for the centaurs' rough treatment of you and your animals," she said, returning to the group. "We had a small pack of your kind pass through the other day, and I'm afraid it riled the centaurs' rather unfortunate instinct for, ah, self-defense."

She indicated Atlan with the term 'your kind.' He bowed his head. "My apologies, Lady Naveen," he said. "It was not our intention to trespass, nor for my people to infringe upon your borders."

Naveen waved him off with a hand. "The world is free, princeling. I claim no control over where others roam."

Hrrghin trotted up from another section of camp, a weathered satchel in her hand. Naveen hopped down the first couple stairs, meeting the centaur half-way as the mare bowed her head and offered the bag. Naveen took it, the pungent mélange of spices within piercing even Atlan's blood-clogged senses. She asked the mare if she would be willing to house their guests, then, when Hrrghin agreed, asked her to deliver their guests' belongings to their housing, thanking the mare again as she trotted away. The kettle whistled, and Naveen left her bag on the steps, retreating once more into her home. She returned with a tray and four clay cups of tea. She sat, the first one of them to do so, and set the tray on the platform beside her. She handed out the cups.

"How do we know it's not poisoned?" asked Mira.

"Mira," Atlan snapped.

Naveen laughed. "Well now, you are one of Eleata's children. You must be, so eager for fighting."

"You knew her?" asked Mira.

"Oh yes. Eleata was my sister," said Naveen, taking the last cup for herself. "I told her not to go on that trip. Having seen her work over the years, I am afraid I was much mistaken."

Atlan shook his head. "You are a constant. You could not have been mistaken."

"You think not, little dog? You do not know how old dwarves are. Even we were young back then." She winked at him, her term for him lacking nothing for kindness. "And even so, elders can make mistakes too, you know. Your uncle, for one, I think."

Atlan blinked, surprised she should mention the king.

Taking a sip of her tea, the constant burned her tongue, raising a hand to her mouth to hide an embarrassed smile and speaking before he could ask her why. "Sorry. It's still a bit hot. I would let it sit for a moment longer." Setting the tea aside, she dug in her medicine bag, the leather supple as a baby's skin from what must have been centuries of use. She retrieved several carefully labeled bottles, which she set beside her on the steps. "Now then, let's see about that back."

She gestured for Atlan to come forward, and he blanched.

"Oh no, I couldn't possibly—"

"Of course you can."

"I—"

"Can and will," she said, pointing to the steps. "Unless of course, you'd spurn my hospitality?"

Atlan sputtered, unable to summon a further defense. He could hardly refuse her with that kind of implication. Face burning, he turned around, sitting on the lowest step.

"My deepest thanks," he said. "You honor me again."

Naveen only gave a dismissive grunt. A moment later, he felt damp gauze on his back, small circular motions buffing the debris from his wounds. The woman was gentle but swift, thousands of years of experience making her hands sure. Kraven drew closer to watch her work, no doubt curious to learn from her expertise. She offered to teach the boy as she went, and when the gauze withdrew, leaves crackled under a pestle, the sharp, woody scent of herbs piercing the air.

"I'm sorry they didn't tend to you earlier," said Naveen, dabbing at the wounds on Atlan's shoulders. "Hospitality is still an area of growth for the centauri people."

The gauze came again, this time wet with medicine. The coolness of it sapped his pain like a sponge drawing water. He could almost have cried from relief. Or embarrassment. Her kindness to him was unfathomable, the height of impropriety given their positions. She encouraged him to try his tea, which he did. Blood washed down his throat.

A couple of centaurs approached the steps, offering care for Batcha and Drake.

"Centaurs no kill Drake? Hurt?" Kraven asked.

"*Non, c'est bien. Aimeriez-vous aller avec?*" she asked, offering the boy the chance to go with.

Kraven hesitated, though in the end it seemed the offer of further education by Naveen—or the duty of watching his feuding companions—was enough reason for him to stay. Naveen asked Mira for approval on Batcha. When permission was granted, the centaur took the beasts away.

"Turn, please," said Naveen, placing a final bandage over Atlan's shoulders. He did, and she grabbed his face, pulling his lips back to examine his gums. She let out a displeased humming sound, wiping her hands on a cloth. She commented on the damage to Kraven, noting a chipped tooth at the back and bruising along the jaw, before dumping the contents of her bowl into a jar and starting again with the contents of two dark bottles.

Mira sniggered, clearly finding his discomfort to be the height of good humor.

Atlan, doing his best to distract the constant from any further humiliations, pressed forward. "Lady Constant, not that I don't appreciate your assistance—I do—but how did you even come to be here? The centaurs haven't welcomed anyone in centuries, let alone let them live among them. And these buildings, the signs. I didn't think centaurs were even capable of building anymore. Or writing."

"I suspect there's a great deal that the centaurs can do that you are unaware of," said Naveen, whisking her bowl. She pointed out a couple of seedpods to Kraven, who crushed them and brushed them into her mix. "Especially given proper direction."

"And they take it?"

The woman paused, smiling as she soaked a scrap of gauze in her tincture. Lifting one corner of his mouth, she jammed the piece of fabric inside, the warm spice of sparrow flower warming his gums a moment later.

"Perhaps direction is a strong term. Instruction might be better, and yes, they do, at least from me," she said. "Kindness goes a great deal towards building friendship, you know. Though I expect with the two of you, that's a lesson you're still learning."

She nodded to him and Mira as she spoke. Atlan staggered

for a response, not wishing to call Mira an unruly murderess in front of the constant despite his feelings.

Mira, having no such qualms, spoke up without hesitation. "He doesn't deserve friendship. Slavers get blades, and he's nearly their king."

Atlan's mouth snapped open, reply ready on his tongue. Catching Naveen watching his reaction however, he forced his jaw closed, sucking on the gauze instead.

Naveen looked disappointed, but let it pass, turning to Mira instead. "Perhaps by inheritance," she said, starting to prod Atlan's nose. "But not by nature, I think."

Mira snorted, unbelieving.

Atlan sucked on his teeth. An idea was forming, solidifying as the constant started pushing the fractured pieces of his nose into shape. As the last shard popped into place, he felt a gush of clotted blood slip down the back of his throat, half of it taking an equally rapid, expulsive exit back out his mouth and nose as he choked. Pain stabbed his sides at the sudden movement.

Naveen gave his back a gentle pat. "Very good," she said. She wiped her hands a final time, then turned her attention to Mira.

Atlan clutched his injured ribs, trying to calm his breath. Careful to keep his head averted, he wiped the blood from his face, taking particular care not to disturb the newly mended bones. Slipping off the bottom step, he leaned forward into a bow, palms to the earth. "Lady Constant, please, a request, if you are willing."

"Just Naveen is fine, and you're going to hurt yourself, but you may always ask."

Atlan swallowed, tasting blood. He sniffed, trying to keep any more from slipping out his nose.

"I believe I may have found a solution to the matter of friendship. The dwarf, you see, is mad."

Mira snarled. "I am—"

Naveen cut her off. "Go on," she said with a nod in his direction.

"Thank you, my La—Naveen. You see, she suffers from gas madness, crazed from the mountains, and if there were any way you could heal her, there would yet be a chance for friendship, and...and at the end of our journey, perhaps I would not have to kill her."

"You would have me fix her?" Naveen asked. Mira's boots scuffed on the wood, the dwarf no doubt ready to attack him, but the constant held her off again.

"I would see her restored," Atlan answered.

"To servitude?"

Atlan's head snapped up, eyes bright. "No. To her normal condition."

There was silence while the woman considered his request. Mira looked ready to chop his head off.

Naveen took a deep breath, letting it out before speaking again. "I have already done a great deal to heal your wounds, little dog. You will undo all of my work if you continue to rest that way. Please, sit up." Wiping her hands free of medicine, Naveen retrieved her cup. "As to your wish, it is already granted. *C'est déjà fait. Elle n'est pas folle.* The dwarf is in her natural state. The madness you speak of does not exist."

Atlan could have swallowed his tongue.

"Ha!" Mira shouted.

"Th-That's impossible," said Atlan.

"Why?" asked Naveen.

"Because, because she's..." Atlan struggled to come up with the words.

"Not in a mine?" Mira sneered.

Atlan looked to Naveen for advice.

"Speak your mind."

"Yeah monster, out with it."

Atlan glared at Mira. If that was what she wanted, so be it. "Because she's terrible," he said. "She's rude, cruel, scheming, a violent cutthroat, and a backstabber. She's tried to kick, slice, or hit me whenever she's had the chance, refuses help, needles me whenever she can, and has made it quite clear on several occasions that if it weren't for a contract we were practically forced into, she'd have my head on a platter, the rest of my race soon to follow. Dwarves are peaceful, agreeable, hard-working, and selfless people. By all accounts I've seen she is none of these things and far worse besides, neither good enough to be a dwarf nor for any intents and purposes even half so good as to have stemmed from someone like you."

Mira leapt for Atlan's neck. Atlan, expecting some sort of retaliation, caught her mid-air, nearly dropping her as his ribs gave a painful jerk. Though it was clear it was hurting her to try to attack, it didn't stop her from trying to scratch and kick.

"Lying monster!" she shouted.

"You asked."

"I'll kill you."

"Animal."

"Enough," barked Naveen.

A crowd of centaurs had gathered around the squabbling pair. Naveen stood at the top of the stairs, hands on hips, expression stern. Kraven looked bleak from his place beside her. Careful not to trigger the contract himself, Atlan set Mira down, resisting the urge to throw her as she hissed more dirty names.

"I said enough," the constant growled.

Drawing himself up from the dirt, body aching, Atlan curled over his knees, nose nearly touching the earth. "I apologize," he muttered.

Mira said nothing.

Naveen re-filled her cup. She took a drink before speaking.

"If you are looking for reasons for her behavior, I can assure you that madness is not one of them. You have said your piece, what you think of her, now let me ask, have you yet invited her to share what she thinks of you?"

"She has not ceased to tell me since we met."

"No less than you deserve," Mira shot back.

"*Desist*, child. Now, perhaps I misspoke. I did not mean if you had asked the results of her analysis, but rather the substance. Do you know why she thinks of you in such disparaging terms?"

"Because she's ma—" Atlan stopped himself. Naveen was convinced Mira was sane, which meant she thought Mira's opinion of him had come from a place of reason, no matter how skewed. He frowned. "She says I am a slaver."

"Are you?"

"No, but..." he stopped, realizing what she had said before. King of slavers...a cold feeling clutched his stomach.

"Mira, perhaps you would like to show him your back?"

"No."

"Obstinacy for obstinacy's sake is foolishness, child," the constant chided.

"Her back?" asked Atlan, head lifting the slightest degree.

Mira glared at him, then Naveen. Then, she relented. Slowly, she turned, loosening the belt at her waist and slipping the cloth down from her shoulders.

Atlan sucked in a breath. "They can't be...that's not...."

Mira said nothing.

Atlan stretched out his hand, fingers crooked. Four long scars stretched across Mira's back, jagged and lumpy with age. Hand hovering a finger's breadth over her skin, he saw the marks matched the gaps between his own claws almost exactly. She tensed at his closeness but didn't retreat. Atlan looked to Kraven and Naveen for help, but Naveen only shook her head, Kraven looking sick. Atlan whined. "An anomaly. A separate attack or self-defense."

Naveen shook her head. "She speaks the truth of her condition. The dwarves are your slaves. Some do live freely, travel and trade, but your people make them work besides, and they punish them if they refuse."

"They are paid."

"Not as much as is owed. And in any case, if they cannot say no, does the recompense truly matter?"

Atlan turned away from the dwarf, drawing his claws back in towards his chest. Mira slipped her vest back over her shoulders, turning to face him as she knotted the cord at her waist.

"Told you," she said.

"I am sorry, Mira. I didn't—"

"Save your breath. You're mine when this contract's over, disgusting excuse for a dwarf or no."

TEN

They were interrupted by a lean, black-coated stallion cantering into camp. He entered by the same arch they had come from and approached Naveen with hardly a glance in the newcomers' direction. He offered the constant a short bow.

"One of their scouts," said Naveen. "Yes, Heirfnn, go ahead."

The stallion delivered a report in Centauri. Atlan tried to follow the meaning, but the scout spoke too quickly for him to understand. By the sour expression that grew on Naveen's face, the news wasn't good.

When he finished, she turned to their group. "I don't suppose you brought along any friends, did you?"

"No," said Mira. "Why?"

"Because according to Heirfnn, there's over a dozen men and elves in the woods, and they appear to be following the tracks of your dragon."

Mira exchanged a grim look with Kraven, who had gone pale at the translation.

"Spider," said Kraven. "He want to kill Mira, Drake."

"Wants," corrected Atlan.

Naveen held up a quieting hand. She paused, then, gathering herself, granted them a tired smile. "Well, you certainly bring excitement with you, don't you? Little wonder, given the combination you arrived in." She let out a breath, then drew herself up, smile regaining some of its usual sincerity. She passed directions along to Heirfnn, sending him trotting back into the woods, then turned back to the group.

"Given the circumstances, I believe bringing the hunters here will only cause trouble. I have asked Heirfnn to politely ask them to leave. The birds will keep an eye on them, and if they insist on intruding, we will be quick to know."

"They're not going to get the same welcome we did?" asked Mira.

A flicker of distaste flitted across the constant's features. "I hope not, though if they insist on intruding, they might." A troubled expression drifted over her features like the shadow of a cloud, but she was quick to cover it with another smile.

Atlan glanced at Mira, but his own guilty feelings were not as easy to shake.

"Come," said Naveen, packing the rest of her supplies back into her bag. "I believe it is time for a break. Tea is good for many things, but a meal it does not make, and now that your wounds are tended, I believe it is time for a story." She handed the mortar off to their medic. "Kraven, dear, that salve should soothe your jaw and that cheek. If it is not enough, I can take a closer look at them later."

She pointed from the mortar to his cheek as she translated, then led the way up the steps. Gesturing to the fire, she indicated that they should sit. She filled a pot with water from the rain barrel and herbs from the bundles hanging from the ceiling and set it over the flames. Drawing several wooden slabs from under a hidden panel in the floor, she followed them up with dried meats, vegetables, and several knives. She mined a few mushrooms from logs under another panel.

Handing two of the slabs off to Mira and Atlan, she separated the meats and vegetables between them, instructing them to start chopping. The third slab and the mushrooms, she took for herself.

"You don't have to do that," said Atlan.

"Then you should be all the more grateful that I am," said Naveen. She winked.

Atlan glanced at Mira, but she had already settled into her work with the same muted determination he had seen before. He had assumed that the healing effects of her rehabilitation had kept her silent before. Now he wondered if it hadn't been wisdom instead. A flicker of something he didn't quite recognize flitted through his stomach. He forced himself to start chopping.

Naveen smiled. "Now then," she said, adding her slow, even beat to the otherwise asynchronous *thok* of the blades. "Who would like to go first?"

It was neither a brief nor collected story. Kraven and Mira did most of the talking, Atlan barely listening and stepping in only rarely to correct Kraven's grammar or Mira's slanderous claims. Despite their difficulties however, Naveen was a gracious host, her croaking laughter chasing Kraven's explanation of the arbitration, regret tracing the centaurs' attack. She tended a fragrant stew while they spoke, ladling out portions with the effortless unobtrusiveness of a practiced hostess when it was finished and barely disrupting the story's flow even when she warned them that it was hot. If the looming threat of Spider or the fact she was hosting Atlan, heir to the slavers, bothered her, she made no indication, treating him as cheerily as she might have treated anyone else the centaurs dragged under her roof. When Kraven finished, hand drifting off towards a nearby centaur by way of explanation for their arrival, she gave them all a firm nod, looking as sated from their story as they did by her meal.

"Well, it has been a long time since I have heard anything so...interesting," she said. "Dear as they are, the centaurs have lost much of their art for telling stories."

She looked to the fading sun, already losing its fight against the tree-lined horizon, then back to her guests. Mira, who had grown increasingly restless as their story continued, fidgeted on her heels.

"We need help," she said. "We're running late."

Naveen nodded. "Yes, I believe you do. More importantly, however, I believe you need rest."

"We don't have time," said Mira.

"There is always time," said Naveen. "The only thing that trims it is hurry."

Mira opened her mouth to argue, but Naveen interrupted before she could speak.

"I understand you are quick to be on your way, but to go off injured and ill-provisioned is not the way to gain time. If you would let me, I would tend your mini hart tonight, let you rest in safety before sending you off in better health and provisioning tomorrow."

"But—"

"There is also, of course, the matter of your pending judgement for trespassing," the constant said, taking another sip of tea.

"You wouldn—" Mira started.

"I would," she said. "Luckily for you, we have come far enough that it is no longer a crime worthy of immediate death to step foot in the centaurs' territory. Luckier still, I am of the sort to exchange a good story for ignorant trespass, a good evening's entertainment for much-needed care. For any other insult the centaurs fear they may have suffered, I think a guarantee that their mercy will be well repaid by the furthered wisdom and caution of their prisoners would be sufficient, don't you? Unless, of course, you'd like to ask them to adjudicate instead?"

She lifted her brow in a teasing challenge, gathering their plates.

Mira scowled, then shook her head.

"I thought you might say that," said Naveen. Getting to her feet, she set the dishes on a tray in the corner along with their cups of tea. "Both Hrrghin and her mate Hrrhrr can understand at least basic Itsrec if you need anything. Per Hrrghin's permission, you may stay in their home for the evening."

Calling over the red stallion from earlier, Hrrhrr, apparently, the constant indicated their gathered guests. Though the stallion's gaze drifted to Atlan, the centaur no doubt remembering that the prince had nearly gutted him earlier that morning, he was quick to relent, nodding and motioning for the three travelers to follow.

Atlan moved to do so, and the constant called him back. "Atlan, if you have a minute?"

"Yes, my Lady?"

"Naveen is fine," she said.

Mira gave them a suspicious look. "What do you want with him?"

"Mira," Atlan growled, but Naveen only raised a hand.

"A private matter," she said. "One best discussed, as most private matters are, alone."

Mira scowled, but Naveen only gave her a gentle smile. She set a hand on her shoulder. "I will not tell him anything that can harm you, make any deals, or sell you off, Eleata-daughter. You have my word."

For a moment, Atlan wondered if Mira would believe her, but Hrrhrr was still waiting, and with some urging from Kraven, the dwarven champion relented, her small form fading into the gathering shadows as the evening began.

Naveen retrieved her medicine bag and gave Atlan a conspiratorial wink. He wondered what she could possibly have to talk with him about, and a small knot in his stomach started to form.

Naveen hefted the bag to her shoulder. "Shall we?"

Atlan nodded.

The last fingers of sunlight were just reaching the top of the encampment's fence, the light fading into ever darker orange and yellow tones. The centaurs had paneled off most of the open-air buildings with the stacks of wall panels, lighting the insides with hanging lanterns taken from posts and roof corners. Naveen led the way down the stairs, waiting for Atlan to navigate them on his still-tired legs, then asked him to take one such light from the corner of her roof.

They struck out for Batcha's pen. The small herd of goats within had taken a cautious approach to welcoming the mini hart, and as Naveen entered, indicating the appropriate post for Atlan to hang the light, it was not difficult for her to scrounge the mini hart out of the group. Hauling him towards the light, she looped his reins over the rail before pulling up a milking stool for herself. Waving to an overturned barrel, she gestured for Atlan to sit.

"I hope you don't mind talking while I work, but his wounds really must be treated."

"Of course." Dusting off the rim of the barrel, he lifted his tail and sat, fingers knitting themselves into a ball in his lap.

"How are you feeling?" she asked.

"Better. Your medicine is wonderful."

"Good." Drawing Batcha's reins a little tighter around their post to keep him from bucking, she ran a hand over the mini hart's side, calming him before starting to work the injured leg and test the joints for movement. The mini hart groaned, and she stopped, running her hand over his coat again and cooing him back to silence.

"So," she said, trying again. "How are you *feeling*?"

Atlan's black ears slanted forward in an instant, fragile skin cracking.

"I think you know the answer to that."

"Confirm for me."

At first, he said nothing.

Naveen waited.

"Terrible," he said.

"And?"

"Stupid. Angry...you must think I'm a fool."

"Really?" she asked.

"You don't?" he shot back. She gave him a stern look, and he dropped his gaze. "Sorry. I just...I should have known sooner. There were signs."

"Give me a hand?" she asked, gesturing to the mini hart. Holding the mount as she instructed, Atlan kept him steady as she gave the bad leg a final pull. The mini hart brayed and struggled, but Atlan held him steady as she felt along the injured joint. Letting go at last with an unhappy *tsk*, she gave the creature several more pats before giving Atlan's hand a few as well to indicate that he could let go.

"Thank you," she said, letting out a small sigh. Stroking Batcha's side, she gave the mount a minute to relax before turning to her pestle. She ground up a few herbs, then added measures from a couple of her bottles. She broke in another leaf, then stirred.

"Atlan, what do you see when you look at Mira?"

He gave Hrrghin's hut a short, furtive look. "You know the answer to that."

"Oh?" she said.

"Yes."

Naveen nodded. Reaching towards the fence, she grabbed a handful of dust from the edge of the pen, mixing it into her tincture until it thickened to a paste. She gestured for Atlan to hold the mini hart again, then rubbed a handful of salve into the animal's side with the heel of her palm, massaging it in with deep, hard circles. Leaving off with a final firm push, she wiped her brow with her arm.

"Only a fool gets angry for not knowing what he doesn't know, Atlan, and everyone hides from the things that will hurt them. To have found out earlier might have crushed you, as it is now, and should, or perhaps even prevented you from taking on this current quest. You have always sought knowledge, as your father did before you. The only question now is what you will do with it." She nodded towards the lead mare's home. "You've got good eyesight, right? I would encourage you to look harder."

He followed her gaze to the hut, eyes unintentionally narrowing against the dark. She laughed, and when he turned back to face her, she rubbed a slick of extra salve on his cheek.

"Your face is already looking better. I am good, aren't I?"

Wiping the rest of the salve off on a towel, she tossed it over her shoulder. She unhooked Batcha's tack and hung it on the post in exchange for the lantern, which she handed to Atlan. She gathered the rest of her supplies, then took his arm with her other hand. "Come," she said. "It's been a long day."

As they walked to Hrrghin and Hrrhrr's home, she kept her pace slow enough for Atlan to match, her arm snugged in tight against his side. When they arrived, she let him go with a careful unwinding of their limbs. She handed him the jar from before. "Put a layer of this on before you go to bed. It will help your skin." Reaching up, she cupped his face, rubbing a gentle thumb on his clean cheek. "Rest well, little prince. Good night."

Turning towards her house, she left him on the ramp, taking the lantern with her. Dragging himself up into the hut, Atlan slumped in the corner. Kraven was already asleep to his left, Mira's form hunched up against the back wall. He could just see the glint of moonlight on her eyes.

"What did you talk about?"

"Nothing that concerns you."

"Liar."

For a long moment, Atlan didn't answer. He wanted nothing more than to sleep, his eyes heavy and body aching, but he could feel the weight of pending words, a readiness that he knew lay just behind her lips.

"Earlier," she said at last. "You saved me. From the centaurs. Why?"

Atlan opened his eyes, surprised at the question. He considered it, the constant's words echoing in his mind.

"Well," he said at last. "It's what kings do."

She scoffed at his words. Of course, she wouldn't believe him. He wouldn't have either, had their positions been switched.

Still, there was a part of him that was hurt that she didn't, not for any personal offense, but because he now knew his words weren't true either. He had always believed in the goodness of his people, that they truly fought for the justice and righteousness that they claimed. Heart and ferocity of the dog, wits and might of a man.

But it wasn't true, at least not anymore. Perhaps not for a long time, if ever. His ears drooped.

Still, there was truth in what the constant had said, too. Hope. He could not believe the words now, not the way things were. But perhaps, someday he could. Perhaps, if he tried hard enough, things could change.

CHAPTER

ELEVEN

When Kraven awoke the next day, his injured face was quick to voice its complaints. His chin, which had been soundly knocked by the centaurs, twinged with every movement of his jaw. His cheek, which Mira had fractured two days previously, was still tender to the touch, the flesh swollen and tender. Stealing outside, careful not to disturb the others, he gazed at his reflection in the nearby rain barrel. He was as dirty as he'd imagined, his chin and cheek an ugly rainbow of reds and purples and yellows. There was even a patch of green. He had never seen Ines look so terrible—at least not before the end—though he had to wonder if she had run into such kinds of troubles before.

Or maybe he was just lucky.

Drake was still asleep, curled up just outside the house. Muted thumps marked the slow passing of centaurs strolling in or out on patrols or taking down the paneling on their homes. Running a hand over the familiar blue scales of the dragon's forehead, Ines' gloves a stark contrast against the brilliant sapphire, Kraven smiled. His good feelings were quick to fade though. He had been astonished to discover that Mira's accusations had been true, that Atlan's people were

117

indeed slavers. He wondered if the bogey was lying or if he really hadn't known. The bogey didn't seem the type to support such a thing, but then again, some people were good at keeping secrets. It wouldn't be the first time.

Rounding Drake's large form to check the dragon's injuries, Kraven was surprised to find Naveen already there. She traced a path along the sea dragon's side with her hand, her fingers dipping down and around to avoid the patched punctures the centaurs had poked in his hide.

She smiled when she saw him. "*Bonjour,*" she said. "*Ça va?*"

"*Ça va,*" he said, returning the greeting with a polite nod.

She nodded but said nothing more. She seemed comfortable with the silence, but he had to subdue the urge to fidget. Kind as she was, there was something about her which unsettled him. A purity or intensity that put him on his guard. He had seen a similar goodness in Ines, a frank openness of spirit that had always both drawn and alarmed him. He had not encountered it in anyone else before.

"The others sleep?" she asked finally, gesturing to the house. She tilted her head, putting her hands next to it, palms together, in the universal symbol for sleep. He nodded.

"Spider?" he asked.

She shrugged, reverting to Fransec. Though the hunters had backed off enough for the centaurs' satisfaction, her birds had reported they were still in the area, tending their equipment and cleaning up camp. With no real way to tell what the hunters were planning, it was troubling news to Kraven, but the constant seemed unbothered, waving the issue aside with a hand.

"I've been meaning to speak with you. Join me for a walk?" she asked, offering translation when he gave her a confused look. She reached for his arm, and, with reluctance, he agreed, proffering the limb. They walked towards the edge of the camp. Naveen bowed her head to each centaur she passed, the centaurs giving brief bows in return. Her power over them and the respect they showed her was remarkable, especially with the pain that still throbbed in Kraven's chin serving as a stark reminder of what the centaurs could do.

He told her he was learning Itsrec. As their conversation progressed, she did her best to speak in simple terms, pausing to let him quiz her on vocabulary at his leisure. For a while, they spoke of niceties, the fine construction of the houses or the excellence of her care. They took a brief detour into medicine, diving deeper for a comparison of the herbs each had chosen for Atlan's rash before returning to their previous topic. They spoke of Kraven's companions and the revelations of the day before only briefly. Kraven did not wish to speak of them, and Naveen, gracious as ever, changed the subject. The conversation transitioned from their current situation to the recent past, how Kraven had left his hometown and the route he had taken.

From there, it was not a large leap to go farther back. He spoke of his family and his home by the sea, how he had rescued and adopted Drake when he found him alone in a sea cliff cave. By then they had left the camp, picking up a basket and two pairs of shears on their way out. They wound their way through the forest to a small garden where herbs and vegetables grew in neat plots and rows. Handing Kraven a pair of shears, Naveen directed him to a coiling patch of terry flower before kneeling in the soil herself.

"It's a strange thing, having one of the Guard come all this way," she said. "Isn't it more usual for you to take on local projects?"

When he captured the meaning of her question fully, he explained in brief his goal of earning his mark by the journey. He did not tell her of his second, stronger goal to understand why he should even want a mark in the first place, nor how

Ines' kindness, how her grace and gentleness toward him even at the worst of his moods, had sparked such an interest in the first place. Naveen was an excellent conversationalist, however, and was quick to sniff him out. She asked how he had come to know of the Guard in the first place, at which point he had little choice but to mention his mentor.

"I see," said Naveen. "And tell me about Ines."

Kraven had expected this, but it was, in a way, a difficult request to fulfill. Because what, exactly, had Ines been like? A happy teenager? A sparkling do-gooder? Yes, certainly, she had been both of those things, but that didn't quite seem to capture it, seemed too shallow a description. There was also a depth to her, a maturity that seemed to well from deep within that he couldn't quite fathom. There was also her kindness and compassion, her unerring devotion to pacifism, and of course, her skills as a healer. She had been much sought after in his village, as well as in several surrounding ones, be it for general bumps and scrapes, coughs and sniffles, or even animal births. It seemed there had been no task too great or small for her to handle, and no person too auspicious or humble for her to help. She had been quick-witted, a star with children, and generous, both with trust and possessions.

She had also been, when she was feeling playful, a pain in his ass, as quick to throw him a jibe as blow a kiss, to tousle his hair as mend his feelings.

The question brought forth a whirl of memories, an infinite blend of emotions.

"She was good," he said at last.

Based on the amount of time it had taken him to supply such a brief answer, he thought the constant would laugh, but she didn't. "Sounds like it would be good to have her back," she said. There was a hint of challenge in her voice, not quite accusation, but certainly a question. He couldn't help but notice a certain attentiveness she suddenly gave him from the corners of her eyes, too, even as her hands kept busy at work trimming a tangle of wild groose. Kraven's lips drew tight at the suggestion, pulling into a grim and thoughtful look he had worn many a time before.

"Yes," he said at last. It was not a unique idea. Many went to the yochni for personal, selfish wishes, of which he knew this was one. Not the most selfish—he knew his family would much rather have had him go and wish for more money and land. But to wish for Ines to come back would squander an opportunity for much good from another, different wish, more even than he thought Ines could do in a lifetime. She would have hated that.

Naveen, still watching him, spoke again, this time going straight for Fransec and only repeating in Itsrec. "The yochni is a powerful creature. Such a wish would be an easy thing."

Kraven stopped pruning, knuckle-deep in a thorny row of strickler. She stared at him, full on, impassive, and he stared back, for once unalarmed by her quiet.

After a moment, he asked her if that was what she was suggesting.

She shook her head. "No, but I am certain you have had the same thought yourself. I am curious as to where such thoughts led."

"You think I...not," he said, after she provided translation.

"Should not," she corrected. Then she shrugged, digging her fingers into the earth. The rich coarseness of her voice felt deep enough to do the same, to root the soil up, turn over its secrets. Her search produced several small clusters of root vegetables as she continued. "What others wish at the yochni is not for me to say. Mira's people exist because of a wish I once denied. Atlan's kind from another. One can never say what will come of the wishes of others."

Scooping the last of the vegetables into her basket, she smoothed over the remaining dirt before dusting off her hands. Cleaning them further with a rather unceremonious wipe on her dress, she got to her feet, offering him first the basket for his harvest, and then a hand to help him to his feet.

"You have great potential," she said, still holding his hand. Her grip was surprisingly firm despite her tenderness. "So do Atlan and Mira. I'll be interested to see how you change the world. I hope you do it together." She released his hand, turning on a heel. "Now come, it is time for breakfast."

He was just turning to follow when their attention was called back by a shrill noise, the screaming, squawking cacophony of dozens of frightened birds all racing in their direction. Naveen squinted, head swiveling as she tried to listen. Then, she looked up.

Kraven was just in time to catch her as she staggered back. The basket tumbled from her hand. The constant's face drained to an ashy gray, weak mutterings dripping from her tongue.

Smoke billowed on the horizon. The hunters were burning the woods.

The first waves of frightened animals were already visible, foxes and deer bounding through the undergrowth, the swiftest birds darting above. Another familiar whistle pierced through the chaotic symphony, and Kraven pushed Naveen out of the way just in time as a volley of arrows thudded into the earth, missing them by inches.

The attack knocked the constant out of her stupor. Grabbing his wrist, she pulled Kraven towards camp, basket and shears forgotten behind them. She was surprisingly spry for her age. Kraven found it difficult to keep up with her through the tangled woods.

By the time they reached the camp, it had burst into a flurry of activity. Centaurs raced to and fro, evacuating livestock and children or gathering weapons to go on the attack. Atlan stood on the ramp of Hrrghin's home, Drake stamping beside him. Mira wrestled with Batcha in a livestock pen. More arrows flew into the woods and camp, a few sharp whinnies letting them know some of the projectiles were hitting their marks.

Drake saw Naveen and Kraven first. Rushing forward, the dragon nearly knocked Kraven off his feet. Atlan was quick to join them, though he still limped from his various wounds.

"Lady Constant, how can we help?" Atlan asked.

Naveen's gaze drifted over the camp, her expression dazed and grieving. She'd worked with the centaurs for over a century. Now, all her hard work was going to go up in flames.

The bogey prince's gaze hardened. "Naveen," he snapped, using a tone far harsher than he had used with her before. It was enough to grab Kraven's attention, too. They turned to face the prince. Atlan continued. "What do we do?"

The words had a centering effect. The constant looked around the camp again, but this time her expression was decisive, strong. "Nothing," she said.

"But, your people—"

"Will be fine," she said, voice firm. "It is hospitality freely given, risks gladly taken. There is a gate at the back of the camp—*une porte à l'arrière du camp*—and passage through the mountains. *Un tunnel.* It will get you to your yochni in time, catch you up with the other champions. Now go. *Allez. Maintenant.*"

Hrrghin galloped towards them, a large spear in one hand and a bow and quiver in the other. Kraven opened his mouth to argue, but the constant cut him off, pressing a hand to each of their cheeks. She had to go on tip-toes to reach Atlan's face. "*Souvenez-vous de nos discussions.* Remember our talks."

Hrrghin arrived in an explosion of clotted, hoof-thrown earth. Reaching down, she handed the bow to Naveen before lifting the constant onto her back. With a final nod from the elf, the pair sprang off, the centaur's hooves finding instant purchase. Before Atlan or Kraven could say another word, they were out the front gate, the last flicker of Naveen's blue dress snapping out of view with Hrrghin's tail.

As he watched them go, another image flashed through Kraven's mind, Ines waving, disappearing into the woods. He wanted to follow, to stop her, but Atlan grabbed his arm.

"No," he said. "We go."

Kraven hesitated, pulling back. He knew Ines would have helped, stayed, but then, with their contract, if he didn't go, none of the others could either. After the beating from the centaurs the day before, Atlan was in no condition to fight, and Mira, despite her ferocity, was little match for anyone Spider would have brought along so long as they protected their knees.

With a final glance back to the woods, Kraven nodded. Ines had been headstrong, but perhaps in this case, even she might have yielded to greater wisdom. Naveen had given them their order. It was time for them to go.

When Atlan saw that Kraven was ready to listen, he was quick to start giving commands. Kraven and Drake would gather their things. He would go after Mira. The bogey loped off for the animal pen. Drake and Kraven went for Hrrghin's home. Thankfully, the dwarf's sorting had already divided their belongings according to usefulness, the most crucial items sharing space in their better packs while those of lesser value snuggled together in more tattered bags and groupings. Kraven waded through a couple of piles, checking for holes or tears and flipping open pack flaps to check contents before grabbing the two best options for himself and Mira, an extra bag of medicinal supplies, and Atlan's massive backpack. The latter was wide enough that Kraven could hardly carry it himself. He handed it off to Drake.

Two flapping, dirty-blond braids and a thick black tail were just disappearing past another house as Kraven leapt off the hut's front ramp. He followed them towards the camp's rear gate.

By the time he caught up, the others were already at the fence, Mira dancing impatiently several feet into the woods beyond with Atlan waiting at the arch. Batcha had been bundled up into the bogey prince's arms, his reins wrapped tight to his body to keep him from bucking. Even so, a new cut shone on the prince's cheek, a corresponding smear of red streaking the mini hart's antler. The fire was moving fast, the late summer leaves making excellent tinder. The first embers were drifting in over the fence at the front of the camp, nestling into the dried thatch and making the roofs of the houses smoke. Soon, they would catch fire, spreading the flames to the roofs around them. A wall of dark smoke marched towards their location.

They ducked through the back gate, the first sounds of distant battle chasing them as they went. The arch was low, Drake having to bend beneath it in order to fit. If not for his narrow body, Kraven wasn't sure the dragon would have made it at all. A path of similarly slim proportions, little more than a deer trail, lay beyond the arch, winding its way up the foothills to a distant ridge. Thick foliage encroached on all sides, the trees forcing the trail up a crooked, stepwise route.

Mira, forging ahead through the undergrowth like a ferret through a snowbank, took the lead. Kraven went next with Drake. Atlan, healing skin already tightening from the heat, took advantage of the path cleared by the dragon. Batcha still squealed in his arms, kicking at his harried captor.

Kraven, catching sight of the bogey's delicate condition, dropped to the back.

The path up was not an easy one. The ground canted ever more steeply the closer they got to the top, with the stone growing ever more uneven and slick. Drake's claws, designed for the sands and stones of the oceans and beaches along the

Coast, shifted on the slippery rock and earth. The blaze from the burning camp, drawing ever nearer, sent rivers of sweat down Kraven's back, the ornamental scales of his silken shirt locking in the terrible heat. His hands felt like they were swimming inside his gloves. Atlan's skin took on an unhealthy, sweaty sheen. Keeping his head down to stop the sweat from running into his eyes, Kraven focused only on taking his next step, on reaching the safety of the ridge.

Mira, quite a way ahead of them and seemingly unbothered by the heat by comparison, made better headway. "Here," she shouted. Kraven looked up. She scrambled up the last few feet of slope, disappearing over a lip. "It's a road," she called.

And indeed, it was. Helping Atlan and the tangled Batcha up the last stretch, Kraven half pushed, half pulled the bogey and mini hart up after her onto mercifully level ground. The road looked as though it had gone unused for as long as the path they had just climbed to reach it had, its wheel ruts long since smudged out by the passage of snowmelt and time. Even so, the surrounding forest had yet to fully overtake it, a low stone wall even lining the sides in root-cracked pieces. Kraven looked down the road in either direction. He didn't see a tunnel.

"Which?" he asked. He searched for the words. "Left or… right?"

"Either," gasped Atlan.

"No," said Mira. "Look. There's a fork there. I can see it."

She pointed along the eastern road towards a broad face of cliff just peeking out from behind another slope. It was still a way off, though if there was space between the two structures, there could be a path.

"Are you sure?" rasped Atlan. The smoke was creeping up behind them, climbing the mountain with the fire.

"Of course I am," said Mira.

"If you're wrong...."

"Then at least I'll know you burned with me. Look, you might know your way around elves and a fancy box with strings, but I know caves. There's an entrance there. I know it."

"But—"

"*Arrêtez,*" said Kraven. He pointed along the eastern path, Mira already inching that way. He hadn't understood most of what she'd said, but they didn't have time to argue.

The bogey prince cast only a brief look down the mountain, then nodded. Batcha was still struggling in his arms, wriggling fiercely. Mira ran. The others jogged after. She reached the corner, then, looking down the forking path, froze.

"Mira—" Atlan started.

"*Yes!*" Throwing up a fist, Mira leapt into the air. Charging forward with a victorious whoop, she disappeared around the bend. Atlan and Kraven exchanged a look. Kraven had thought something was wrong when she had stopped, that perhaps there hadn't been a further path. Clearly that was not the case.

They were almost to the corner. Kraven reached it first. Atlan, close behind, pulled up short beside him.

The prince's response was not nearly so enthusiastic as the dwarf's had been, his sweating face going slack with despair. "No. No, Mira, wait!"

The problem wasn't that the cave wasn't there. In fact, it was magnificent, the entrance soaring to nearly thirty feet at its peak. Massive pillars lined its maw like ribs on a snake. Statues spanned the gaps between, each exquisitely carved hero unique in its pose and armament. Not only big enough to shelter them all, the cave was also far enough back from the woods that it was doubtful the fire would even reach it.

No, the problem wasn't that the cave wasn't there.

The problem was the size of the statues. Though clearly carved at larger-than-life scale, their childlike proportions made their race abundantly clear even at a distance.

The cave was dwarven, and Mira had just disappeared inside.

CHAPTER

TWELVE

The magnificently pillared entrance to the dwarven cave lay at the bottom of a long gravelly slope. By the time Mira heard the others call her, she had already reached the bottom, her momentum carrying her all the way down and past the statues and several yards into the dark. Cool air swirled around her, tightening the sweat pooling on her skin. Even from a distance, she could feel residual heat pouring down the slope, pressing in from behind. Sparks and ashes fell through the air outside like snow, bits of burning leaves scudding down the path or rising on gusts of hot air, but the slope was long and rocky enough she knew they would be safe inside.

She lifted her hands to either side of her mouth. "Hello? Hello?" she called.

No answer. Atlan and Kraven skidded down with Drake and Batcha behind her.

"Stop, Mira, don't," wheezed Atlan. Rolling Batcha down his shoulder, he passed the mini hart to Kraven, the boy nearly tipping over as the frightened creature bucked. Drake came quickly to his master's aid and the two of them got the

129

mini hart safely down to the ground, though not without a handful of dirty looks in the bogey prince's direction.

Mira ignored them. There still hadn't been an answer, though if the dwarves had seen the bogey, she could see why they wouldn't speak up.

"Hey, we're here! Help," she tried again.

Atlan lurched to reach her. She lifted her hands again, and he slapped them aside.

"Stop it," he snapped. "Be quiet."

"Don't touch me."

"Then stop."

She glared at him, but didn't speak again, listening instead for the telltale thunder of boots, the clank of armor, cries to attack.

Nothing. No sound beyond the roar of the flames outside, the unhappy moans of the animals, and their own rasping breaths. Atlan glared at her, clutching his wounded ribs. What fur hadn't been eaten away by his rash was glossy with sweat, his swollen face making a sucking sort of hiss with every breath.

"Stop that," she said.

"I'm breathing."

"Then don't."

The bogey scowled, forcing himself up to his full height with a groan. He peered into the darkness, swollen snout quivering. No doubt he could sense far more than she could, though to what result, she couldn't say.

"We go around," he said. "Wait until the fire dies down, then go over the range instead."

"On hot ash? Are you crazy?"

"Better than going through here."

"Why?" she sneered. "Are you scared?

"Yes. As well I should be if anyone here behaves like you," he said. He tugged his shirt back into order with a huff, then gave his pants and tail a light brushing for soot, dusting up small billows of black in his wake.

Kraven, having finally wrangled the animals, stared back up the slope. His expression was a strange tangle of bitterness and grief, wrath and pain. For a moment his muscles twitched between the various emotions, but in the end, grimness won the lot. It looked familiar on his face, as if it had often been there before. "That was...bad," he said, Batcha letting out a mournful groan as if in agreement.

"No kidding," said Mira. She pointed deeper into the cave. "Now, things can get better."

"*No*," said Atlan.

"Why not?"

"Because your people will kill me if I do."

"You're more than welcome to burn."

Kraven let out a sharp breath and put up a hand, arresting the argument before it could get any worse. Pointing to the animals, he shared a brief exchange with Atlan. The bogey argued at first, but it was clear between the animals' poor condition and their need for swiftness that he did not have a choice. Drake, leaning heavily against the cool walls deeper in the cave, looked as though he would not survive another hour outside in the heat. Batcha, drenched in sweat and wobbling, was not much better. Eventually, Mira heard the word "Naveen," and, after a last few weak remarks, the bogey surrendered.

"Fine," he said. "But we'll need to find a torch."

Mira grinned. Sconces lined the entrance to the cave. Most had long since burned past any usefulness, but they managed to find a couple that still had some life left. Kraven got them out, then lit them with his flint. He offered one to Atlan, the bogey the natural choice to carry it for his greater height, but the prince only shook his head, pointing to Mira to take it.

"Coward," she said.

"Madling."

"*Arrêtez*," said the boy and handed her a torch.

The pillars stretched for the first quarter mile or so. Arches connected each pair, ribbing the ceiling until the roof eventually lowered into neat, squared-off corridors. Though Mira's clan had attempted to flee the bogeys by digging smaller tunnels in their caves—the bogeys likely as not to crack them open like badgers after ants regardless, structural damage or no—it was clear that the halls they were in now were older, shaped and constructed before the slavers had taken full control or perhaps even back when the monsters were welcome. Intricate stonework and murals of dwarves or Eleata covered the walls, and thin veins of gold still lined most of the arches, only a few broken with the gold removed.

All around them was silence. They found a few rooms, guest quarters, and what appeared to be a larder. What little remained inside each was broken or ransacked, sleeping under a shroud of dust. So far as they could tell, the entire place had been abandoned.

They walked for nearly an hour before Atlan re-entered Mira's pool of light, his shadow looming large ahead of her in the flickering glow of Kraven's torch. By that time, her entire body was buzzing, her mind racing through the possibilities of what could have happened. When he reached her, he said nothing for several minutes, merely matching her pace. His presence chaffed against her, burrowing like a bug under her skin.

"What?" she finally snapped.

He closed his mouth in an embarrassed grimace of a smile, having just opened it to speak, and his gaze drifted off to the walls, eyes tracing the chiseled ridges of a finely etched carving.

"It's beautiful here," he said.

"So?"

"So nothing," he said. He paused. "So, uh, are dwarven caves always like this?"

"Dead, you mean?" she asked, shooting him a sharp look. She softened the slightest degree, memories of home turning her maudlin. "No. Not before your kind shows up anyway."

The bogey shouldered the blow in silence. His expression was hard to read from below, the low lighting casting him in monstrous tones, though even she had to admit his countenance didn't hold a candle to others she'd met. Certainly, none had ever saved her life. Her scars itched.

His gaze slid down to her, one yellow eye catching the light. "Is it like this where you're from? Your...cave, I mean?"

Her head whipped towards him, green eyes glittering, and he flinched. She glared, and his black ears drooped, swiveling to the side.

"No," she said, looking back to the tunnel ahead. "We serve a purpose, so some of us are allowed to live."

The bogey paused, letting the comment soak in. She could still see him from the corner of her eye. He looked away, studying the cave walls, then down at his feet. "Is it nice there?"

This time her look was angry, but he didn't look away, already braced for backlash. She searched his face for some hint he was looking for information, a way to trap her or her people, but there was none, at least that she could see.

"Yeah, it is," she said at last.

"It sounds nice," he said. "Worth protecting. Look, Mira, I—"

"Stop."

"But—"

"No, stop." She could see something up ahead, different than the doors and arches they'd already passed. Running forward, she raised the torch, the small orb of light illuminating her discovery.

It was a door, the bottom two thirds of it crumbled to pieces. Lying in the rubble, rotting to dust, was the corpse of a bogey.

Atlan shot her a horrified look, but she hardly even saw it. Dashing forward, she scrambled up the pile of bones, breath catching as she saw the carnage on the other side.

She knew now why they hadn't seen any of her people.

They'd picked a fight with the bogeys.

The other side of the door was piled with bodies, dwarven and bogey alike. Sprung traps pinned the invaders to the walls, axes or spears nailed others to the floor. There had to be over a dozen corpses, the once fine corridor transformed into a massive death trap.

Faded brown paw prints streaked further down the blood-stained hall. The bogeys had broken through.

Mira shot Atlan an accusatory look, enough venom in her eyes to poison Drake.

"Worth protecting, huh?" she said. "Right."

"I would nev—"

But she was already turning, sliding down the bogey bones.

The footprints stretched farther than her light could reach. The more she saw, the faster she went, pace increasing rapidly from a walk to a jog to a run. How far did the carnage last? How far had the bogeys gotten?

Atlan, struggling to keep up from his wounded body and more delicate path through the bones, called after her to stop. Mira ignored him. Something creaked and twanged behind her. She heard him bark in pain. Still she ran.

"Mira," called Kraven. "Wait."

Mira didn't wait. She had to know. She had to—

Atlan's voice rang out sharp and sudden behind her. "Mira, no! Don't!"

Too late. There was a door ahead, half-open with an overturned table barricading the gap. She could feel the floor vibrate as he charged for her, almost feel his arms reaching out, but she put on a final burst of speed. Leaping over the makeshift barrier, she felt the air swish past her braids as Atlan caught up, as his claws just missed the back of her vest. Torchlight filled the chamber.

Mira pulled up short.

Drake's claws and Batcha's hooves clattered to a halt, the table screeching as Atlan slammed against it. Kraven's soft gasp floated on the air.

Cold air. Empty air.

Dead air.

Gathered in the center of the grand hall, surrounded by the last of the overturned tables, was a massive pile of charred bones, a metal crown half-buried on the top.

Mira dropped the torch. She staggered forward, soot and ash spinning around her feet like snow in the flickering light. She picked up the crown. Atlan climbed over the table.

"I'm sorry, Mira, I tried to warn—"

"You knew?"

"No! The smell...."

He stopped, and Kraven climbed over the table as well. Lifting his torch high, the medic revealed more of the wreckage. The dwarves had taken their last stand in the dining hall, the tables that had once served as barricades overturned and thrown aside in the bogeys' fury. Piles of furs and blankets served as final beds, smashed boxes as the last reserves of supplies.

A message was scrawled in soot on one of the pillars, the black smeared through with deep, dark brown. Kraven brought the torch closer.

Atlan read the words. "Here lies the last of the dwarves of Gulied Mountain…Beware of gases. High prince…Rufius."

"Your father?" Mira snarled.

"No," he said, ears drooping once again. "He's my uncle."

Mira looked at the bones around her ankles, most thin, fragile, or small.

"The elderly. Children," she said. "Anyone who couldn't work in the mines."

"I'm sorry, Mira."

"Children."

"I didn't know!"

She sprang from the ashes. Advancing on him, she lifted the crown. He stepped back. She swung. Pain bit through her arm—an effect from their contract—and the metal whinged back inches from his sweet spot.

"Stop it," he said.

She tried again.

"Stop it," he repeated, and this time retreated, holding up both hands. She came forward, swinging harder.

"Murderer," she said, crown swinging back. "*Murderer.*"

"Mira, I—"

"Murderer!" Running at him, she kicked and punched, lunging at anything close, trying anything to land a blow. Kraven tried to stop her but couldn't get near. Atlan's foot caught on a stone, and he fell back, hitting a table.

She swung for his face, hands flinging back again and again as she screamed.

He didn't resist her.

With a final anguished yell, her hands stopped, crown gripped in both just shy of his nose. Flames of pain poured down her arms from the effort.

He met her gaze, yellow to green, and her grip faltered. Blood trickled down her palms in twin half-moons, oozing out around the metal.

"I'm sorry," he said. "I'm sorry."

"Aaaaaaaggggghhhhh!" Mira screamed again, throwing the crown across the room. Tripping over his leg, she fell, grit and ash smearing into her wounds.

Squeezing her fists around the slick, red curves on her palms, Mira sobbed, fury and sorrow so thick as to nearly choke her. Of all the people to be stuck with, of all the people to find this place with, it had to be him.

And she couldn't even kill him, couldn't avenge their deaths.

Couldn't do anything.

Animals, she thought. Murdering, slaving, animals.

Atlan didn't move, letting her sob. His leg was still pinned under her ankles. She could feel it every time he moved, feel every muscle pinch, every uncertain twitch. His hand hovered over her back so close she could feel it, though he didn't touch her.

Then, he withdrew. Pulling his foot out from under her, he stood. She heard him retreat and root through their packs. He said Kraven's name, then an order in Fransec.

A moment later, Kraven crouched before her, a roll of gauze in one hand, his gloves in the other. She heard more noise from the bogey, the thin slither of leather on leather, the familiar click of popping latches. Stone scraped as he sat on a table, and then came the delicate tuning of strings.

Kraven took her hands, his bare fingers cold on her skin. She jerked back on instinct, but he only grabbed her hands again. When she stopped fighting, he began to wrap them. The tuning stopped, silence filling the room like a breath.

Then, Atlan started to play.

A soft, sad melody, it started as a single, quavering spiral, searching and alone. Adding more strings, chords, he built on the sound, molding a deep, rich landscape, a village of sound. Joyful notes sprang across the instrument's face, shouting from one to another, calling back and forth in a communal chorus. His fingers flashed, danced, building up to a wild crescendo, and then the melody changed. A thrumming march paired with discordant harmonies, bringing with it loss, terrible loss, age and time and the crumbling of strength. The onslaught of armies on innocent lands. Notes crashed in violent dissonance, working in strange in-between tones Mira had never heard. Strings shrieked. Halting runs ended in drop after drop. For several minutes, the music seemed to swirl in a dizzying tumult of loss and confusion, spiraling down until only the first small melody remained, wounded and limping on. The strongest, harshest song she'd ever heard, it seemed to cross centuries of time in moments, lifetimes in minutes.

Kraven's hands stilled, leaving off in their work.

It was the most beautiful thing she'd ever heard.

The melody recovered, regaining some of its joy before trailing off in a sad sort of whimper. The bogey prince continued to play, something softer, easier, but his fingers slipped, notes bowing. With a grunt of pain, he dropped the melody. He caught it, barely, and brought it down to something simpler still, something easy. Kraven resumed his work, and Mira realized she was no longer crying.

Easing off like a bell tolling in the distance as Kraven tied off the last of the bandages, Atlan finished playing. As the last notes buzzed into echoes above, he set his palms on the strings, cutting off the sound.

When he lifted his hands, Mira caught sight of his fingers.

They were covered in blood.

THIRTEEN

The music left Kraven spellbound. He had heard live music in his village back home of course, had even been dragged out onto the dance floor by Ines on more than one occasion, but what Atlan offered...Kraven had no words. Even with his injuries, the bogey had not been exaggerating his prowess. The effect was mesmerizing. Even knowing Atlan's injuries, Kraven was tempted to ask him to play again.

A glance at the motionless Mira, however, a stark reminder of where they were, who Atlan was, and what the prince's people had done, was enough to quell the instinct.

Atlan's family had killed the dwarves. Slaughtered them in their own home. The thought made Kraven sick, and a sudden urge to move or get away swept over him.

Atlan moved first. Their last torch was flickering like a man's last breath from its place propped up on a metal plate. As Kraven moved to stand, the bogey spoke. "Kraven, go find a new torch. *Une nouvelle torche.*"

Kraven pulled a face, in no mood to be ordered around, but another quick glance at Mira reminded him now was not the time to argue. And the bogey was right. They needed light if they were going to continue. He drew on his gloves, standing to leave. Then he saw Atlan's hands. The bogey had a wound on his arm as well, a dust-clogged trap having misfired when they'd chased after Mira. Kraven hesitated, then started pulling his gloves back off.

"It's alright," said Atlan, catching the motion. "*C'est bon. Prends la torche. S'il te plait.*"

Kraven frowned. The bogey needed treatment. On the other hand, perhaps the bogey's injuries were not the only thing to be mended. Atlan, face drawn into a tight and thoughtful look, stared at Mira, his hands slowly bleeding into his lap. Mira, staring at her own bandaged hands, didn't move. Neither spoke, but there was something to their shared stillness, a kind of tension or bond. It felt like a crack in a sea cliff, a fissure ready to shear off a chunk.

Kraven decided it was best to give them a moment. If something did break between them, Kraven did not wish to be there when it did. Handing the gauze off to the prince, he left the room, Drake, as he always did, following behind. Kraven took the remaining torch, knowing that Atlan would be able to see by the scattered luminescent moss dusted across the ceiling and the dim light his torch supplied from the hall. As to Mira, well, perhaps it was better for her not to see.

As he left, he felt some pressure within himself release, and knew it was good for him to get away, too, to leave them to their quiet. Kraven could not stand the sight of the room, no, tomb. He was, of course, not unfamiliar with death. He had trained as a physician even before he had joined the Guard and had seen more people die than most his age. Infirm old men and women he'd been tasked to sit with, those injured in accidents or sick with various maladies or disease.

Each witness had been terrible in its own way, but this was different. This had not been the natural march of time ushering someone into the dark—or light, depending on what one believed. This was not cruel accident or fate robbing a life of its unmarked minutes.

This had been wholescale slaughter, completed with malicious intent, and the very thought of it made his gut roil and his hands tremble with rage.

It was just as the bandits had done. Just as it had been with Ines.

Kraven stopped, forcing himself to catch his breath.

The bandits who had killed Ines were dead. They couldn't hurt anyone anymore. He squeezed his fists, felt her gloves around his hands. She wasn't entirely gone, he thought, even though she was.

Drake nudged Kraven's shoulder, reminding him of their current task, and he forced himself to continue. Only then did he realize his brow was cool with sweat. Drake let out a worried coo.

"*C'est bon*, Drake. *C'est bon*," he muttered.

But he was not okay. Not really. Because Atlan was heir to the bogey empire, and beautiful as the music had been, as difficult as it was to think that the bogey might have known—as much as Kraven *didn't* believe he had known—that didn't change what he had seen in that room or what the bogeys could really do.

Kraven knew that he had treated Mira poorly now, too. Naveen had confirmed the truth of Mira's accusations, Mira herself even providing proof with her scars. And still, the truth of the matter had seemed far off, somehow separate from their lived reality. Even at his most assumptive or self-important, even at his most imperious or know-it-all-ish, Atlan had also been kind and polite, far more tolerant towards Mira than Kraven would have expected from a slaver or even just a regular royal. Compared to Mira, with her near constant venom, her exhausting paranoia, and extreme alacrity in the art of insults, Atlan had surely been the party more in the right, the one preferable both as ally and friend.

But now...now the true reality of the bogey prince and his people, realities Kraven had tried to push aside in the chaos leading up to and after the attack on the centauri camp, had come into sharp, undeniable focus. Kraven could tell from the bones that many of those killed had been elderly or children. With the advantages Kraven knew bogeys had in both size and strength, it would have been a massacre even had the dwarves all been soldiers.

His shoulders sagged. Annoying or mean as Mira could be, he now knew he should have treated her kindlier. Ines would have been disappointed.

And of course, now that he knew, what was he supposed to do about it? Atlan was next in line to a kingdom of horrors. If Kraven helped him, wouldn't he be helping them, too? What if he brought the bogey to the very brink of the yochni itself, hand-delivered the prince to the yochni's door? He didn't want to kill Atlan, but if they went on like this, if he or Drake or Mira were only forced to kill or be killed by the bogey later, surely it was better to end things now. Why put off the inevitable if he was only going to get more attached? Why take the risk?

He wondered, not for the first time, what Ines would do. Surely the right thing, if there even were such a thing. She had always seemed to know what to do, even when she hadn't. Even when she had been puzzling through something or suffering, there had always been an assurance about her, some kind of internal compass or confidence that she would find the right way, that she would make it through.

Kraven wished he had the same self-assurance himself. He'd been so sure he'd made the right decision when he'd come up with the arbitration. It had saved all of their lives, benefitted them all. He had done the right thing, hadn't he? Done what Ines would do?

But maybe he'd gotten it wrong after all. Or maybe it was just time for something new. Maybe it was time to move on.

He had the ability to cancel the contract. Atlan was well enough to walk on his own, and now that they were in the cave, surely Mira was safe from the hunters as well. They were safe, he could continue his journey, and if Mira and Atlan tried to kill each other after he left, well, that wasn't really his problem, was it? He couldn't be responsible for every spat between every group of combatants, nor could he be there to pull every argument apart. If he cancelled the contract now, he could simply walk away. Surely, he was far enough down the corridor that he wouldn't even be able to get back in time to stop them when the inevitable violence began....

Several more excuses ran through his mind, but even as they did, he knew they were weak, and getting weaker with each iteration.

Because, of course, he did know what Ines would have done.

She would have helped them both. Just as he had done when he'd made the contract. And just as, now, he knew he ought to do again. At least if he meant to follow her path.

Not, of course, that Kraven knew exactly what helping both of them was supposed to look like or how to do it. He sighed, rubbing a gloved hand over his face. There was, it seemed, only one way to find out. Perhaps Ines' ways really were rubbing off on him.

He and Drake reached the next room along the hallway, and Kraven, returning to his earlier task of finding a new torch, looked inside. He had already checked a few other rooms with little reward, the torch flickering dimmer with every step. Now, at last, he found what they needed. It was a storage room, several moldering sacks and boxes lined up against the wall. He saw evidence of wear, tiny holes where rodents had chewed through and the shriveled remains of vegetables which had long since sent out roots and, finding nothing, died. In the corner, under a series of buckets and tools hung from pegs on the wall, was an oil barrel, several torches poking up from the flammable liquid.

Kraven grabbed one, carefully rotating the wood as he lifted so as not to send rivers of liquid fire dribbling back onto his glove. He lit it, the room coming to life with a cheerful glow, then extinguished the last one before grabbing a couple spares. Leaving the rest of the supplies, he turned to exit the room.

He was just stepping into the hall when he heard it.

A soft noise, like the shuffling of a boot, almost too quiet to hear. He stopped, wondering if he'd misheard, but Drake was looking farther down the corridor as well. Kraven lifted the torch.

"*Bonjour*? Hello?"

Nothing. Kraven waited, but no further sounds came, no shapes shifted in the dark. Drake's nostrils flared in the slow, steady way they did when he was scenting, so different than Atlan's rapid-fire quiver, but if the sea dragon smelled anything, the scent appeared to be weak. When Kraven touched the dragon's leg, Drake turned and whuffed his master's hair, acting for all the world like a puppy who had been only momentarily distracted. Kraven frowned, but let it go. It was time to get back to the others.

FOURTEEN

When he entered the stillness of the great hall, Kraven found Mira and Atlan waiting, clearly alerted to his approach by the light and the sound of his call. Both of them were on their feet, Atlan with his claws poking out from the tips of his new bandages, Mira with her axe in hand. Her tears had dried on her cheeks, giving her face a strangely streaked appearance in the fiery glow.

"*C'était quoi?*" Atlan asked, nodding towards the hall outside.

Kraven gave a dismissive wave. "*Désolé.* Sorry. I thought I..." He stopped, cupping an ear to indicate sound.

Atlan frowned. "What did it sound like? *A quoi ça ressemblait?*"

Kraven shook his head. For all he knew, it could just have been Drake or a figment of his imagination, unlikely as Drake's reaction made that seem. He explained as much to Atlan, though when he saw the bones again, he found it difficult to face the bogey heir head on.

Atlan, trained as a diplomat since youth, fell silent for a long moment, then asked, "*Vas-tu bien?*"

Kraven was not okay, but he only shrugged, giving a weak

gesture to the chamber around them. Atlan's features grew drawn, but he kept quiet, perhaps mindful that Mira was still listening even if she could not understand.

"*Je ne tolérerais jamais cela,*" he said, voice soft. "*Je ne ferais jamais rien de tel.*"

"*Je sais,*" said Kraven, though he couldn't entirely keep the mistrust from his voice. The bogey was claiming innocence, that he would never tolerate such behaviors, but of course, even if he had known about the massacre ahead of time, even if Atlan himself had ordered it, Kraven suspected the bogey's answer would have been the same.

The bogey pursed his lips but didn't push any further. "We'll keep an eye on it, look harder if we hear anything else," he said. "Mira?"

Kraven opened his mouth to scold the bogey, certain it was too soon to push her, but the dwarven champion was already on her feet. She retrieved the ash-covered crown. Brushing it off against her pant legs, she shoved it into her bag.

She thrust the table aside, then took the lit torch from Kraven. Stepping into the corridor, she turned to the right, away from where the noise had been. Kraven watched her go, too surprised to even follow at first, but then Atlan touched his shoulder, nodding towards the corridor. Kraven headed out after Mira but looked back to find Atlan checking the tunnel's left branch, his snout to the air. The bogey didn't seem to find anything, and soon he followed as well.

They walked through nearly unending tunnels. Atlan stayed in the back, Mira serving as de facto guide in front with Kraven and the animals filling an uneasy gap in between. With each lost in their own thoughts, nobody spoke, even the animals seeming to pick up on the dreary mood.

Phantom sounds and scents seemed to follow, too.

Though Kraven never heard or smelled anything else, Atlan continued to stop and sniff, his black ears swiveling and twitching as if tracing miniscule sounds and whispers. Several times, he pivoted, posture going as straight as a pointing hound. But each time, he only turned back, ears drooping as if disappointed. Or afraid.

Mira was not open to the idea of a follower. The first few times Atlan stopped, she froze, axe half-raised. By the tenth time, she no longer so much as looked back. By the twentieth, her shoulders were so scrunched with irritation she was practically walking with a hunch.

Kraven was astonished she made it to the thirtieth, though it proved to mark her limit.

"What are you *doing*?" she snarled. "And would you *stop*?"

"I can hear something," Atlan defended. "I think there's something there."

"That's just your imagination."

"It's not my imagination," he said. "Drake is reacting too."

"He's probably reacting because you're reacting. You're being paranoid."

"It's not just the noises. It's the scents, too. They're too... young, new."

"That's me."

"No, it's not. I know what you smell like. This is different."

"So *what*?" she snapped. "What difference does it make? Even if there is someone here, what are you going to do about it? Hunt them down? Chase them? Ki—?"

She stopped herself, but she hardly needed to for them to know what she meant. Even Kraven, who had struggled to follow most of the conversation, couldn't miss the accusation. Except, where he might have expected her to finish her sentence, she had stopped, and where he would have expected to see her usual scowl, he saw a mouth that twitched with indecision, eyes that carried a look he could almost swear was doubt. For a moment, Mira's gaze bored into Atlan's, but then, whatever she was feeling, she forced it down, burying it deep inside.

Drake shuffled on dry feet, letting out an unhappy coo. The sea dragon was not meant for such arid conditions, his scales already starting to peel.

Kraven stepped between the feuding pair. "We go," he said.

He pointed to Batcha and his dragon to make his point clear. Neither of the animals were doing well—as if any of them were—and they needed to keep moving, find water or an exit. If they didn't, well, they might not make it at all.

Dropping back into the shadows, Atlan did not speak again for the rest of the afternoon.

They pushed until Kraven felt like his feet would rub away into nothing inside his boots, but eventually had to admit they weren't going to get out in a day. Mira, reluctantly, found them a place to rest, a storeroom where she found Atlan's presence least disagreeable to rest in. Barrels lined cobwebbed shelves along two walls, the other two bare. A large barrel in the corner held stagnant water. What the others contained Kraven could neither tell nor care. The weary troop shuffled in, leaving Drake and Batcha—who had developed a surprising affinity for the dragon—to settle in the hallway outside. The three companions slumped to the floor.

For a moment, Kraven closed his eyes, breathing deeply. It had been an exhausting day, and he only wanted to sleep. Still, if only for the sake of keeping the torches burning, he knew they'd have to set a watch. Perhaps he could convince Drake or—

"Kraven," said Mira, sounding concerned.

Kraven opened his eyes, his gaze following her pointing finger to Atlan. He was breathing heavily—heavier than he should have—and a long dark streak had smeared the barrel beside him. The bogey's arm was still bleeding.

Kraven frowned. *"Il saigne toujours?"* he asked. He'd dressed the wound properly on one of their earlier breaks, and it should have stopped bleeding not long after that. Now, Atlan's dark sleeve was soaked to the wrist, the silk heavy with red.

"You should have said something," said Mira with a strange edge to her voice, almost like a scolding mother.

The bogey opened one eye and forced a tremulous smile to his lips. "You didn't seem like you wanted to talk," he rasped.

"Stupid," she started, then stopped, folding her arms. She looked aside. "You're bleeding all over the floor."

"Would you like me to get a jar?" he asked.

"Atlan," Kraven scolded. But the anger he had seen flash in Mira's eyes was already gone, quelled by what Kraven thought might be actual concern. With no time to investigate the sudden change in her demeanor, he handed her the torch.

Crouching beside the bogey, he took off his gloves. Atlan gave a pained hiss when Kraven prodded the wound, and the medic gestured for him to unbutton his shirt. Atlan did, peeling it back from his arm and shoulder.

"Mira, *mon sac*," said Kraven. He pointed to his bag, snapping and gesturing for her to bring it over.

She did, though she almost missed his fingers as she handed it off, her gaze drifting to the prince.

"De l'eau," said Kraven. *"De l'eau."*

"Water," gasped Atlan, providing translation.

Mira shook her head as if clearing her thoughts and scuttled off to grab their canteens. As Kraven started his work, she brought him the first one, then filled another from the barrel.

The wound had seemed innocuous enough. Shallow and clean-edged, it wasn't even that long, about the length of one of Kraven's fingers. Compared to Atlan's size, it should have been an easy fix, the simple stitches he had applied earlier more than enough to seal it closed.

But it wasn't. Blood still pulsed weakly out between the stitches, steady as if Kraven hadn't treated the wound at all. There was only one reason he could think of for the wound to still be bleeding.

"*Du poison,*" he said.

Mira looked up sharply, the pronunciation of the word perhaps similar to its Itsrec translation, but when Atlan caught the motion, she only looked away. Moving to stand by the door, she set her gaze out into the dark, away from the bogey prince. Kraven asked Atlan if he had any other symptoms.

Atlan didn't, other than feeling a little weak. Kraven shoved an extra crust into the bogey prince's hands and ordered him to eat.

"*Pouvez-vous faire quelque chose?*" Atlan asked after a small bite. "*Aide?*"

Kraven frowned, rubbing his temples with one pale and bloodied hand. In truth, he wasn't sure what he could do. The problem was twofold. First, without knowing exactly what was causing the bleeding, it was difficult to know the cure. Second, and more importantly, even if he did know how to fix it, without access to greater supplies, he wasn't sure he could. There was one sliver of good news though, thin as it was. He passed it along.

"What did he say?" asked Mira.

Atlan grimaced. "It didn't hit any major veins, so I'm not in any danger of bleeding to death. At least, not yet."

She turned back to the hall again, her reaction difficult to read. Whether it was because she was worried Atlan was going to live or going to die was difficult to say.

"Can you slow it down at least?" asked Atlan. "*Pouvez-vous ralentir le saignement?*"

Kraven gave an uncertain shrug, digging through their packs for something that might help. He found a small jar of glue used for binding bandages. It wouldn't fix the underlying problem, but it might buy them more time. He smeared the glue onto the wound.

Atlan asked how much time he had. Kraven frowned, tilting his head as he considered. As before, it was difficult to say. He had never met a bogey before, let alone treated one besides Atlan. Without knowing how much blood the bogey prince had to lose, it was impossible to guess, though, thankfully, Atlan didn't seem to be bleeding particularly fast. If they were lucky, they might be able to exit the caves before things grew too severe; whether he would be able to tend him after that was still unknown. Kraven offered his prognosis.

"Great," said Atlan. "Thanks."

Kraven nodded and started wrapping the wound. Mira turned back to the room, wandering to a corner from whence to watch his progress. Atlan watched her in return, though neither of them spoke. Eventually the bogey's eyelids started to droop.

Kraven drew out Johann's knife, cutting through the strip of gauze. He pressed the end down lightly against the rest of the bandage, sealing it with the sticky layers underneath. He glanced at Atlan's face. The bogey was asleep.

A shadow fell across his patient, and Kraven looked up to find Mira.

"Is it done?" she asked. "Finished?"

Kraven nodded, wiping his hands clean before pulling his gloves back on. Her expression was difficult to read. Something had changed.

"You are okay?" he asked. "The room...."

She grimaced and shook her head, her dirty blond braids

slipping against her shoulders. Her gaze returned to Atlan, however, and she neither rebuffed Kraven nor retreated as he had expected. She bit her lip. "It's terrible, what they've done. Bogeys murder dwarves. Enslave dwarves."

Kraven, who managed to catch most of her meaning thanks to their previous conversations and lessons with Atlan, nodded. He watched her a moment longer, studying the pained lines dimpling her normally child-smooth features. Though she had spoken of the bogeys' cruelty, he couldn't help but notice the worry in her face, her gaze directed at the bogey prince.

"Mira...you are...afraid..." He thought hard, wanting to make sure he chose the right word. "For Atlan?"

The surprised expression on her face told him he had chosen correctly.

"No," she snapped. "Maybe. I don't know. It's confusing. And annoying."

Kraven, who struggled to follow what appeared to be her rather contradictory set of phrases, pretended he had understood her perfectly. He had not seen Mira open up in this way before—or at all, really, and while he could not trace her every word, he was curious to decipher what he could.

"You really think Atlan bad?" he asked.

Her expression slammed into an immediate scowl, though it seemed more defensive, less sincere, than he'd usually seen.

"Yes. I think." She shook her head. "He's a bogey. He has to be."

Kraven, fairly certain he'd understood despite what was obviously flawed logic, considered this. "He..." he mimicked strumming on the harp. "For you."

"So what?" she growled, though that, too, seemed insincere.

Kraven thought again, then said, "I think Atlan help. Or, want to help."

She gave an annoyed sniff, her voice regaining much of its usual mutinous tone. "Yeah? And what about you? Kraven still help?"

The question took Kraven off guard. He had not mentioned his internal debate about whether to abandon the squabbling pair to either of them. Perhaps he was easier to read than he thought. Or perhaps, he thought wryly, going back on his promise of help was simply the logical response. The non-Ines approach.

He sighed. "I help. Atlan and Mira. Both."

She watched him, her green eyes sharp in the light of the torch. Her gaze fell to his gloves, and he couldn't help but pull them away, out of her sight.

"Mira," he said. "Your wish. You will...?"

Before she could answer, a noise caught their attention—a small, glassy clink, almost like a toast of glasses, followed by a barely audible grunt.

Kraven and Mira hopped to their feet, exchanging a look. Drake gave a low warning hiss outside, Batcha letting out a low moan. Mira jogged Atlan's arm, rousing him from sleep, and the bogey blinked at them with slow, sleepy eyes.

"What—?" Atlan started. His nose quivered. His eyes went wide. "*No.*"

Too late.

Footsteps raced in the hall outside and a clay ball about the size of Kraven's fist clattered into the room. A small fuse sputtered and cracked, and thick, caustic smoke filled the air. The smell of rotten eggs choked the chamber, the fumes burning at their eyes. More smoke bombs bounced and rolled into the room. Crossbows fired in the corridor. Drake and Batcha shrieked.

Before any of the trio could react, a dozen figures swarmed the room. Not one of them was over four feet tall.

CHAPTER

FIFTEEN

The dwarves made quick work of their ambush. Atlan didn't even have time to get to his feet before one of them slammed him in the sweet spot with the back of their spear. Fiery pain coursed through his stomach, dropping him to hands and knees. The dwarves washed over him like a deadly wave, dragging him to the ground and wrenching his arms behind him. He tried to shake them off, to swipe out in defense, but there were too many, their grip too strong. He cried for mercy, yelping in pain, but they paid him no mind. Yanking his head up by the ears, they forced a belt around his snout, cinching it tight against his tender flesh. He didn't even have time to bite. Somewhere beside him, he heard Kraven crying out. Mira shouted in alarm. Drake's initial roars quieted to painful whimpers. What had happened to him and Batcha, Atlan couldn't tell.

Within two minutes, it was over, every member of their party securely bound or handled. Lying flat on his stomach with six or seven dwarves spread out along his back and legs, it was all Atlan could do to move his tail, even that resulting in the weapons that ringed him pressing closer in. Two spears snugged up against his cheeks, the cool eye of an axe pinching

155

the back of his neck. Kraven and Mira, similarly restrained though less securely guarded, lay on their stomachs to his left. Atlan tried to catch Mira's eye, to gauge her response, but she looked as startled as the rest of them, a stunned, hollow expression painted across her face. Atlan's sweet spot burned with pain, and nausea bit at his stomach.

The dwarves wore bandanas or scarves with dark-tinted goggles hanging from their necks or propped up on their fore-heads. Jars of pale luminescent blue moss hung from neck-laces or shoulder clips for light. With their prey well and truly bound, one of them stepped forward, drawing down a dirty scarf to reveal a dark and wiry beard, twin lightning strikes of gray flashing through it to match the ones at his temples. His forehead was high and craggy under his goggles, his dark mud-colored eyes shining with a hatred deeper, older, and angrier than even Mira could have managed. Atlan wondered if he should attempt to ask for a voice as the dwarf approached, to signal a desire to speak, but something told him to make the attempt would do more harm than good.

For a moment, the dwarf stared at him, his gaze drilling through Atlan's skull. "Do you have him?" he asked, looking to the dwarf holding the axe on Atlan's neck.

"Yes."

"Are you sure?"

"Yes."

"Good." The elder dwarf's shoulders relaxed as he let out a breath.

Then, whipping back with a force and speed the bogey prince would not have expected, he kicked Atlan right in his mending nose. Atlan let out a shrieking yelp, even the impro-vised muzzle not enough to fully smother the sound. Jerking back and away, he cut his cheek on one of the spears. The dwarf on his shoulders shoved his head back down to the floor, and the rest resettled along his back like disrupted birds on their roosts. Kraven tried to argue in Atlan's defense. Atlan heard the boy receive his own kick, followed by the sharp snap of the damaged bone in the medic's formerly healing cheek. Kraven howled in pain but soon went deathly silent. Blinking through tears, Atlan looked over to see a knife newly settled along the boy's throat. Warm blood dribbled out of Atlan's nose.

Mira lay motionless past the boy, still stuck in whatever thought had caught her first. Atlan could tell her mental gears were trying to turn, but that they'd been jammed by the dwarves' sudden appearance, their unexpected but very real survival.

He wasn't sure what would knock her out of it, but then the dwarven headman, having had his fill of torture for the moment, walked down the line to stand before her. She gazed at him, eyes vacant, and then, something clicked. Atlan could almost imagine her thoughts shifting into place. A dwarf. A real dwarf. Alive. And then, yes, the bloom of new thought. The dwarves—at least some—had survived. Her body relaxed, and a warning knot started to coil in Atlan's stomach.

The headman glanced between his two prisoners and Mira. She paid neither Atlan nor Kraven any mind, and after a moment, the leader gestured to the dwarf that was pinning her down. "Let her up," he said.

The dwarf did so, shoving Mira forward to meet the headman. From his position on the floor, Atlan saw her gaze flit briefly to Kraven and himself. There was a hint of doubt, no, regret, perhaps, in her features, but it didn't last long, snuffing out as quickly as the wick of a candle. She turned back to the dwarven headman and from then on paid her companions no further heed. The worried knot grew.

"You're alive," said Mira. She made a show of rubbing her recently freed wrists. The dwarven leader, watching her with wary eyes, was not impressed.

"Who are you?" he asked.

"Mira," she said. He waited. "Goldfist. Dwarven champion." She said it with confidence, but he raised a brow, clearly still suspicious.

"From?" he said.

Mira's gaze flicked briefly to Atlan, as if she were still afraid to let the name of her home slip in his presence, then answered: "Haufin."

"Mira," interrupted Kraven, trying to draw her attention. One of the dwarves holding his hair tightened his grip and the boy flinched in pain. "*Mira.*"

She was careful to keep her expression neutral. Atlan didn't even bother seeking her attention. He knew it wouldn't help.

The dwarven leader continued as if Kraven hadn't spoken. "Haufin, eh? I have cousins there." He spat, just missing Atlan's eye. "Or at least, I did. Hard to know if they're still alive."

Mira gave a commiserating nod.

"It's strange for a dwarven champion to be traveling with their kind," said the headman.

The dwarf with the axe resting on Atlan's neck leaned as the dwarven leader spoke, the blunt eye of the weapon pressing painfully in. Atlan tried not to react, though when it started pinching his nerves, he couldn't help but let out a low groan.

The headman watched Mira.

"There were...circumstances," she said.

The headman's expression drew down into an even craggier frown. "I see. And the boy?"

Mira hesitated, then said, "He's the circumstances."

Kraven, who was clearly unfamiliar with the word, looked to Atlan for translation, ever careful not to slit his own neck. Atlan had no way to speak with his muzzle and no way to move with the twin spears resting against his cheeks. Even if he could have, it would not have helped.

The dwarves had taken their supplies when they attacked, dumping out Kraven and Atlan's things and rifling through Mira's. Atlan was careful not to react, even when they started scraping at the locks for his harp. Kraven's expression boiled with rage at the indignity.

One of the dwarves found the metal crown Mira had pulled from the dwarven ashes.

"Soom," she said, handing it over.

The dwarven leader held it up, giving Mira an expectant look.

For a moment, her cheeks reddened, as if she had been caught with her fingers poking into the pie. "I was going to return it. I had it for the next of kin."

Soom nodded, though whether he actually believed her wasn't clear. He rubbed his fingers over the delicate inlay, then brushed off the rest of the ash and blood. He settled it reverently on his crinkled hair and let out a satisfied sigh. "My father's," he said.

He gave the group a measuring look, lingering on his prisoners the longest, then gestured from his people to Kraven and Atlan. "Gag him and get them up. We'll take them to the forge." He turned to Mira. "As for you, I think you've got a story to tell. Better hope for your sake it's a good one."

Atlan knew any story Mira would have to tell would not go in his favor. He tried to catch her eye before she left the room, to beg mercy for himself and Kraven, but she would not meet his gaze, and he could tell by the look on her face that the scales had already tipped. He shared a look with Kraven, the boy's face flush with wrath and fresh bruising.

So much for making progress.

The dwarves had ringed both Kraven and Atlan's necks with spear tips, keeping a close eye should either one try anything funny. Two more prodded Atlan's legs with their spears once they were both standing, and the dwarves and their captives stepped out into the hall. Batcha seemed unharmed, perhaps shielded by the dragon or simply missed by the bolts. Drake swayed on wobbly legs, side and chest pin-cushioned with crossbow bolts. No doubt they had been coated with some kind of sedative, given the dragon's woozy expression. Kraven's eyes narrowed with rage at his dragon's injuries, though with their new restraints, there was little either of them could do.

The dwarves prodded them again, forcing their captives into motion, and Mira began her story.

It was exactly as farcical as Atlan had expected. Though she made very few accusations against him directly, she made little effort to hide anything about him either, keeping no secrets about how they had come together or his position as bogey champion, heir to both the Gulied clan's slaughterer and the bogey throne. Of the time he had saved her life, she said nothing at all, nor his music in the dining hall, saving Batcha from the fire, or even his many and earnest apologies on behalf of himself or his people. Dodging every possible chance to mention his more redemptive qualities, if anything, she picked up steam as she went, her depictions of him growing more grotesque by the minute. Towards her own flawed qualities, she was equally elusive, Kraven practically an evil mastermind by the end of it for having forced them together.

Atlan was disappointed to find he was surprised. The feeling quickly soured to anger.

By the time she started winding down, he could have ripped her in half. Even with Soom's clearly pre-set inclinations towards Atlan's guilt, he knew she could have done more to convince the dwarven headman of his innocence, or at least not have bulked Kraven in with his lot. She could have at least tried to help the boy, but, he supposed, being helpful —or showing any kind of mercy, apparently—just wasn't in her nature. Not for the first time, Atlan wished Kraven had never rescued her from the hunters.

Thankfully, however, even Mira's fount of deceit had its limits, and while her steady stream of half-truths made their journey through the tunnels seem unending, eventually her fable did come to an end. With it, so too did the surrounding darkness. Pale yellow light bloomed at the end of the tunnel, replacing the luminescent blue of the dwarves' moss-filled jars. As Atlan readjusted his arms again, ever wary of slitting his throat on his new collar, the echoing roar of a giant water-fall and the undertones of a gathering crowd rumbled down the hall. Faint scents of iron and fire, oil and coal floated on the drifting air. Wherever their destination was, it was huge, both scents and sounds muddied with echoes.

Something tickled at the back of his mind, some book or scroll he had read, and then, as he caught his first distant glance of their destination, he understood.

Of course, he thought, stepping out from under the lip of their tunnel. This was no small smithy tucked into abandoned halls. No, this was something far, far greater.

Fanren's Forge.

Or at least, what was left of it.

One of the oldest smelting operations in the world, and one of the largest, it was a massive cavern nearly half a mile across. High, banded walls of red, yellow, and iron gray stone rose to a ceiling nearly a hundred feet above them, their sides scalloped out into a giant, terraced bowl. Side rooms for individual forges lined tier after tier, slanted, dormant chimneys poking out from the walls to siphon smoke into central chambers and distant vents. Minecart rails ran along several tiers with rotting platforms, switches, and bridges for delivering ores and metals crisscrossing the wide, open distances between. Elevators as small as Mira to as big as Drake ran up long shafts to the luminescent moss-dusted ceiling, and grand carvings of Eleata and her children danced over the walls. Some fifty dwarves of varying ages gathered on the tiers below them, though their own expressions were not so merry.

Atlan had read volumes about the place. If he weren't so sure he was about to be murdered, he'd have been exploring everything in sight. But he was going to be killed, and not all of the history books and knowledge he'd gained in all his life was going to change that. Luckily for him, he had more tools at his disposal than books and scrolls.

Readjusting his fingers again, he gave the ropes another scrape with his claws. He'd already managed to saw through the first strand during their trip through the dwarven tunnels. If he could cut through the other two, there was a chance he could still live.

Walking out into the yellow light of the cavern, Atlan was met by the jeers and boos of several dozen dwarves. Dwarf-sized tunnels now lined the walls of the forge like the haunts of ground bees, perhaps last lines of defense or shelter in case the bogeys came again. He wondered briefly if this was where they lived now, but the scents were too faint, the darkened forge too run down and coated in dust. Of the dozens of chandeliers and chains of lanterns strung across the massive cavern, only a half dozen or so were lit. The tanks and water-wheels meant to catch and divert the waterfall spilling from some eighty feet up the wall lay stagnant and waterlogged or rotting, the sluice gates, levers, and pulleys to work them clogged with decades of dust.

Starting down a wide, curving stone ramp, Soom led their group towards one of several large plateaus spread across the cavern's center. They appeared to serve multiple purposes, both as convergence points for the mine cart rails, stopovers for traveling across the cavern, and, as appeared to be their current purpose, oratory platforms for events. Three massive ore crushers took up most of the rest of the floor. Slanted conveyer belts and shoots led from one to another and on to waiting furnaces. Thankfully, none of the furnaces were lit, each sleeping under a thick blanket of gray dust and soot. Reaching the plateau, the dwarves nudged Atlan and Kraven forward, bringing them both within inches of the edge. From above, Atlan could see the fanged gears lining the crushers, waiting to mince them both into jelly. He slowed his pace, steps shrinking as he drew nearer, and the crowd gathered around him laughed.

"Turn around," growled Soom.

Atlan did, his heels biting the platform's lip. Kraven shot him a worried look, and Atlan redoubled his efforts behind his back, sawing furiously at the rope's second strand. He hoped the dwarves on the tiers wouldn't see it snap. Lucky for him, it seemed Soom was ready to turn their executions into a show. Hopefully the headman would be long-winded enough to save their lives.

As if on cue, Soom turned to the crowd, a wicked grin smeared across his face. "Brothers, sisters," he said. "Tonight, we mark a grand occasion. It is with no small sense of irony that I tell you I am happy at last to have a bogey among us. Though our suffering has been great, fortune has smiled on us at last, bringing us not just any slaving mutt, but the nephew of our great persecutor himself."

A raucous cheer burst from the crowd, some members throwing stones or debris. None came close enough to hit Atlan, but he could hear them clang against the crushers and break on the floor. Kraven, whose former anger had long since melted into fear, stared at him in horror. Atlan sawed harder, his fingers bleeding through the gauze. Mira looked anywhere but at them.

"Not only that, but our fortune doubles," Soom continued. "For he is not only their heir, but also their champion, and he travels with a champion of our own. We have received a great gift!"

Grabbing her wrist, Soom lifted Mira's hand high to a thundering round of applause and cheering. Her reaction was difficult to read, snagged somewhere between victory and looking ill.

Atlan ignored her. The second strand had just snapped. He twisted his wrists against the third. Soom, if he noticed, didn't care. Lost in the rapture of his victory, he looked out to the gathered dwarves.

"Death," the dwarven leader said, voice now quavering with emotion, the weight of his grand purpose. "We are most of us not strangers to its cold visitations, have suffered the great grief of having those we loved taken—ripped—from our grasps. We have suffered not only under the great curse of the bogeys' oppression, but of those, too, who have aided them, who have stood by and watched us crumble even as they've helped the bogeys' further their evil cause."

At this, he pointed at Kraven. Atlan glared at Mira, but she didn't return his gaze.

Soom continued. "But our suffering is near an end. We will strike down those who would see us enslaved, and with this death, these deaths, we will rid ourselves of the bogey threat. With this one, final push, we will end their empire."

Grabbing a spear from one of his men, Soom twirled it in his hand, pointing straight for Atlan's ribs. He looked to a cluster of dwarves standing near the controls for the sluice gates. "Start the crushers!"

Atlan went rigid at the command, nearly forgetting to keep cutting the ropes. He was getting close, his bloody wrists now wrenching against the fibers. Behind him, he heard the creak of old gears, sluice gates clattering open, and chutes and pipes shrieking and clanging into place. A symphony of gurgling water and splashing streams crashed into being behind him, the diverted water racing down towards the wheels that would start the crushers, the gears that would grind his bones.

He was out of time. Shooting desperate looks to Kraven and Mira, he begged silently for their help, some kind of intervention. But Kraven was still on the edge himself, and Mira, though now looking his way, was pale and silent. It was too late. She wouldn't help. She was going to let him die.

Stepping forward, Soom lifted his spear, aiming for Atlan's sweet spot.

The headman lunged.

The final strand snapped.

Ripping his arms free, fragile skin shredding against the coils, Atlan side-stepped just in time, one leg spinning out and over the chasm behind him in a dangerous arc. The spear, thrust forward with enough force to have killed him even without the crushers, missed him by inches.

Atlan grabbed the weapon, the dwarven leader still clutching the other end. Swinging the spear like a scythe, bowling half a dozen dwarves off the platform's edge in the process, Atlan whipped Soom out over the crushers, the force of the motion sending the headman's metal crown spinning off and away. Atlan loosened his grip, ready to send the dwarf and spear flying.

"Father!"

Atlan slammed his fingers shut. Soom swung forward then back from the momentum, and found his level, dangling at the end of the spear like some oversized turkey's wattle.

A new dwarf had entered the scene. He stood at the top of a ramp, his hands clutching his knees. His chest heaved from exertion.

Soom grunted from his position at the end of the spear, hanging over the hungry gears.

"Kill them," Soom ordered. "Kill them!"

Atlan heard the shuffling of boots. His head whipped towards the sound, but he was a second too late to remember he wasn't the only one being guarded. With Soom at the end of his spear, the dwarves were hesitant to attack him. The same did not apply to Kraven. Aiming for his face and chest, the dwarves thrust forward with their spears.

Jerking back, the boy took a step. There was no ground waiting beneath it. With a look of sheer terror, Kraven fell over the edge.

CHAPTER

SIXTEEN

Drake, eyes still glazed from the sedative, leaped after his master like a dog after a stick, following the boy's body down and into the rumbling gears. Atlan heard the grunts of impact, a furious screech of metal.

Atlan ripped the belt from his face with his free hand, his other hand still grasping the headman's spear. Ducking down to grab one of the spears that the dwarves he'd knocked off the edge had dropped, he brandished it in front of him, warding back those who remained.

"Kraven," he shouted. "Kraven!"

The boy did not respond.

"Kraven!"

"*C-C'est bon! C'est bon. La couronne*, it stopped the...." The boy's voice trailed off, and Atlan risked a glance over his shoulder. Both boy and dragon had fallen into one of the crushers, the crusher's gears quaking as they struggled to grind. To the boy's left, he could see the twisted metal of the dwarven crown, hear the high shriek as it drew down into the serrated teeth. It had jammed them just in time.

Scooping up more dropped spears, Atlan threw them to the boy. They wouldn't stop the gears for more than a few

167

seconds, maybe not even that long, but perhaps they could help. Perhaps it could be enough. Thankfully, the crushers had not yet gotten up to full speed.

"Get out. *Maintenant,*" he said. To Soom, "Stop the water."

Soom laughed.

"Now!" barked Atlan.

"Never," grunted Soom. "You're going to die."

Atlan turned to the other dwarves. "I'll throw him in."

"Don't do it," countered Soom. "Kill him."

"Enough," came a third voice, the newcomer from before. Trotting down the ramp, he kept his eyes on Atlan. "Stop the water."

The gates clattered back into place. Below, Kraven urged his somnambulant dragon to move as the gears ground down to stillness.

"Arge..." Soom warned.

"Enough," said the dwarf.

The newcomer reached the platform.

At a guess he was in his mid-twenties, though with dwarves it was always hard to tell. His face held much the same structure as Soom's, though it was softer and of a more thoughtful cast. His hair was dark brown, tied back and smoother than the others'. Unlike most of the rest, his face was clean shaven. As he crossed the platform, his attention never left the high prince.

Mira, meanwhile, cowered against the other dwarves, her blond hair a pale flame amidst the others' blacks and browns.

Nice try, thought Atlan. Now that there was at least one dwarf who could see reason, the tables were about to turn. "Get them out," he said.

"No," said Arge.

"Kill him!" shouted Soom. "Do it, Arge, now!"

Atlan gave the dwarven leader a warning shake. His

wounded arm was starting to burn from the weight of the spear, the shaft digging into the back of his arm, but he held it steady, unwilling to let the weakness show. "Get them out," he repeated.

The dwarven heir looked unphased, almost curious. For a moment, he said nothing, then, "You're not as terrible as I thought you would be."

Atlan's ear twitched. "A bold thing to say when I've got your father dangling over a cliff," he said.

"Maybe," said Arge. "And maybe if you wanted to kill him, you would have done it already."

Atlan's tail, waving back and forth in a slow, angry arc, stopped. Clearly, the dwarven heir wasn't as stupid as his father. Or as blood thirsty. The dwarven headman muttered another threat, and Atlan shook him again. Arge kept his gaze steady.

"You were running," said Atlan. "Why?"

The dwarf's expression soured a degree, defenses rising.

"I think you know the answer to that," he said.

"I am certain I do not," said Atlan.

Arge glanced past Atlan to his father, who had managed to hook his legs up onto the spear, and, from what Atlan could tell, was trying clumsily to shimmy his way down.

"Come any further and you drop, dwarf," he growled.

Soom froze.

Arge didn't flinch. "There are men in the caves," he said, loud enough for all to hear. "Headed this way."

A whisper of dread buzzed through the crowd.

Atlan tried not to drop the spear.

"I'm certain they're yours," Arge continued.

Atlan looked to Mira. She was still trying to look as small as she could against the crowd. If he wanted to out her for lying, now would be the time. Spider and his men—and more importantly the fact they had chased them nearly all the way to the dwarves' doorstep—had been as cleanly downplayed in her story as Atlan and Kraven's kindness.

Satisfying as it would be to show her for the lying traitor she was, however, it wouldn't help him get out. And, murderous captors though the dwarves were, he didn't want their blood on his hands if he could avoid it. Not after what his uncle had done.

Letting out a huff, he lifted Soom's spear, hefting it to his shoulder so the dwarven leader hung from the shaft like a wanderer's pack.

"Slaving...*gojan*..." Soom muttered.

"Keep talking if you want to drop," said Atlan. Turning the conversation back to Arge, he continued. "They aren't mine. But I think I know who they might be. I can only assume my friend will be ground to paste if I do not return your father unharmed. Worse, that you'll all kill me as soon as I give him back. I propose a trade."

"Don't," said Soom. "Kill him. Just—"

Atlan let the haft slip up to the top knuckles of his fingers, the dwarven leader dropping nearly a foot before the spear caught. "Those men won't wait forever."

Arge's mouth twisted, his keen eyes running over the gathered dwarves, Mira, and his father before narrowing in on the bogey heir. "What do you propose?

Atlan stopped just shy of taking a deep breath, though he was sure Arge could see the relief in him all the same. He re-adjusted the spear to a more comfortable position and raised his voice loud enough for the whole forge to hear. "It has come to my recent attention that gas madness is a myth, a fact of which I had not previously been aware. My uncle's unconscionable crimes against your people are also a recent discovery. I do not wish to repeat the matter, nor to have my own life snuffed out. The deal is simple. Let me chase off the men, and if I succeed, we go free."

"Liar," cried Soom. "Whatever he's telling you—"

Atlan dropped the spear. The dwarves let out a collective gasp, but the angry grunt as Soom smacked into the gears below and the lack of subsequent screams told Atlan he had made his mark. The dwarf had landed after the gears had stilled. Atlan set the butt of his second spear against the platform. "I don't think we really have time for that kind of talk anymore, do you?" he asked.

There were two more spears lying at his feet, the one he held poised for fatal action. Even with the remaining dwarves surrounding him, if they wanted to take him down, it would not be easy or without cost.

Arge's features pinched, studying the bogey heir. Below, they heard a series of clangs, Soom scrabbling about in his crusher while Kraven slipped again in his. The medic let out a sharp bark of pain and Arge's eyes lit with a sudden cunning.

"We cannot take your word on its own. We need collateral, proof that you will keep your word. The boy," he said. "And the dragon."

Atlan's ears gave an irritable twitch. The dwarven heir was smart. Still, Atlan could hardly have hoped for better. He knew he would have had to give something in return, some proof of his good intentions. He glanced to Mira, curious as to her reaction, but she hadn't looked up from the ground.

"Fine," he said. "Anything else?"

"Only one," said Arge. "You don't go alone. We go with you."

"No."

"One."

"No."

"Me."

Atlan glared at the dwarf, but the look on Arge's face told him that the dwarven heir would not back down.

"You take me," the dwarf repeated. "If I don't return safely to confirm your success within the hour, my people kill the others. If you succeed, if the men leave our caves permanently without discovering our existence, you all go free. When you go, you tell no one of our existence and your people do not trouble us again."

Atlan scowled. The dwarf was lying of course. Or, if not lying, at the very least making promises he couldn't keep. Atlan knew the dwarves would kill him whether he scared the men off or not. Any talk of hostages or time limits was simply colored smoke. Still, the dwarves' duplicity hardly changed Atlan's intentions to follow through with his promise. He didn't want to repeat his uncle's mistakes and would do what he must to make sure that he didn't. If he failed to make a deal now, his only other options were to fight his way out or cut a deal with Spider when the hunter arrived.

"Fine then," he said. "Tell me what you saw."

SEVENTEEN

Arge gave his hurried report. By the time he was finished, Mira was certain that the men in the caves were Spider and his crew. Though their number had dwindled from their fight with the centaurs, they still had some of the additions they had picked up after Kraven had helped Mira escape, their number holding steady at seven or eight. Arge had been left behind as rear scout in case Atlan had brought any friends. When he had realized which direction Spider's men were going, he'd no longer had time to stop to get an accurate count.

Still, what information he did seem to have, he gave freely, confirming that Johann, with his single arm, had managed to survive, that the group was a mix of elves and humans, and that each one of them was still armed with nets, spears, or blades.

Atlan, getting care for his wounded arm from a dwarven attendant at his request, listened with the same cool patience he used when he explained things to Mira. If he noticed her presence at all, he ignored it. Mira scowled. She had, quite simply, miscalculated. Now, she was paying for it.

"And what would you suggest for me to scare them off?" Atlan asked.

The dwarven heir shrugged. "I'm sure your species' reputation precedes you. I'll lead you to their location, and when we reach them, you go ahead. By tooth, tongue, or coin, convince them to abandon their course. If you succeed, we return and I confirm your completion of our deal, releasing the lot of you to go free. Fail or fail to return in time, and we proceed with our original execution as planned."

Atlan's gaze drifted to Kraven and Drake. Already pulled from their prison at Atlan's demand and very unhappy to be serving as hostages, they stood on the platform with the groups' belongings, awaiting the success or failure of Atlan's mission. Whether Mira and Batcha's fate was to be tied in with Kraven and Atlan's was an area which, to her at least, still seemed largely legally gray.

The salve the dwarven attendant was using had a pungent, fishy smell. The old and broken trap that had struck Atlan before they'd found the dwarven tomb had been tipped with the same poison the dwarves had used against Drake during their ambush, the soporific effects the bogey might otherwise have suffered had the trap been newer lost with time. The dwarven attendant finished tying a cloth over the noxious solution—the scent no doubt ten times worse for the bogey prince's more delicate olfactory senses—and Atlan shooed her away.

"I'll need my things," he said, giving the bandage an exploratory examination with his hand. The dwarves exchanged nervous glances, with a few shooting questioning looks to Mira, though most turned to their new impromptu leader Arge. Atlan gave them a tired look. "If you want me to play monster, I need to look the part. Keep your word, and you've got nothing to fear from me."

Whether his eyes stopped on Mira, or she just imagined it,

was hard to say, but she could feel his anger all the same. Her stomach gave an irritating pulse.

"Do it," said Arge, nodding to two of the dwarves.

Dragging the bogey's pack forward, they laid it at his feet. A third offered his whip with shaking hands. The prince checked for his harp, then shouldered the pack. Finally, he took his whip. Letting it roll loose, he gave it a light slap against the ground to get out the kinks before re-coiling it into three neat loops and knotting it at his side. Whether the small, self-satisfied quirk at the corners of his mouth was because of how it made the dwarves—including Mira—jerk or something else was impossible to tell. He turned to go.

"Wait," said Mira.

Both Atlan and Arge turned, Arge's expression curious, Atlan's one of wrath.

"Yes?" said the dwarven heir.

"Take me with you," she said.

"No," said Atlan.

"Please."

"Why?" The bogey's voice was nearly a snarl, but she pressed onward.

"I...I want to help."

Atlan gave a derisive snort at that, but Arge looked thoughtful.

Mira pressed her case with the dwarf. "Please. I've no reason to get in your way or reveal your location. I won't do any harm. I just...please. I want to come."

Arge shot a curious glance to Atlan, perhaps seeking his opinion.

The bogey shrugged. "Whatever," he said, tone cold. "It makes no difference to me."

Arge gave the bogey a scrutinous look, then nodded, gesturing that Mira should join them. He led the way up the ramp from which he had come. Atlan went next, Mira trailing behind him. Soom, still being helped out of the crusher below, howled at the dwarves not to trust the bogey, to shove him off the edge of the ramp, but none complied.

The tunnel the dwarven heir had come through had twin doors, since closed. As the newly formed trio approached, two dwarves cracked them back open.

"Be careful," one of them whispered to Arge. She looked away when Atlan glanced down at her, as if pretending he wasn't there might make him disappear. The bogey huffed.

Arge only gave her a gentle smile. "Don't worry," he said. "I'm sure he will keep us safe."

The bogey champion's shoulders rippled at the remark. "Don't try anything funny," he growled and stepped into the dark.

The doors closed behind them with a grinding moan, the pale blue of the moss in Arge's necklace jar brightening in response. They had agreed not to take torches lest the men be alerted to their presence. With only the jar and a faint dusting along the ceiling for light, Mira couldn't see more than a few feet ahead, though she knew Atlan could see nearly as well as if it were a sunny day. He leaned his spear against the wall, the dwarven weapon—though surprisingly long for its usual wielder's size—of little use in their coming ruse. Arge had promised them that an hour of time was more than enough to reach the men and chase them off, but the prince kept them at a fast walk all the same, Mira and Arge nearly having to jog to keep pace behind him. He didn't ask any questions, Arge pointing out the turns without prompting.

The bogey's attitude to Mira was as indifferent as if she didn't exist. It bothered her that she cared. She tried to ignore it, but by the end of the first ten minutes, her frustration had built to a point she could no longer ignore. "Atlan," she said.

He paused, looking down at her over his shoulder. "Are you injured?"

"No."

"Then keep walking," he growled.

"Stop," she said.

He did. "What?"

She hesitated, her fingers tight on her axe. "Why did you let me come?"

He looked over his shoulder, yellow eyes thin glints in the dark. "You *asked* to come."

"I didn—" she said, voice going sharp. "You could've said no. If you're just going to ignor—"

"What are you, jealous?"

"No, I just—aren't you worried that I'll do something? Try something else?"

He turned fully towards her then, expression dark.

"No. You know why? Because you're a rat, Mira. And the thing about rats is, they always cling when they're going to drown. These people will die without my help—*your* people. So no, I'm not worried. At least not now. Whatever else you try later, I'll deal with as it comes."

It was impossible to miss the threat in his voice, the near promise of violence if she endeavored anything else. As they resumed walking, Mira drifted farther behind.

They padded on for another ten minutes, the only sound the shuffing of their feet or Arge's directions. At last, Atlan slowed, eyes narrowing to pale jewels in the bluish light. He stopped to smell, then jerked his head towards the tunnels forking off beyond.

"I can smell them," he growled. "Put away the light."

Mira, trailing behind, had nearly fallen out of the pale, luminous ring. As Arge tucked the jar back into his vest, she reluctantly pulled up alongside. Wiry fur swept them both as Atlan swatted them lightly with his tail.

"Hold on. Let go when you can see."

Mira grabbed the bogey's tail, Arge's form close on Atlan's

other side. His fur was softer than she expected, thick where it had managed to survive the rash. In the faint light of the ceiling moss, she could only vaguely make out his form, a mountainous shadow against the faint smokiness of the blue. It was the silhouette of a monster, his faint snuffing as he scented the dark the sound of nightmares. All the same, she could feel him guiding them both, keeping them from scuffing stones or bumping corners.

Stealing forward, feet almost silent now against the stone, they made their way down another two hallways with little more than the sound of Atlan's sniffing. The red dagger pattern on the back of his shirt rose and fell in a constant huff, nose buzzing at the end of his snout. Realizing with a jolt that she could see it, she let go, Arge doing the same. The faint glow of torchlight illuminated the intersection ahead. The shuffle and clank of equipment drifted around the corner, as well as the rumbling voices of Spider's party. She heard low grousing from their leader, Johann's patient reply.

Atlan's face curved into a fountain of downward angles, his feature's coming into ever greater detail as he approached the next corridor. Drawing up to his full height, he stepped to the corner, black ears peaked. Then he was gone, slipping around it and out of sight. Mira heard several startled shouts from the men, then the bogey's low and angry growl. "Who are you?"

"Wha—Spider, the name is Spider. These are my men, Joh—"

"What are you doing here?"

"You don't know? I was sent here."

"By whom?"

"You. Err, one of you, at least. Your champion, I think."

Mira nearly swallowed her tongue. Arge's gaze darted to her in the semi-dark. There was a slight pause from Atlan, one so brief she wouldn't have caught it if she didn't already know him. The bogeys only ever sent one champion. Atlan had assured them it was him.

"Our champion sent you here?" he growled.

"There was a dragon. He didn't have time, so he paid us the money for the dragon and the dwarf."

"Competitors," Atlan growled.

"Mmhmm. He said he'd pay good money for their heads and dragon parts sell so well...."

"I see, and you followed them here?"

"We smoked them out, followed their tracks."

"That was you," the bogey said.

"Yeah, well, ah, there were centaurs."

"Yes, I know."

"We killed a fair share of them, chased the rest off with the fire."

"I was their *guest*."

Spider didn't answer right away, and Mira heard the clanking of shuffling gear.

"There was a dwarf," Atlan said.

"And the boy?"

"Him as well."

"Where are they?" Spider asked.

Mira froze. If Atlan were intending to betray them, hand them over for what she'd done, now was his chance. The bogey paused, and she wondered if he was considering it. She knew she would have. A wash of guilt stirred in her stomach.

"The girl was mad," said Atlan. "I killed her myself not ten minutes past. I found the boy dying earlier. As a mercy, I killed him too."

"The dragon," Spider insisted.

"Already dead. It was badly wounded in the fire. I had to kill it before the boy."

"Is there nothing to claim?"

"I ate what I would. There is little whole remaining."

"The skin...."

"An excellent cloak in the making. Unless you would attempt to lay claim?"

She could almost hear Spider's knees knock.

"N-no, I wouldn't do that. Just trying to fulfill my duty. I was hired by your kind after all," the hunter said.

"How admirably dutiful of you," Atlan sneered. "You may return to your master and tell him the job is finished. The creatures you sought are dead."

"What if he doesn't believe me?" Spider asked. "Is there no proof I could bring? A sliver of scales perhaps?"

"I somehow doubt it would reach them," said Atlan with a knowing growl. He paused, the popping of the hunters' torches filling the space between. "Tell them Atlan has sent you. I am sure they will know what that means."

The hunters hesitated.

"Now would be the time."

With a clattering of gear and smattered thank yous, the men fled. The torchlight faded, and silence replaced their frantic boot stomps. A moment later, she heard the soft shuff of bogey feet, accompanied by the faint clack of claws on stone and three gentle taps against the wall. It was their signal that Atlan had returned. The taps came again, closer, then again, only a few feet away. She reached out a hand, feeling before her.

"Here," Atlan whispered, and his voice was no longer angry. He nudged her palm with his knuckles, and her fingers latched on to him like a death grip. He chuckled softly in the darkness, his usual laugh, normal, kind.

"Were you frightened?" he asked.

"Shut up," she said. "Yes."

"I can smell it on you, scaredy-cat."

She smacked his hand, but he didn't laugh, voice going somber.

"If it makes you feel any better, it was stronger on them."

Arge pulled out his glowing jar, and Atlan stood, padding forward into the shadows. The darkness swallowed his expression as he walked, and his tail swung, a slow arc of thought. The two dwarves fell in beside him, the trio starting back for the forge, and his chin found roost on his fingers.

"You were a monster," said Mira.

Atlan inclined his head, considering. Then his gaze settled on her.

"Perhaps a similarity between us," he said.

She looked away. "Maybe. But that doesn't make us alike."

He paused, expression once again losing to shadow. "We both want what's best for our people."

Arge looked between them as Mira considered. "Atlan, are you really their champion?"

Atlan stopped, flinching at the question. "Yes, I am, and the high prince."

"Then who is the other bogey?" the dwarven heir asked.

The high prince's voice took on its former, huskier tone. "I don't know."

EIGHTEEN

The group walked in silence for a while, each lost in thought about who the second bogey could be and, more importantly, who, if anyone, had sent the second champion.

They were running out of time, however, and they all knew unpleasantness would be waiting for them when they returned. The dwarves would not suffer Atlan to live. Mira wasn't sure how much of their hour they had left, though she thought she was beginning to recognize some of the halls and murals. They were getting close.

Atlan pulled to a stop, then turned to face them, broaching the subject first. "I don't want to hurt your people, Arge."

The dwarven heir studied Atlan for a long time, then nodded. "No, I don't think you do."

"But they will kill me."

"Yes."

Atlan's shoulders sagged, though they all knew it was only confirmation. He was silent for a moment. Then, "The boy and the dragon. They'll kill them, too?"

Arge nodded. "Our greatest asset is our secret, the fact the outside world believes we are dead. Were the boy to tell anyone, we would be ruined. Father, particularly after the boy's treatment thus far, will not take that risk. The dragon, likewise, will serve little purpose to us after the boy's death. We would, perhaps, set the creature free, but if it were to strike at us again, we would destroy it. Or perhaps save ourselves the trouble and do it right away, harvest the scales and claws."

Atlan glanced down at Mira at the remark. She had, of course, understood the importance of secrecy when she had lumped Kraven in with the bogey earlier, known that the dwarves would not let the boy live no matter what she said. A guilty twitch stirred in her stomach at the bogey's reproving look, however, and she knew she could have tried harder to plead the medic's case.

For the moment, the bogey let the issue slide. "Whoever the other champion is, we have to stop him. If the empire sent someone besides me, they either thought I was dead or wanted to replace me. If it's a stray bogey who chose to go on their own, that could be even worse."

"I agree," said Arge. "But what do you propose?"

Atlan looked Arge dead in the eye. "To convince your people to let me live."

Mira's stomach clenched. It was, of course, the obvious choice—who better to take on one bogey champion than another? But still, the residual fear she had for his people was not easy for even her to deny. She could not imagine what such a task would be like for the Gulied dwarves. It likewise did not address what would happen if she and the others in her group succeeded, what a danger it would pose if Atlan was set free and allowed to travel all the way to the yochni's cave.

All the same, Kraven, she knew, was not as forgiving as Atlan despite his altruistic deeds. Even if she and Arge could convince the dwarves to let the boy and his dragon live, which she doubted, she doubted even more that he would help her stop the other bogey. Not if Atlan died. That meant no dragon for transport or for battle, and while she had always known she might have to try, she was not confident of her ability to kill a bogey on her own. She needed help, which in no uncertain terms meant keeping the high prince alive.

Something deeper tugged at her gut, another reason she wanted Atlan to live, but she shoved the feeling down, squelching it down so far she thought it would leak out her toes. She was not ready for that thought yet, and they had work to do.

Arge shook his head. "My father will never allow it."

"I know," said Atlan. "But I'm asking you all the same. Please."

The dwarven heir frowned. He rubbed his jaw, his surprisingly soft-looking hand swallowing the lower half of his face. He studied Atlan, mental gears clicking behind the dark orbs of his brown eyes, then looked to Mira.

"What do you think?"

Mira's eyes fell to the floor. She felt Atlan's gaze upon her, though when she looked up to meet it, she found his expression placid, neither pleading nor incriminating. Simply waiting for her answer. She rubbed her arm, considering. "I think...a deal is a deal," she said at last. "He's fulfilled all the terms of your agreement, so you should let him go."

Neither Arge nor Atlan gave any immediate physical response. Atlan watched her for a moment, expression inscrutable, then switched his gaze to the dwarven heir. Arge locked eyes with the bogey for a long moment, then sighed, crouching to draw in the dirt.

"There's a ramp. It branches off from where we'll enter, running down the forge's side..."

Ten minutes later, Mira hung in the darkness, Atlan's

chest hot and firm against her back. Arge hung beside her, the bogey's arm sealed over both their stomachs. The dwarven heir's jar lit up the inner side of the door before them. The door that would lead them back to the forge. Atlan gave a nervous sniff. He picked up the spear he had left behind.

Their plan was straight forward. Atlan, as the primary target, would charge the dwarves, distracting them the best he could. Mira, moving with Arge, would take the side ramp, getting a head start towards the forge's elevators. Atlan would help Kraven escape with Batcha and Drake, their group would catch up with Mira at the elevator, and they'd escape up the shaft and out the mountain's side.

Mira's stomach hummed, nearly as tight as the bogey's grip.

Atlan stepped forward and knocked.

Doom. Doom. Doom.

The knocks boomed through the stone. Atlan's arm squeezed tighter still. Mira squirmed against him, hating the feeling of his claws at her stomach, but he didn't relax his grip. He stepped back, further into what would soon be shadows, and his low growl thrummed against her back.

Hinges creaked. Stone grated. Two dwarves opened the doors.

They hadn't been wrong.

True to Atlan's prediction, the dwarves had prepared while they were away. A low barricade was set up at the bottom of the ramp leading up from the central platform with rows of armed dwarves pointing crossbows and spears at them over its top. Kraven, hands tied, was stationed with Batcha and his dragon at the plateau's far side, a row of dwarves pinning them all in place. Many of the dwarves who had gathered for the execution still lined the tiers, waiting to watch the fight. Atlan's growl deepened. He stepped forward, the moss in Arge's necklace fading in the light of the dangling lanterns and chandeliers.

Soom, seeing his son hanging as a dwarven shield over Atlan's sweet spot, snarled. "What is the meaning of this?"

"I could ask you the same thing," said the prince.

"Traitor."

"No," said Atlan, voice sharp. "The traitor is you. I have returned within the hour, both returned safely, and the hunters gone. Arge, Mira, did I complete my task?"

Arge nodded. Mira hesitated, then did the same.

"Good. Kraven, let's go. *Allons-y.*"

The boy raised his hands to remove the gag. The dwarves lifted their crossbows, their shoulders tensing as they took aim.

"I have fulfilled my word. Release him," Atlan snarled.

"No."

A steely silence charged the air. Drake started to rumble, a low warning bubble of a hiss pressing through his chest.

"There has been a development," said Atlan. "Something you should know. Will you even attempt to listen?"

Soom's hand found the bottom of his crossbow, already steadying it to lift.

"You'll kill them," Atlan warned. "Fire your arrows through them to me. Your ally. Your son."

The other dwarves' aim wavered, but Soom didn't so much as flinch.

The bogey prince tilted his head down to his wards, face equal parts angry and sad. "I'm sorry," he said.

"Fire," shouted Soom.

"No!" Atlan dropped down in an instant, body curling over the two dwarves as the crossbows fired. He let out a sharp yelp, two arrows finding root in his arm and shoulder while the others soared overhead. Mira heard another order to fire, Drake shrieking as the crossbow bolts flew. Rising to a knee, Atlan threw Mira and Arge towards the second ramp. The bogey prince surged to his feet, spear in hand, and chaos erupted on the plateau.

With a mighty sweep of his tail, Drake swiped the group surrounding his master. Several dwarves flew off the plateau, their shrieks cutting off with ominous finality or breaking off into wounded moans. Those that remained thrust their spears or aimed their crossbows. Kraven ducked and wove, scrabbling to grab the rearing Batcha without getting skewered by dwarven weapons.

Atlan charged down the main ramp, shouting in Fransec. He threw his spear sideways, tangling dwarves in the weapon's shaft. It didn't buy him a lot of time, but it was enough for him to reach the bottom. Leaping over the barricade, he landed waist deep in a ball of dwarves, blades, and crossbow bolts, his claws and jaws swinging like scythes through the panicked huddle.

Mira, just gaining her feet, hesitated, but then Arge grabbed her arm. Atlan had promised not to hurt the dwarves if he didn't have to, and it seemed that the dwarven heir believed him.

"The ramp," said Arge. "Go."

Mira fled with the dwarven heir, forcing herself not to second-guess her and Arge's decision. With Kraven's arbitration, none of the original group members could leave without the others, not unless the others were dead. If Kraven and Atlan were going to make it, Mira had to reach the elevators.

Still, it was hard not to look back or slow down as fear for her people pulsed through her veins. Dwarves screamed as Drake shrilled and struck, as claws or teeth met flesh and bone. A glance back told her more dwarves were massing, too, that her companions were being swarmed. Batcha brayed, Kraven shouted, Atlan yipped and howled. The bogey was disarming the dwarves as he fought, throwing spears and crossbows over the edge at every opportunity, but it didn't stop the onslaught. When he threw away spears, the dwarves drew knives. When he tossed aside knives, they tackled and dragged. He was tough, as all bogeys were, his thick, wide bones protecting much of what might otherwise have been vulnerable to say nothing of his almost unmatchable stamina, but even for him, the tide of little nicks and bruises had a cost. The dwarves were trying to take him to his knees by force of numbers. If something didn't change soon, they would succeed.

With a sudden swing of his arm, Atlan cleared a swathe. The dwarves fell back, if just for a moment, and he reached for his waist. He unfurled something long and dark and terrible from its place at his side.

No. Mira's lungs caught as he raised his arm. She opened her mouth to scream for him to stop, but it was too late.

Crack!

The sharp snap of the whip rent the air like a clap of thunder. The dwarves skittered back, retreating like bees from a thrown bucket of water. Mira's knees nearly buckled. Atlan raised his arm again, his face plastered with a snarl so terrible she almost didn't recognize him. It was the face of the slavers, generations of bogeys who'd fought and killed her people. Mira couldn't breathe, her lungs clogging at the sight, the sounds. This was the bogey who'd frightened the hunters. The one who had called her a rat.

He had lied. He was going to kill them. He would kill them and her and—

Arge grabbed her arm. "Look!"

He pointed to the prince's whip. Mira traced its arc. Every crack made her skin jump and crawl, made her scars itch along her back. She could barely make herself look. But then sweet relief—air—filled her lungs.

The whip wasn't landing. Snaking in and out of the

dwarves' ranks with pinpoint precision, the whip kept them at bay, but never seemed to strike. She looked over the edge, below the platform where Atlan fought. Though several dwarves had fallen from Drake, and crossbows and spears littered the floor like so much kindling, there were no fallen dwarves around the prince. From his position, he could have easily booted several of them over the edge, caught them up with his whip. But he hadn't. Instead, he pushed and swept them aside, snapped them back in strategic waves. He was clearing a path to Kraven and Batcha. Making an exit for them to escape.

Atlan had told the truth. He wasn't attacking, or at least not enough to really hurt.

Mira turned to Arge, her lungs still juddery with fear. The dwarven heir nodded and increased his pace to a jog.

"H-how can you believe him?" she asked, forcing herself to resume her pace.

"I'm not sure that I do," he said. "But I know that whoever sent those men was worse, and that if that other bogey makes it, we may never be able to leave these caves. And, if all else fails, if he's not really who he says he is," he said with a nod back to Atlan, "we've got you to protect us. Finish him off. I believe, for all he said, that you'll protect us, that you'll do what needs to be done."

The dwarven heir pulled to a stop. They were about halfway down the ramp, their path cutting down across the various tiers along the cavern's walls until it met the gentle upward slope of the cavern's floor. There were no dwarves ahead, all of them focused on Atlan and Drake. Arge pointed to the elevators ahead, singling out the largest of them. Like many of the others, it was free-standing, its shaft reaching up like a pillar to pierce the ceiling far above.

"That's the one you need. I have to go back, join them, but that will take you up to the top, out of the mountain. You'll be on the northern side of the range. Travel northwest, and you'll reach your path. Be careful, Mira, and keep our people safe."

He looked her in the eye, then thundered back to join the fray. In the chaos Atlan was causing, she doubted anyone had noticed Arge giving her a head start. Even if they had, he was only helping one of their own.

Kraven was almost to the edge of the platform now, hauling on Batcha's reins. Drake surrounded them like a shield, fighting off any who got too close. Tapping the sea dragon's foreleg, Kraven gestured for Drake to grab the tinier mount. Then, with Batcha safe in the dragon's front claws, the boy gave a last kick out at the dwarves and swung up on the sea dragon's neck. Drake leapt off the platform's edge. It was at least twenty feet to the floor, though for the dragon, it wasn't nearly as dangerous of a fall, his massive legs and almost cat-like agility absorbing most of the landing's blow.

The only one left on the platform was Atlan. He was still fighting and holding back the dwarves, throwing or kicking every weapon he could over the edge. One arm was already half-useless from the first bolts the dwarves had fired, the tips no doubt poisoned with the venom they'd used on Drake. But if he could hold out long enough to reach the edge, to jump, they could all go free. Drake could catch him, or at the very least soften his fall. Mira turned to run.

Atlan screamed.

With the others gone, the dwarves had redoubled their efforts. A small squad of them had managed to scrounge up a handful of crossbows and fired on him. Three bolts were now buried deep in the bogey prince's back. Whirling, he scrabbled at the embedded bolts, trying to wrench them free. He whipped at the dwarves with his other, weaker hand, but the whip's tip only slapped limply against the stone. The squad fired again. Two more bolts slammed into Atlan's chest, only barely missing his sweet spot. He staggered from the impact, nearly falling. He lifted his whip in defense, but Mira knew it would not be enough. Not if the dwarves hit him again.

"Atlan!" Kraven called from below. "*Cours*. Run!"

Drake pawed at the cavern floor, ready to return and catch the prince, but Atlan waved them off. "Go," he howled. "Go."

Mira tried to push herself into motion, reminding herself this was the best way forward. He was still technically her enemy, despite his help, and if he died here, it was the best way forward, the best opportunity to have her problems solved. If he died now, it wouldn't be her fault. It would be the dwarves'—and Atlan's for not retreating in time. Kraven wouldn't be able to blame her then. And besides, she had to reach the elevator. She had to make it for any of them to survive.

The dwarves lifted their bows again.

Keep our people safe.

Mira was running before she even realized what she was doing. Farther up the ramp, three ropes ran through metal anchors bolted to the wall. They were connected to the chandeliers. If she could just snap them in time, create a distraction....

Atlan looked over his shoulder, scanning the cavern for his companion's progress. He looked wobbly, about to fall, but still he managed to find her, to see what she was about to do.

The dwarves rushed him, making their final push. He opened his mouth to tell her to stop.

Too late. *Crack!*

Mira slammed her axe into the wall just as the dwarves made contact, shoving Atlan off the edge. All three of the ropes snapped, practically smoking from their speed as they whistled through their pulleys. Atlan was going to hit hard, she knew, but if he survived, if Kraven and Drake reached him in time, they could still get out, could *all* still get out. With the chaos the fire would bring, the dwarves would be distracted, and nobody else would have to get hurt.

Or at least, they wouldn't have, if Mira had remembered the lanterns.

She was just turning to shout for Kraven and Drake when she realized. The chandeliers were hung above the lantern strings, leaving no way for them to fall except through the oil-filled web. Atlan slammed into the floor. Arge, hearing the whistle of the ropes, looked back to her from his position on the larger ramp. He had almost reached the main platform. The horror on his face said it all.

It was like sending down a rain of fire. Slamming onto the floor and into the crushers, two of the chandeliers burst into instant flame, burning pools of oil racing out from the wreckage. Lanterns fell in and among the dwarves. The third chandelier fell directly into the open chimney of the forge, years of old oil and dust igniting in an instant. Dwarves screamed as they tried to dodge hot metal and running oil, as they were splattered in flaming liquid. Some scrabbled to rescue injured companions. Others shouted orders to put out the flames.

Kraven looked up at her from the floor, his face gone pale with horror. Mira could only stare at the conflagration. She had done this. *She* had done this. She nearly dropped her axe.

The dwarves did not give them long to recover. Fresh shouts of rage mingled in with the cries for help.

Mira forced herself free from her stupor. She called down to Kraven. "Run. Run!"

Her shout startled him into action. He sprinted forward for Atlan with Drake. The bogey heir was barely twitching, his body riddled with bolts.

Mira turned to make her own escape, but Arge caught her eye. The dwarven heir was still staring, shock and betrayal plain on his face.

"I'm sorry," she mouthed, knowing there was no way he would be able to hear her over the popping shrieks of burning metal and dwarven screams. He didn't respond, only turning back to help his people. She moved to go as well, but then the dwarves made a mistake. Startled into action by the fire, some of the younger dwarves on the tiers took the initiative to act.

Unfortunately, their solution was to turn to the waterfall. Opening the sluice gates, they turned the chutes onto the flames. Mira shouted, begging for them to stop, but it was too late.

It went as badly as she knew it would.

Flames erupted in gigantic, searing gouts as soon as the water touched the flaming oil. Thick, black smoke billowed up in caustic plumes, and a tide of dirty water swept across the floor, flaming islands of oil scudding along the top. Dwarves screamed as the hellish flood caught them up, droplets searing through skin or setting clothing afire.

Kraven and Drake, still dragging a mostly useless Atlan, put on a frantic burst of speed, just making the slope in the cavern floor before the water slapped up and back to level. Flames licked the high prince's feet and Kraven leapt forward, batting the flames with his gloved hands.

Realizing their mistake, the dwarves on the tiers redirected the water's flow, but it was already too late.

Mira could barely breathe. She ran, air fouled with smoke tearing through her lungs. Each breath felt like a knife in her chest. Everything in her wanted to scream and go back to help the dwarves, to reverse some of the damage she had done, but she couldn't stop, had to keep running. None of her companions could escape if she didn't reach the elevators.

She made it just behind the others and helped Kraven shove the animals and the nearly unconscious Atlan into the elevator cab. She could hear the frenzy of the dwarves behind them, screams of the wounded and terrified youths. She tried not to listen, to ignore it the best she could.

But then came a scream she could not ignore, a thunderous bellow of rage. Mira turned. It was Soom, the pent-up hatred of hundreds of years vented in his single, terrible sound. He was coming for them, and he wasn't alone.

A half dozen dwarves—each as sooty and singed as Soom—had managed to rally around their leader. Each one still had their crossbow, some with bolts already loaded, others well on their way.

Mira slammed her weight against the elevator's gate, helping Kraven click the latch into place, then ran for the elevator's controls. The dwarves were closing in fast, but maybe they were still out of range. Maybe they would miss. The first two fired, and a bolt bounced off of Atlan's ribs, the other just missing her. She glanced behind and saw that the next batch were nearly ready, the dwarves finishing loading or taking aim.

Mira threw the controls, heard the release as the counter-weight fell from above. She leapt for the guardrail, stretching out a hand. Kraven caught it, drawing her into the tightly packed cab.

"No!" shouted Soom, lifting his crossbow. "Fire!"

The bolts flew seconds before the elevator's cable went tight. Mira jerked away, expecting death.

The bolts missed, some hitting the elevator's gate as it jerked into motion, others simply firing astray. One slammed into Drake's chest.

Unsettled by the elevator's sudden movement, Atlan started to tip, his top-heavy body leaning heavily over the rail. Mira grabbed his chest. Kraven grabbed the back of his shirt. Together they hauled him back to safety, even Drake squeezing back to give them more room, though there was precious little to spare. Soom frantically reloaded his crossbow, slamming the bolt into place as they shot up from the floor. Bolts chased them up through the cavern, but none of them met their marks.

Soom spat and snarled, throwing his crossbow across the room. "Slave trader," he screamed. "Slave trader!"

Mira slumped back against Batcha in the crowded cab, her and Kraven's fingers still wound tightly into the motionless bogey's clothes. Soom continued to scream at them from below, howling the epithet over and over as they rose.

"Slave trader" was a term used only for dwarves that worked with the bogeys, who sold out their own for the bogey's gain. It was the worst possible insult the dwarven leader could have given her.

The worst part though, was that now it was true.

NINETEEN

The elevator rattled up the shaft with alarming speed. Smoke swallowed the flaming wreckage as they ascended so that only hot orange embers of light shone from beneath. Screams rose up through the smoky veil. Mira clung to Atlan, her stomach souring with every breath of smoke, teeth gritting with every scream or sob. Kraven's black-gloved hands had nearly disappeared into Atlan's dark silks as he helped her keep the top-heavy prince from falling over the rail. Beneath the soot, the medic's face was as pale as the dead, pinched with pain as he looked down over the smoke.

Mira closed her eyes, breathing through her mouth to avoid the seared flesh smell. She had done this. Ruined her people. Their destruction was all her fault.

Sliding up into a stone shaft in the ceiling, the elevator knocked against a hidden lever, slowing the rest of their ascent. As they reached their final mooring at a stone and wooden platform, the ropes began to tremble with the telltale strikes of axes. Mira pointed from her axe to the rope and swung her arms to mime this information to Kraven, who promptly kicked open the gate, shoving Mira and the unconscious Atlan out ahead of him. He had said nothing during their rapid rise and was equally quiet now. Drake unfolded from the cab with an unhappy coo, setting down a shaken Batcha.

Behind them, the elevator dropped several inches, the remaining ropes straining as another one snapped. Mira didn't care. Crumpling down beside Atlan, she buried her hands in the bogey's sleeve. "Is he okay?" she asked, voice numb. "Alive?"

Kraven felt for the bogey's pulse. It took him dangerously long to find it, but eventually, he nodded. His gloves had been burned in broad patches when he'd slapped out the fire on Atlan's heels, the leather melted against his skin. For once, he didn't try to remove them as he tended his patient. Instead, he rustled in his pack, bringing out a small ball of gum paste to jam the holes as he yanked the bolts from the bogey's flesh.

"*Les blessures*...hurt. Bleed," he explained, voice tight. He flinched with every bolt he removed, his burned fingers already glistening with ruptured blisters.

Between bolts, he gestured to the original, poisoned wound on the bogey's arm. Though they'd seen the strong, fishy paste the dwarves had applied to it before to stop the bleeding, they had no way of knowing what the dwarves had actually used to make it, nor any way to get the materials even if they had. In sum, if the poison on the bolts was the same as what had been on the spear that had cut Atlan's arm before, if Kraven's gum didn't plug the bleeding, the bogey would bleed to death.

Mira would have ruined her people for nothing.

The elevator screeched as the last rope snapped, wood and metal crumbling as it tumbled down the shaft. Black smoke plumed up in its absence, choking the air out with soot and gas.

"Drake, *ici*," said Kraven, calling his dragon. Suffering the effects of the bolts he had taken himself, the sea dragon let out an unhappy moan. He limped over on unsteady feet. Kraven flopped the bogey's chest over his dragon's shoulders, instructing Mira to pull from the other side to help get him on. Kraven threw her up top with his patient after, ordering her not to let the bogey fall. He urged Drake to his feet, then took Batcha's reins, stretching out a hand to find his way through the faint smudgings of luminescent moss and smoke.

Thankfully, there was only one path to exit the mountain. According to Arge's previous explanation, the way out was only a half mile long, the tunnel straight as the rails it sheltered with no connecting intersections or rooms. Hopefully, in crashing the elevator the dwarves had also destroyed their best ability to catch up. Maybe, with everything else that had happened, they would even give up the chase.

Thinking back to Soom's face, the sheer hatred he'd held for the bogey prince, Mira doubted that they would.

It was a hatred she now recognized in herself. She had never realized how ugly it was. She'd never realized a lot of things. Like the fact that if Atlan died, she would be sad, and not just because she would not be the one to kill him. Or the second, perhaps more disturbing natural fork and conclusion of the first thought, that if he survived, she would be happy.

Though logically she knew it was insanity—that if he persisted in his own plans for reaching the yochni, she would have no choice but to kill him when they reached the chamber—she also knew that the frantic trembling in her chest was not merely nervous energy or battle fatigue, not simple surprise at her own survival. No, it was all of those things and more, including relief that the bogey—no, Atlan— was still breathing and the fear that, if they did not act, if Kraven's plugs didn't work, he might not continue to do so, might in fact backslide from the land of the living into the final and murky depths of the dead.

Which led her to her third and final conclusion, the worst of them all. That if all these other things were true, she, Mira Goldfist, Champion of the Dwarves of Haufin Mountain, was friends with a bogey.

Slave trader. The words echoed in her mind. *Slave trader.*

The slur was still making laps through her mind when they reached the end of the tunnel. As Drake stepped out from under its lip, she looked back, dreading what she was almost certain she would see. And there it was. Thick clouds of black smoke billowed from the mountain in at least four places. Any champion, bogey, or bounty hunter for miles would be able to see that something had happened and know that something, someone, was there.

The fire would not have killed all of the dwarves, but for those that survived, their location had been revealed. Their one defense against the bogeys was now gone.

Mira retched. She turned just far enough to avoid Atlan's toes, her fingers tight against the buckles of his pack. His bag felt softer than it had before, the rigid wood of his harp case no longer holding its form. He'd fallen on it when the dwarves had pushed him. She wondered if the harp had splintered.

The unconscious bogey, still hanging over Drake's shoulders, started to slip. Rushing to Drake's side, Kraven pulled on the high prince's arms, helping to draw the unconscious bogey back into position as the last of her hulching subsided.

Even now the medic didn't face her. Clutching Atlan's wrists with a grip so tight it turned his burned knuckles white, he only stared at Drake's side, unmoving.

"Kraven?" she asked.

"What?" he said, voice flat. He didn't look at her.

"Kraven," she said, voice quavering. "Please."

He looked up then, eyes so angry she almost wished he hadn't.

"Kraven, I'm sorry," she said. "I'm so, so sorry." And with that, at last, the tears came, welling up fat and multitudinous on her cheeks. Spilling down onto her grimy vest, they overflowed onto Atlan's soot-stained pack, rolling off to water the ground below.

Kraven didn't answer. With a final check that Atlan was secure, he turned on his heel, yanking on Batcha's reins and resuming the long walk down the mountain's side.

"*De l'eau,*" was all he said.

Whatever venomous effects the sea dragon was fighting, he still knew the command for water and how to find it. Though it took him nearly an hour to do so, at last they emerged on the shores of a small pond fed by a converging stream. By then the moon had reached its peak. A dusting of clouds drifted against the smoke-smudged heavens, blotching the starlight from the sky. Batcha's antlers, hanging low, dragged against the brush. Kraven staggered alongside him. Drake, catching sight of the pool, sloughed Mira and Atlan off like unwanted cargo before slipping into the shallows. Mira, hands still loosely knotted into the bogey's silks, didn't let go as she fell. Atlan landed on her legs, but she didn't move him. Her cheeks, long since dried from her tears, felt tight and stung from the salt and smoke.

For a long time, neither she nor Kraven spoke, she still under the bogey's weight, Kraven at the water's edge. The bogey's skin was now fiery hot with fever. Though the putty Kraven had used to plug Atlan's wounds had stuck throughout the ride, neither the bogey's pulse nor his breathing had improved. Without greater supplies or knowledge, they both knew there was nothing else that could be done.

The moon was well on its way to setting when Kraven finally moved. His burned hands had been resting in his lap, and at last he moved to heal them, peeling the scorched gloves from his hands and picking melted leather from his wounds. Shooing Drake from the shallows, he dipped his hands in the pond, hissing and sighing in pain and relief as he began the arduous process of cleaning the burns. Mira watched him in silence, her own fingers hot from the heat of Atlan's shallowly rising chest. Only days before, she would have rejoiced to have him so near to death. She'd practically prayed for it when he'd been injured with the skin fang. Now...now....

With some assistance from Drake, the still woozy dragon faithfully bringing him whatever tools or herbs he pointed out from their supplies, Kraven made a salve for his hands. Smearing it on in thick, pungent layers, he coated his hands nearly down to the wrists. Then, wincing at every pull and tug of his injured muscles, he bound them up with gauze, pulling the knots tight with his teeth. When he was finished, he gave the remains of the burned gloves a long look. Then he shoved them back into his bag. He moved to Drake. They'd squandered the vast majority of their supplies on Atlan, and with his injured hands he couldn't stitch any of the dragon's wounds closed, but he did the best he could, washing the wounds out with bunched up fabric before covering them with what gauze they had left. It wasn't much.

Kraven pressed his hands and forehead against the dragon's cool scales, his entire form as still as the dead. He stood that way for a long time, and when he finally turned to face her, there was a hollowness to his gaze, an expression she didn't quite recognize glinting softly in his moonlit eyes. He took a step towards her, and something in his look sent shivers down her spine.

"*Drake, ici,*" he said, voice flat. Mira knew it was a

command to come. Something tightened in her chest, and she realized that, of all of them, only Kraven could break their contract. Only he could annul their terms. Take revenge for what she had done.

She had sold him out to the dwarves, been willing to let him die with Atlan. She'd hardly considered it when she'd told her tales, thought of him only as collateral damage in her personal war. Except now, with him looming above her, the dragon just behind him, she realized she had made yet another mistake. The boy had said he wanted to earn his mark, to prove himself a real physician. But if he killed her now, nobody would know. Nobody had to know.

He started muttering in Fransec, eyes picking up the unearthly, pale blue glow they had when he used his arbitration. As when he had made the contract, she didn't need translation to understand what he was saying.

Kraven was annulling their deal.

"Kraven, Kraven, don't. Please. I'm sorry, I'm sorry," she begged. Was it just a trick of the night, or were Drake's eyes shining with malicious intent? His teeth glittering in the light of the moon? She scrambled back, kicking out from under Atlan's fevered body. Kraven advanced, backing her up against a tree. He'd drawn Johann's knife. She covered her head. "No, Kraven, please. Please, don't."

And then she felt it. A simple snap, small as a breaking thread, deep within her chest.

She looked up, Kraven's form half-blocked by her lifted arms. His bandaged fingers were tight on his knife. She waited for him to strike. But then, slowly, he eased his grip. His glowing eyes, though still angry, started to fade, the glittering light winking out through rims of tears.

She waited, breath held, for him to speak. Drake let out a nervous coo. Batcha skittered on his lead. Then, at last,

Kraven let out a long and shuddering breath. He sheathed the knife.

"I am going *home*," he said.

He glanced down at the bogey, and a look of pain, almost regret, crossed his features. Then, expression hardening, he turned away. "*Ici, Drake. Viens.*" Stooping to pick up his pack, he turned west, towards the Confluence. It was the main network of roads to the yochni's cave, the paths ever converging until they reached the mountain that housed the yochni itself. It could take him to the creature's very doorstep. Or, as it seemed Kraven intended, home.

Mira looked at Drake, the sea dragon seeming just as confused as she did.

"W-what?" she managed. "You're leaving? What about Atlan? The yochni? The Guard?"

"I do not care."

"Yes, you do. That's what you wanted, right? To earn your mark? And Atlan, h-he'll die."

It was unclear to Mira how much Kraven was picking up from her side of the conversation, but it was clear when he stopped, when his shoulders tensed and bunched, that it was enough.

"Yes. He will," he said. He whipped out a hand to point to the bogey. "You do this. You kill Atlan. Kill dwarves. I do not. I go home."

"B-but your mark."

"I do not want the mark!" the boy shouted. "I do not want the Guard. I do not want the mark. I *want* Ines. To know...to be...I wanted to be like Ines." His voice crackled and twisted with pain, writhing with it like a living thing. It was a pain Mira had not seen in him before, and she wondered that it could have been lying there underneath all this time.

"B-but, you said..." she started.

Kraven cut her off, face twisting into a terrible, wrathful

sneer, the mutinous grimace of an injured beast. "I wanted to be like Ines. I am *not*."

With that, the medic turned on his heel, back towards the road that would take him home. Drake, a fountain of nervous trills and whistles, followed, casting several nervous looks between the various members of their party as he went. His chirpings became ever more imploring, but Kraven did not respond. The pair crested a hill, and, for a moment, the medic paused. Hope rose in Mira's chest, the faintest spark that he might change his mind, but when he looked back, his stony expression told her it was for naught.

"Atlan is sick," he said. "Will die. You want to kill Atlan, kill Atlan. Is better for both. Goodbye, Mira."

Kraven turned again, and the pair disappeared from sight.

For a moment, Mira could do nothing but stare. The boy was gone. He had abandoned her, them, and now that he had, Atlan would die. She could not save him on her own, nor had she the strength to carry him. Without Kraven, the bogey would die.

Mira shook her head. He couldn't give up. *She* couldn't give up. Not when they were so close. Not when Atlan would die.

Mira jumped to her feet, running for the hill and scrambling through the leaf litter to its top. The boy and his dragon were making good progress, but she could still see their retreating forms, and they were still within range to hear her.

"Kraven. Kraven!" she cried. "Stop!"

The boy didn't look back.

Mira slid down the other side of the slope, giving chase. He sped up. She ran faster. Drake, still struggling from the poison and reluctant to leave, looked back at her, twittering, but still Kraven continued.

"Stop," she cried. "Please, Kraven. I'm sorry, just wait."

And the boy did. Or at least, she thought he did.

But when she caught up, the face he turned on her was cut into a terrible, unforgiving snarl. "Leave," he said.

"Kraven," she said, trying to grab his arm.

He smacked her hand away. "*Leave.*"

"Atlan..."

"Atlan will die. I am *not* here to help. I *will* not help. *Leave.*"

He pointed back to where she had come from, expression clear. She had pushed him too far, done too much damage, and she knew there was no way he would forgive her now. No way that he would help. Kraven would leave. Atlan would die. And it was all Mira's fault.

Drake let out a sorrowful coo, but Kraven snapped out a hand to silence him. "Drake, *nous partons. Allons-y.*"

The sea dragon gave her a mournful look, but he did not disobey his master. Kraven turned again, and the dragon, though clearly unhappy, followed.

Mira slumped down to the earth, staring after them until long after they disappeared. She waited, but they didn't return. The pair had truly left.

For long minutes, she sat, wishing the earth would simply swallow her whole, that some monster would come and eat her, that she would fall into an ocean and drown. Nothing was too ill a fate. Not after what she had done. Destroyed a friendly clan, doomed her own to destruction. She had not killed a bogey but saved him, and in so doing ruined her own chances of reaching the yochni in time.

She had failed on every level.

And there was still another bogey. She'd nearly forgotten in the chaos. Kraven didn't know about the other bogey. Would her yelling bring it near? Would he meet it on the road?

She didn't know, but then, even if she did, what difference could it make? Even if she wanted to help him, she was not strong enough to do it. Assuming Kraven would let her get near to him in the first place, there was no reason he would believe her. Even in this, she had failed.

She sighed. Kraven was not coming back. Both of her feet had fallen asleep beneath her, and though some part of her still hoped the medic would return, she knew deep down that he would not. It was time to move.

Forcing herself to her feet, she shuffled to the top of the hill. Batcha was in the valley by the pond, staring up at her. Atlan lay, still splayed where she had left him, barely breathing.

For a moment she considered Kraven's suggestion to kill the bogey. Atlan was sick, dying, after all, and to let him live now might only prolong his suffering. Or worse, if she left him behind, perhaps he would be found by the dwarves, healed only to be killed later in a worse and more gruesome way. She could not leave him to that fate, nor had she the time, strength, or will to try to bring him with her.

He's the high prince, she reminded herself. That won't change even if he lives, or what will happen if he gets his wish. If either bogey gets their wish.

She paused, peering down at the helpless prince. From her current position, he looked small—or at the very least small for him. Weak. He was alone, defenseless. Now was her chance. The opportunity she'd been waiting for all along.

It was for the best, she thought, fingers tightening on her axe. She couldn't leave Atlan. Couldn't take him. The second bogey had to be stopped. Even if it killed her, even if she didn't make it in time, she had to try. She took her first step down the slope. It was time to fulfill her duty.

Something crashed in the woods.

Batcha started like a hare, squealing as he tugged on his reins. Mira dropped to the earth, instincts sharp even if her mind was not. Letting long years of training take over, she stilled herself to listen. It had not come from the direction Kraven and Drake had gone, west, towards the Confluence, but from ahead, to the north. She heard thumping, a rhythmic plodding and another crash. Trees groaned as the mystery entity approached, their branches creaking as they bent out of pose. She could see a faint glow from the direction of the noise, the same kind of light the dwarves had used. She wondered briefly if it was them, but surely they couldn't have come so quickly, especially from the opposite direction.

Whatever it was, it was headed straight for them, though whether it had been drawn by the smoke, Mira's cries, or Batcha's ongoing screams was impossible to tell. She froze on the hill, wondering if she should leave. Atlan was a goner already, after all, and though Batcha had been a strong and loyal mount, she was close enough now that she could perhaps make the yochni on foot if she escaped. The mini hart shrilled on the end of his reins, head bucking so fiercely she thought he might snap his own neck.

Mira growled to herself. Then she slid down the hill, dead leaves slicking under her boots as she descended. She had had the mini hart since she was a child, and he had always been faithful, even at the height of his skittishness. He had followed her all this way, and though she had failed at everything else, she wasn't about to let him get eaten alive or killed by whatever it was that was coming. She would cut the reins, set him free, and then run. There was no saving Atlan, his form too heavy to lift and too out in the open to hide. But Batcha. At the very least, she could still save Batcha.

Hitting the bottom of the hill, Mira took off sprinting, scooping her axe from the sand as she ran to the mini hart. He bucked and kicked, thrashing his head in a panic, but she twisted and ducked around him, smooth as a dancer in her ripostes. The glow was nearly upon them now, the clustered light swelling well over ten feet tall. Leaves rustled in a rushing wave towards the edge of the clearing, spreading out from the creature like the roots of a tree. She grabbed Batcha's reins, raising her axe to cut him free.

Shapes burst out from the forest, more than a dozen all at once. They were short—no taller than Mira, but swift, skittering over the sand like a swarm of beetles.

Mira blinked and dropped her axe. *No. No.*

TWENTY

Kraven kept his eyes fixed straight ahead as he stormed through the woods. His hands stung under their gauze, and pus was already oozing its way through some of the cloth. Drake nudged his back with a nervous whistle, urging him to ride, but Kraven shook his head. He didn't want to be sitting right now. He wanted to move.

Mira had sold them out. After all they had been through, the centaur attack, the fire, Atlan's song. He'd even thought things had started to change between her and the bogey prince. But no, Mira was the same as she ever had been; and though Kraven had done nothing but help her, even saved her life, she had still handed him—all of them—over to the dwarves.

And then the mountain...the mountain...screams echoed in Kraven's mind, flashes of fire, the smell of burnt flesh.

Kraven kicked a floor nut, sending it skittering through drifts of dead leaves. Squelching down another wave of nausea, he squeezed his bandaged hands, beat them against a nearby tree.

They had ruined the dwarves. Though he knew many of

them had been safe on the tiers above the fire, that even those on the floor could have survived, he also knew many was not all. He had heard the screams, the frantic splashes, mortal moans.

He had gone on his journey to help others. To save lives. Now he had helped to end some.

Atlan's face flickered through his mind, slack and covered with blood, and Kraven's stomach lurched. If he didn't turn back, he'd be responsible for the bogey's death, too. He'd done nothing to prevent it. Had practically told Mira to kill him. Even if she landed the final blow, Kraven knew it would be at least partially his fault, too.

Ines would have been ashamed.

But it didn't matter now. Ines was dead, and Kraven was nothing like her. He had tried to do the right thing, tried to understand. He'd thought he had been doing the right thing when he'd saved Atlan and Mira, thought he'd done right when he'd made their deal. He had saved their lives, forced two enemies together.

But no, Mira had still hated Atlan, and Atlan had still disdained her. The prince's people had killed the dwarves in the mountain, and given the opportunity, the dwarves had tried to do the same to Atlan in return. Even when the prince had offered the dwarves a peaceful way out, they'd betrayed him, and in making their escape, Kraven and his group had doomed the dwarves in return. It was a cycle, an endless cycle, and there was nothing Kraven or any of the rest of them could do about it.

Ines had died because she'd been a fool, and Kraven knew nothing he could have done would have changed that, nor what had happened here. He could not change the hatred these people shared, and he was no longer willing to try.

It was time for him to go home.

Drake nudged his arm, offering a mournful coo. The dragon's ongoing kindness, his undying affection for him, was enough to move Kraven at last to tears, and for a moment he pressed his face against the dragon's smooth scales. Alarmed at his master's sudden outburst, Drake nuzzled him back, then more urgently nudged his chest. He lowered his head, offering one of his horns as grip, and Kraven, after drying his face with dirty wrists, at last consented to ride.

It was mid-morning by the time they reached the Confluence. An ever-narrowing network of converging roads, it was the main series of paths by which potential champions reached the yochni. By the time champions reached Blood Pass, the main canyon that cut through the mountains, the Confluence was already down to three or four paths. By the time they exited—if they exited at all—it was down to one. From there, the road took a relatively straight path to the yochni's mountain. Or, if traveling in the direction Kraven and Drake would be, home.

They stopped just inside the tree line, and for a moment, he considered turning north. If he took that route, he could reach the yochni himself, perhaps wish Ines back to life, for her to undo all he had done. Surely if anyone could do it, it was Ines. But no, that was a road of blood, of killing any who stood in his way. He'd known that since before he'd left home, and now, having experienced the caves, he would not put more blood on his hands, not for a fool's errand, nor even for the sake of Ines.

Kraven turned Drake south.

The road was wide, perhaps wide enough for six men to stand abreast. While he knew it would be safer to walk the road itself—most groups sticking to the less visible paths through the forest alongside for the sake of stealth or ambush —he also knew that if he took those same less visible paths, he could find stragglers or loners, people who, in exchange for his protection or some of his supplies, might help.

He would find bodies, too, and, if the stories were true, lots of them. It was an unpleasant thought, his stomach still woozy from the fire in the caves, but in their current circumstances, even the dead could be helpful, grant them the supplies or medicine that both he and Drake desperately needed.

For a moment, he wondered if he might even find a Guardsman or an apprentice like himself. Such an occurrence would be helpful indeed, though he doubted the odds. Even those who had granted him permission for his journey had warned him against the dangers and foolishness of his quest. The closer champions got to the yochni, the more ruthless they became, and the idea that some might masquerade as Guardsmen to further their cause was neither a foreign nor even unlikely idea. No, anyone he found now would almost certainly be an enemy, or at the very least treat him as such. Outside of the company of the dead, Kraven was on his own.

He felt a pang of loneliness, and for the briefest moment, Mira and Atlan came to mind, a stab of regret quick to follow. It wasn't too late to turn back, after all. Maybe if he tried harder, he could help Atlan. Find a cure or solution. Carry him to get help. After all, helping Atlan wouldn't mean helping the bogeys at large, right? Not if he didn't take the bogey prince to the yochni's cave? And, despite her hatred for his people, Mira had wanted to save Atlan, had even been willing to waste the time in getting the bogey aid. She hadn't run off as soon as Kraven had cancelled the contract, and, he suddenly realized, she had even gone back to help the bogey when the dwarves had betrayed them. Though she wouldn't have been able to leave him behind by the terms of their contract, she hadn't had to intervene to help him. Left on his own, the bogey would have been killed, freeing the rest of them to continue on their way. Without Atlan, perhaps the dwarves would even have let them go. Maybe even helped them, or at least her.

For the first time, Kraven pulled Drake to a stop, looking back. He remembered how Mira had begged him to stay, to not leave Atlan behind.

Perhaps she really had changed.

Kraven's gaze caught on the streaks of red slipping down his sea dragon's side. He thought again of the mountain and the fire and screams and banished any redemptive leanings from his mind.

Ines' way didn't work. To try anything else would only end in more heartbreak.

He prodded Drake with his heels.

As they continued, Kraven allowed Drake to keep carrying him. He wasn't sure how his extra weight would impact the dragon in his wounded state, but he also knew that if he walked, they would be limited by his human pace. It would be a long time before they reached a human settlement again, and while Drake certainly had more blood to lose than Atlan and the wounds were slow to bleed, he didn't want to take any more risks than he had to. They had to find help fast.

Except, there didn't seem to be anyone on the road. Kraven knew that the number of surviving champions dwindled considerably once they reached Blood Pass, its narrow confines a breeding ground for ambushes and betrayals, but even so, he felt certain that at least some champions would still be headed their way. But Drake trotted along for an hour, and they found no one. Not even a body.

Briefly, Kraven wondered if they were too early, but the woods surrounding the yochni were protected by the Guardians, wish-crafted creatures of shadow that kept anyone from approaching too soon. It was said they would kill anyone who tried to sneak past, but then, if Kraven wasn't seeing them—or, more accurately, being killed by them—that had to mean they had already disappeared for the age. He wondered if he was too late, but of course if that were the case, he'd be seeing the dead. It was as if the champions had simply disappeared.

Kraven decided it was time for a break. Though Drake never complained about his weight, Kraven wanted to be careful of working the dragon too hard. Leading Drake into the middle of the Confluence, he directed his friend to lie down. Though it would make them easier targets for anyone hiding in the woods, Kraven knew Drake would be imposing enough to scare off most attackers even at their healthiest, let alone wounded and dirty as most champions would now be.

He checked the sea dragon's wounds. Though it was difficult to gauge the damage accurately with the caked blood that had dried around them, the bleeding did seem to have slowed, the poison perhaps lessened by the rinse in the pond where he had left Mira. The wounds Drake had sustained when the dwarves ambushed them had been tended before Mira and Atlan left to chase off the hunters, meaning the dragon's condition was less severe than it might otherwise have appeared.

That didn't mean that the remaining injuries would not become problematic given more time, however, and that thought troubled him greatly. Even as they rested, dark, rusty patches of mud formed in a dotted outline along Drake's flanks. They were small, yes, but even dragons had limits on how much blood they could lose. And, of course, the longer Drake bled, the weaker and slower he would become. It was a race against time, a race in which Kraven didn't know when the clock would run out.

Kraven drew out his book of medicines, skimming

through the pages now that he had the time and light. His fingers burned and stung with every flip of a page, every bend to grab them, but he knew the matter was important. There was something about the wounds that stuck in his mind, some vague memory he felt he ought to remember. The book itself, perhaps the heaviest thing in his pack, was a compendium of salves, powders, tinctures and more. It was, in essence, the collected knowledge of generations of Guardsmen. An abbreviated version, of course, but extremely valuable all the same. If there was an answer to Drake's condition, odds were high it was in the book. Kraven searched, looking first by symptoms, then local plants, fungi, animals, and more.

Nothing. Still, though, the thought scratched at the back of his mind. There was something he was missing. Something that he knew. Whatever it was eluded him, but he did not have time to wait for his mind to catch up. He couldn't afford to spend all their time resting and reading. He'd have to think about it on the way.

Wincing as he gripped the heavy volume, Kraven put the book back into his pack, then urged Drake to his feet. An early fall breeze rattled the trees, shaking leaves down to the earth. Drake scented the air, looking unsteady on his legs, then shook his head and sneezed. He looked farther down the road, eyes narrowing, but whether the dragon had sensed something, was being further affected by the poison, or was simply tired was difficult to tell. Kraven decided he would walk for a while.

They made it until almost lunch, still without seeing champions. Drake grew ever more skittish as they traveled, side-stepping and pawing the ground like a nervous pack animal. Kraven, who neither saw nor sensed anything save the usual sights, smells, and sounds of the forest no matter how many times he stopped to check, tried to coax his dragon along, until finally, Drake planted his feet, letting out an obstinate bray.

Kraven, careful of his burns, set his hands on his hips. "Drake, *nous devons partir. Allons-y,*" he ordered.

Drake, giving a rebellious whistle, laid down, pointing his great snout down the road.

Kraven frowned, but when his friend's whistles turned into whimpers, he relented. "*D'accord, d'accord, je vais voir,*" he said, moving to the dragon's side. He decided he would check one more time, noting that he would need to consider the additional symptom theory more seriously if his final search still proved fruitless.

Drake, sensing his master's intentions, readied himself to stand. Kraven climbed up onto the dragon's shoulders, and Drake rose, granting Kraven a better view. The dragon huffed, pointing his snout and stamping his feet. Kraven patted the sea dragon's neck and, shielding his eyes against the sun, followed the direction of the creature's nose. He studied the landscape ahead.

His heart sank. As he'd feared, there was nothing there. Forest spread to either side of the road, undisturbed; ahead, he could see the great curve of the mountains they had traveled through, the giant cleft of Blood Pass slicing them cleanly through the middle. He could see no indication of champions ahead, no smoke from fires, no glinting metal, or even a cloud of displaced dust. The Confluence was barren.

Except—a sudden claw of nervousness snagged his gut, tugging at Kraven's insides like a cat with a thread. There, just on the hazy cusp of the horizon, a dark, rippling shape. The nervous claw pulled harder. A strange spur distinct from the larger mass poked out near one end of the mysterious shape. Kraven strained his eyes to see.

Then, in an instant, it came into focus, the rest of the

shape—or rather, shapes—coming into sharp and terrible clarity.

Kraven twisted on Drake's shoulders, vomiting over the side of his dragon.

The spur was an arm, the rest of the shapes butchered bodies. Not all of them were in one piece. They were also, none of them, human. Neither were they dwarven, elven, or even centauri. The lot of them were massive, tailed, and covered in fur. Kraven had found a massacre, and all of the victims were bogeys.

No wonder he hadn't seen any champions before. Anyone who could take on a pack of bogeys could surely slaughter a human. Or, for that matter, anyone else. Including, perhaps, a dragon.

With effort, Kraven forced himself upright, wiping his mouth on a sleeve. Fear quivered in his chest, his senses now stretched to their limits. Was the killer—or killers—still around? Hiding in the trees or buried amidst the undergrowth? He strained his ears, trying to tune out the wind and what he hoped was only the usual rustling of the leaves to hear anything, *anything*, underneath. He sensed nothing. He checked to see if Drake detected anything more, but it seemed that he did not. Kraven waited several minutes, but still nothing. Perhaps the danger had passed.

Either way, Kraven knew they couldn't stay where they were forever. Home lay to the south, past the massacre, and while a detour around it would certainly save his more delicate sensibilities, it would lose them time, to say nothing of losing the opportunity to gather any supplies the bogeys had carried. It also increased the risk of running into whatever it was that had killed them. He urged his dragon forward, Drake more willing—though still reluctant—now that he knew his master was apprised.

The sight—and smell—grew only more gruesome the

closer Kraven drew. Whatever had killed the bogeys had not been kind to their organs, and several of the same lay split open and drawing flies in the sun. The putrid smell of offal clogged his nose, traveling all the way down to his throat. Kraven could tell neither how long the bogey bodies had been there nor who or what had murdered them. All he knew was that it was not a place to stay for long. The bogeys' belongings had gone untouched. Covering his nose with an arm, Kraven began rifling for supplies.

He was halfway through when he heard it. Or, rather, caused it. He was side-stepping a particularly gruesome pile of gore on his way to the next pack when he tripped on an arm. He stumbled, boot slicking in a thickened, rusty red puddle, and something whimpered behind him.

Kraven yanked Johann's knife from his boot. Drake, who had stayed on the perimeter, let out a warning whistle. Kraven turned, knife raised, but there was no one there. Or at least, nobody new. Or dangerous. Not anymore.

It was one of the bogeys. She was the smallest, her fur once a mousey brown. Several deep claw marks sliced through her chest. The wounds were rimmed with congealing blood, flies buzzing around the streaks. Her hands, half-lifted, twitched in pain, and Kraven winced, knowing she was already too far gone to help. Had he never woken her again, it would have been a mercy. For a moment, he hesitated, wanting to flee, but then she spoke.

"P-please," she whimpered, reaching out and turning her head in his direction. Her eyes were glazed and filming. Whether she could see him or not, he couldn't tell.

He dropped beside her all the same, taking her hand in his own. She squeezed with a frightened, iron grip, fingers sealing around his burns, but he forced himself not to cry out, gritting his teeth against the pain.

"Ç-ça va, ça va," he said. "I am here to help."

The bogey shook, head juddering as she turned fully to his voice. Her breath rattled in her chest, sucking through the holes.

"W-where?" she stammered, blind eyes searching for his face.

"Here," said Kraven. "I am here."

She swallowed and nodded, though Kraven knew she could see him no more clearly than she had before.

"H-he," she started. Kraven put out a hand to stop her, pressing it against her shoulder, but she shook her head, forcing herself on. Her breath was barely a whisper. "The pass...it was a blood bath. We fought. Were clear. Nobody else...made it. He promised we would...but then...he betrayed us. Killed. It was so sudden. W-we, didn't expect..."

Kraven scowled, her broken grammar confusing, words unclear. She was crying, short hiccupping little gasps.

"W-who?" he said. "What?"

If the bogey knew he couldn't understand her, she made no indication. Her eyes began to pearl. "He, he promised...the empire...forever. Stop..."

Kraven drew close. "Who?" he demanded. "Who?"

But the bogey didn't answer. Her head rolled back, and her sightless eyes stared blankly at the sun.

She was one of seven, assuming Kraven's count was correct. Every one of them dead. And not just killed. Shredded. This was not the work of a killer who prided themselves on efficiency or cleanliness. Not even speed. No, this was the work of a true monster. Of someone who enjoyed the work. Pools of blood clotted the road. Entrails snaked across the dirt. The excess was abominable.

Kraven looked away, trying to catch his breath, and his gaze caught on something new. Bloody footprints leading from the massacre. Towards the yochni.

Peeling back the dead bogey's fingers, Kraven untangled

himself from her grasp, burned hands stinging as they scraped against the rough skin of her palm. Rising to his feet, he approached the edge of the bloody scene. He put his foot down on the first print, studying the four long marks stretching out past the tip of his boot. He had seen prints like this before, walked alongside them for the past several days. The killer was a bogey. And it looked like he had a wish.

CHAPTER
TWENTY-ONE

The dryad was tall, his upper branches swaying some twenty feet above the earth. Mira sat nestled in his upper boughs, not more than six inches from his craggy face. Batcha, uncomfortable and complaining, hung from one of his massive hands. Atlan, unconscious and sweating, lay across the dryad's opposite shoulder, his blood slowly leaking onto the creature's bark.

Below, the small army of saplings that had swarmed their group as soon as they'd burst from the undergrowth wove in and out of the foliage like hyper-active squirrels, squealing out every discovery and question that came into their green little minds.

Cavore, the dryad who carried them, walked well the line between patient answers and plain patience. He had come to investigate the smoke. Though Mira had threatened him with her axe—even chopping off the hand of one of the saplings in her initial panic, the dryad had seemed unperturbed, simply asking if she had been the one to set the mountain on fire.

Mira had dodged the question, explaining that it wasn't the mountain itself that had burned so much as the inside.

When the dryad had pressed, she'd admitted she'd had a hand in it, though she'd insisted the woods were safe.

The dryad had taken this news in stride, seeming both concerned that anyone should want to set anything on fire and satisfied she hadn't harmed the woods. His attention had then turned to Atlan, the bogey's form already hopelessly prodded and poked by the curious saplings despite Mira's most vehement threats and axe waving. In between trying to ward them off the dying bogey, she'd explained their situation.

Not long afterward, Cavore had promised to take them all to Oosek.

"He will know what to do," the giant tree had insisted.

"And graft my hand?" asked the sapling she had wounded, whose fascination with her seemed only to have grown with the injury.

"And graft your hand," Cavore agreed. Then he had picked up the bogey.

Now Mira interrogated the dryad for answers: Would Oosek be able to help Atlan? Could they still reach the yochni in time? Where did the dryads live?

"If anyone can help your friend, it is Oosek. As to the Eye," he said, using their unique name for the yochni, "it is difficult to tell. We never know when it blinks. Not until after. As to where we live, we live here."

"What about the Guardians? Don't they attack you?"

Cavore shook his head. "We live like the trees. Slow, unchanging. We do not seek the Eye, so the shadows do not bother us."

"Are they still here?"

"No," said Cavore. "They left two suns before. They did not disappear any pilgrims this year. There have not been many through the woods."

Mira nodded, considering. If the Guardians had left two

days previously, that meant the other champions would have begun their final approaches to the yochni. She was behind. All the same, the dryad could cover considerable ground with a stride longer than even Drake's, and if she could convince him to help her, she could make excellent time, more than enough to catch up, and perhaps even enough to wait for Atlan to awaken. Assuming, of course, that he awoke at all.

She looked across to the unconscious prince. She had no idea what he would do even if he did wake up. Help her? Blame her? Exact revenge? Now that their contract was over, there was no reason he shouldn't abandon her, let her reap the wages from the damage she'd sowed. She shook her head, pushing the doubts from her mind. She'd just have to cross that bridge if—no, *when*, she reminded herself—they came to it.

The sun was high by the time they reached the dryad camp. Cavore's pace was leisurely in comparison to his size, but even so, they covered miles of land. They traveled north, parallel to the Confluence and a little to the east. By the time they reached their destination, she thought she'd saved perhaps half a day of travel, to say nothing of the much-needed rest for Batcha.

The camp lay at the bottom of a shallow basin centered around a waterfall and a pool. A small beach had formed on one side with damp leaves churned into the sand by thousands of star-shaped sapling footprints. There were even more of the young dryads in the camp, those that had traveled with Cavore racing forward to meet the onrushing wave of their peers with tales of adventure and glory. Over the general din, Mira heard mention of a sapling person—perhaps a reference to herself with her small humanoid stature—a wintering dog man, and a blazing fire. The details, she surmised, were readily exaggerated.

The camp was not simply a nursery however, and while

the saplings swarmed and ebbed like a murmuration of star-lings, several older dryads approached to greet Cavore and his guests. The dryads came in varying shapes and sizes, some as old and craggy as trickthorn trees, others thin and supple as orpek sprays. Some were tall and tree-like like Cavore. Others were shorter, with smoother bark and more humanoid features. From what Mira could tell, there was no clear hier-archy between the two categories, though some within each group were paid special deference. A short, humanoid dryad with eyes like squallnuts and smooth, mouse-brown bark was given the most respect of them all, the others parting to give him passage. Cavore set Mira down, then introduced the dryad as Oosek.

"Hello, Oosek." Mira offered a small, nervous bow of her head. At first she couldn't place her anxiety, but then Cavore set Atlan's body down and it struck her. If this was Oosek, he was the one who could help Atlan. If he couldn't....

The elder dryad smiled, his features creaking as he did. "Hello. Welcome to our camp. And welcome home, Cavore."

Cavore nodded, explaining his recent expedition and discovery of their guests. Oosek listened, expression going grave as Cavore's story turned to the bogey. Shooing the saplings away, the elder dryad pressed carefully pruned fingers against the bogey's neck, checking for his pulse. He opened one of Atlan's eyes, examining the dilated pupils before listening to his weakening breath and feeling his fevered forehead. Mira's stomach tightened as the dryad frowned. He let out an ominous hum.

"It has been a long time since I have seen wounds like this," he said, voice a caramelly rasp. "How was he injured?"

"We were in the mountain. There were other dwarves. They attacked," said Mira, voice quiet.

Oosek nodded. "This sickness is the work of the sucker

hands. If the little ones attacked you, they must have collected the sucker hands' poison."

"Sucker hands?" said Mira.

Oosek rubbed his chin, fingertips scraping against the bark. "I believe the humans call them sirens. They were created by the Eye, though many of their kind have died since they were born. We have killed all that live within our woods, though some still live deep within the mountains in pools or along the coasts where they were born." He gestured with his hands, indicating a creature not quite as long as Mira was tall before pointing to his palms. "They carry mouths along their palms, the teeth of which are coated with a perilous venom. It dulls the mind, supplementing their blissful songs with hallucinations of the same nature. Simultaneously, it makes the blood flow free, preventing the wounds from closing. Once they have that, they can feast at will, suckling all too willing hosts."

A shudder of rustling leaves swept through the ubiquitous saplings at the description, their trembling sending their foliage aflutter.

"It doesn't work on trees," said Oosek.

"Can you help him?" asked Mira.

Oosek continued his examination, this time letting out a more optimistic hum. "Perhaps. I have seen only seven creatures escape the sirens' grip. Of those, only two woke from their eventual poisoned sleep. How many others the sirens have taken, how many I have not seen...."

Mira did not want to know. "How can I help?" she asked.

In the end, the saplings did most of the work, darting off into the woods with a few of the more reliable dryads to hunt for mushrooms while Mira helped Oosek grind herbs and pond shrimp shells. When the dirty work of ingredient preparation was complete, their fingers reeking of fish and earth, Oosek set Mira to mopping Atlan's brow with a mossy compress, taking over the finer work of portioning and mixing to finish off the salve. As the dryad worked, Mira's expression grew ever darker, a pending sense of helplessness welling up inside. What if Atlan didn't make it? Or what if he did and no longer wished to help her? Could she fight the second bogey alone? Would she even make it to the yochni in time?

She tried to think of more positive things, reminding herself that it wasn't too late and that the dryads would help her regardless of what happened to the bogey prince. And of course, fighting off other champions—including, perhaps, a bogey one—had always been the reality. Whatever happened to Atlan, that truth would remain unchanged. Nothing, she told herself, would have changed.

But she knew that wasn't true, and her forced optimism did very little to hide that fact, even from herself. Things had changed between her and the prince, and now everything was different.

"Done," said Oosek at last, interrupting her thoughts. The salve was gray and pulpy, with half-mashed mushrooms and shrimp shells peppered through with shredded green. The elder dryad shooed a group of inquisitive saplings aside, then removed Atlan's tattered shirt and extracted the plugs Kraven had used to stopper the bogey's wounds. Using a handful of leaves plucked from his own shoulder, he spread the salve over Atlan's injuries, using the same leaves and moss to seal the wounds when he was done. He looked up at her with a smile, then, frowning, took the bowl. He passed it to a sapling for refilling, then peeled the moss from her hand, passing it to another sapling and asking the leafy youth to take over. He pulled Mira gently to her feet.

"You walk the line of sickness yourself," he said. "Come. Rest." His skin was coarse and surprisingly firm for its flexibility. He tugged her towards the little beach, the quiet roar of the waterfall lulling her closer to sleep with every step. Save for a brief doze while Cavore had carried her, she hadn't slept since the night in Naveen's camp. She looked to Atlan, unwilling to abandon her post, but Oosek shook his head, insisting.

"In harming yourself, you harm him too," he said. Saplings approached carrying food and water for her, and Oosek redirected them to a sandy spot by the pool, gesturing that Mira should go there also.

"His burns," she said weakly, pointing to the bogey's damaged feet.

"I will tend them. Please. There is nothing else you can do for him now. You did well to bring him here."

Mira wanted to resist, but she knew the dryad was right. There was nothing else she could do, and whether or not the bogey survived, she still had work to do, work she could not finish without first taking a rest.

The dryad whom she'd injured, who had introduced himself as Brushek during their journey to camp, nuzzled under her arm, propping her up with his short, stout body as he helped her to the sand.

"Look," he said, wiggling a vine- and leaf-wrapped hand. "Nannan grafted it on." He gestured to a slender dryad with peeling white bark dotted through with brown. Nannan waved, and Mira nodded a vague assent, her footsteps slowing to an almost stagnant pace. Slow, foggy thoughts circled in her mind, Atlan's health, her future path, but she couldn't focus on any of them. The full weight of her exhaustion hit her suddenly, and her feet staggered on the soft earth. She fell and didn't get back up again. Voices chattered around her, a mix of chirrupy sapling babble and the calm, steady thrum of the elders. She could no longer make any of them out distinctly, and soon heard nothing at all.

The next thing Mira knew, bright sunlight was shining

through the trees, searing through her closed eyelids. Firm structures crowded over and around her, pinching her into place. Fear that she had been bound and captured gripped her and she jerked to get free with a yelp. But no, it wasn't her enemies. It was the saplings. As her eyes adjusted to the light, she realized she was lying in a pile of them, several more circling the clustered group.

She heard a round of titters from the tiny trees twined around her, the saplings she had thought had been sleeping all smiling and giggling up at her. One of the nearer dryads, Nannan, Mira thought, smiled as well.

"They are unfamiliar with night winters. They were determined to try it." Nannan tilted her slender head towards several roving bands of saplings chasing each other in packs around the pool before nodding back to the smaller pile. "Some of them made it."

Mira nodded, looking down at her unlikely brood. As her senses oriented to the morning and the fact she was not in danger, she couldn't help but smile. She rubbed grime from her eyes with hands still dirty and smelling of shrimp. When she opened them again, she saw Oosek approaching from the water's edge, a bowl of fresh fish in his hands. Water shone in beads along his now barer branches, his bark dark with moisture. Several more dryads stood under the waterfall he must have come from, washing dying early autumn leaves and dirt free from their bark and branches or collecting fish or plants from the water.

"How are you feeling? Did you sleep well?" asked Oosek, offering the bowl. She noticed he didn't use the word 'winter' for 'sleep' as the others did. Of them all, he came the closest to Itsrec vernacular.

"I did," she said. Then, smile disappearing, she remembered. Scrabbling free from the dryads, she ran towards the bogey prince. He was still covered in leaves and moss and salve. Long thin leaves and vines had been wrapped around his feet. "Atlan?"

"Lives," said Oosek, following her with a more measured pace. "I have not treated his kind often, and they are rare to take the help even when offered. They are hale beasts, though, and survive much that others would not."

"When will we know?" asked Mira.

The dryad shook his head. "Today? The next? It is difficult to tell. His fever broke in the night. It is a good sign."

Mira nodded. The bogey still looked terrible, though his breathing did seem to have improved.

Oosek extended the bowl again. "You should eat."

"Do you have a fir—" She cut off, realizing her near mistake. "Uh, I don't eat them raw."

"Ah, yes, of course. It has been a long time since we have had visitors of your kind," said Oosek, looking embarrassed for his mistake. One of the fish gave a twitch. The elder dryad handed the bowl off to one of the saplings, instructing her to take them back, and Brushek miraculously appeared in her place, this time bearing fruit. Mira, who had not realized just how hungry she was, took a handful of berries and an apple and started munching.

"What will you do now?" asked Oosek.

Mira swallowed—the small swarm of saplings around her oohing at the fancy of her doing so—and looked at her feet, then Atlan.

"I don't know. I was hoping he would, that *we* would have a decision. Or, not a decision, but, an outcome, this morning. One way or the other."

Oosek nodded. "I see. He is your friend?"

"Yes."

"But you go to see the Eye."

She nodded.

"It is rare for friends to make it this far. You would leave him now?"

She looked up sharply, then back down. "It's complicated."

Oosek tutted, an uncharacteristic distaste coloring the sound. "With pilgrims, it is always complicated."

Her frown deepened at his rebuke, but she wondered if he wasn't right. In her sleep-fogged delirium of the day before, everything had seemed so clear. Save Atlan. Rescue her friend. Stop the other bogey. It had made sense at the time, been a near singular focus for her to latch onto in her distress. But now, in the light of a new day, it seemed perilously naïve. Atlan was still the high prince after all, near king of the empire that had enslaved her people. Even if they stopped the other bogey, that would not set her people free. Nor could she think of a way to ensure her people's safety outside of the bogeys' wholesale execution.

It was not a pretty solution, but she could not see another alternative. What choice did she have? Perhaps things were not so complicated after all. She looked down to the bogey prince, his body still covered in leaves, dried salve, and moss. His feet were shod with leaves and a dark red paste administered after she'd fallen asleep. His fur, still patchy from the skin fang and cuts from the dwarves, stuck out from his skin in off kilter angles, his entire coat and black and red silks filthy with soot and blood.

"Can I help clean him off, at least?" she asked. "Get him some water?" She was eager to be on her way, but if there was any small kindness she could do before she left, she wanted the opportunity. Oosek gave her a wary eye, then moved to Atlan's shoulders, indicating she should carry the prince's feet.

They were almost to the water when Mira heard the startled squawking of birds. A terrible crashing of wood and leaves thundered through the woods, barreling in their direction. She'd left her axe by their things and wouldn't have time to reach it before the whatever-it-was arrived. For a moment, fear gripped her chest, even the peaceful dryads rising to full alert, but then she saw a flash of brilliant, blessed blue.

Mira dropped the bogey's feet.

"Kraven!"

TWENTY-TWO

As the camp came into view, Kraven heard Mira shout. Through the thinning veil of trees that still shrouded her from view, he saw her running full tilt towards him from her location beside a waterfall-fed pool. Trees dotted the sand and water, and dark, shrub-like forms raced along a sandy beach. Kraven couldn't tell what they were from his distance, though based on her tone, he didn't think they were dangerous. As they reached the tree line, he pulled Drake to a stop and dropped to the earth. Mira crashed into him a moment later, her arms sealing so tightly around his waist he thought she might crush his organs. The shrub things followed right behind, surrounding them in a rustling mass of just-turning leaves and scratching twigs.

"M-Mira?" said Kraven as he staggered to catch their weight. The shrub things, which had broken upon them like a wave, swirled around them in excited eddies and whorls. Mira, looking suddenly embarrassed and red-eared, released him.

"S-sorry. It's just...you came back," she said. "I thought you were gone."

Kraven, catching most of her meaning, frowned, his

previous anger difficult to forget even despite his current intentions. It was not impossible to overcome, however, and soon his grimness left him, his gaze shifting first to the surrounding creatures and then on to the larger camp. The majority of the creatures were tall and tree-like, some smaller and humanoid while still smaller ones scurried about the camp in packs and groves, their highest branches reaching no higher than his chest. He'd heard rumor of such creatures, though their territory did not extend to the Coast. It seemed Mira had found the dryads.

Interesting as they were, however, they were not the main focus of his search. Kraven looked past the leafy creatures. Then, he found Atlan. The bogey was propped up in a shallow basin of sand and rocks along the pond's edge, his head resting against the shoulder of another dryad. For a moment, Kraven thought he was dead, but then he saw the bogey's chest lift. Kraven sucked in a relieved breath.

"He is alive," he said. He jogged to the water, Mira right behind him. He glanced at her axe, still lying near the shallows. "I thought you...."

Mira lowered her gaze. "Me too. I was going to, but then they showed up. Or, Cavore did. That one. And some saplings. They saved him from the bleeding, but now he's asleep and we don't know if...."

She stopped, perhaps noticing his clouding features, and attempted to clarify. After several more rounds of pointing and gesturing, she managed to get her message across. They had been rescued and Atlan saved. At least for now. Mira introduced the dryad Atlan was leaning on as Oosek, and Kraven offered a short bow, passing on his thanks.

As he straightened, Mira's eyes widened. She pointed to the dark brown patches staining his bandaged palms.

"Kraven," she said. "What happened?"

Kraven flinched. In the flurry of his arrival, he'd nearly

managed to push aside his gruesome memories. Now the images of the murdered bogeys came flooding back. Oosek, still propping up Atlan, gestured to one of the taller dryads and they brought over a rock for Kraven to sit on. The saplings wheeled a chunk of log over for Mira as well before settling or scattering as they pleased. Many of the saplings still hopped at Drake, the dragon doing his best to keep away without stepping on or crushing their smaller forms like some old hound dealing with pups. Kraven, though he might normally have tried to assist his dragon, ignored them. The memories were still too strong. Too terrible. He stared at the water. He ran a hand over his face, then, finding it still dirty and stained, pulled it away. Mira set an encouraging hand on his knee, but he found he couldn't even bring himself to acknowledge the gesture, let alone thank her. He looked at her hand, expression blank, and she pulled it back into her lap, waiting for him to speak. He closed his eyes and drew in a deep breath. Then, he opened them again. "There is..." He paused, searching for the word. He held up two fingers. "Two bogeys."

Mira looked up. "The second champion."

"You understand?" he asked, brows raising.

"Yes, well, we were going to tell you, but then—"

He shook his head, cutting her off. Now that he had started, he needed to finish, to get all the memories out. "There are..." He held up several more fingers. "Many. Dead. Many..."

"A pack?"

Kraven, recognizing the word, moved to snap his fingers, then, flinching in pain from his burns, waved his hand and nodded instead. "Two bogey—"

"Second bogey."

He nodded. "Second bogey kill pack. Kill champions."

The dwarf frowned, puzzling through his meaning. Then

her eyes went wide, the pieces clicking. The second bogey had killed the other champions. And then he had killed his pack. Which meant unless there were other champions who were either very fast, very hidden, or very far behind, the second bogey was the only one left.

She jumped to her feet, boots shuffling in the sand as she started and stopped, pacing in a tiny circle. He could practically see the gears spinning in her skull, running over the various iterations of options ahead. Then, a new spark flew high from the rest of her mental bonfire, and she looked to him.

"Kraven. You were going to leave. Go home. And Drake —!" She looked to the sea dragon, the giant creature still doing his utmost to avoid being overrun by the saplings. She scanned the sea dragon's sides for injuries, but the wounds were no longer bleeding. She turned back to Kraven, amazed. "He's okay. How?"

Kraven dropped his gaze, feeling sick. He had figured the question would come up, though he had hoped that it would not, that he would not have to discuss the slaughtered bogeys any further. Releasing his gathered hands, he tapped the handle of Johann's knife, then made a jabbing motion towards his palm. He made a sort of plucking motion with the fingers of his other hand, trying to suggest something spiky coming up through the skin, then, when that didn't work, laid his knuckles against his palm, wriggling his fingers.

"One bogey," he said. "Bones were broken. Up. Through." He tapped his head, before pointing to his pack. "I...think. Medicine book. Sirens."

Oosek, who had listened quietly throughout save to silence an errant sapling or two, nodded. "He means their teeth. If he is from the Coast, it is reasonable that he would know of the sucker hands." He bared his own teeth, tapping them with a finger before pointing to his palm. Kraven, following the gesture, nodded.

"They are not...many. But I...understand them. People talk about them. Medicine."

Mira seemed to understand, and for a moment she sat in silence, brow furrowed in thought. Kraven could practically feel her next question brewing, but waited for her to reach it herself, for her to choose her own words to ask.

As ever, when it came, she was direct. "Kraven. Why are you here?" She pointed at him, gesturing to the space around them and repeating the word "why."

He winced, gaze dropping to the sand.

Mira pressed. "You were going home."

Kraven's frown deepened, but he didn't deny her the answer. He sighed, then gave her an apologetic look. "Ines... have helped. I was bad about Ines. Before. Second bogey is bad. Ines have helped."

It was not exactly right grammatically, though Mira seemed to catch his meaning. "I'm sorry," she said. "About earlier. Before. I shouldn't have betrayed—hurt—you and Atlan. Lied. That was bad of me, wrong, and I'm sorry. And for what it's worth, I think you are like Ines. Well, I think. I guess."

It was, in some ways, a useless sentiment. Mira had never met Ines and was thereby unable to make any kind of legitimate comparison. She seemed to realize her mistake, too, backpedaling even as she said it. But it was sincere and kind and something Kraven very much needed in that moment, even with the few snatches he had not been able to parse. In essence, it was enough. He smiled, the first since he had arrived. "Thank you," he said.

Mira smiled, but before they could get any farther, a sound interrupted them. It was weak and soft, little more than a truncated whimper. The two of them shared a look, then sprang towards the water.

Atlan was awake. Mira splashed in up to her knees, taking the bogey's hand. Kraven waited on the sand. Atlan groaned and opened his eyes to narrow slits. The usually bright yellow of his irises was dull with sickness, his expression equally blunted. He looked between them to his grasped hand and back again and gave them a single, wondering blink.

"Hi," he said.

"Hi," said Mira.

Kraven, a little surprised by Mira's suddenly affectionate behavior, waved. Atlan smiled weakly in return.

"I feel terrible," he managed. "Like I've been sleeping for days."

"You have been," said Mira. "Almost."

The bogey nodded. "Ah. I had the strangest dreams." He swallowed, eyes closing again, then sat bolt upright, nearly upending Mira as he did. "The yochni. Did it—?"

"You're fine," said Mira. She spread her feet to steady her weight. "We're not too late."

Atlan frowned, looking down at the hand she had held. Confusion clouded his features.

"Atlan," she said, "There are things you need to know."

The bogey's eyes narrowed in concern, questions racing over his face. He was still exhausted and weak, however, and needed to rest. Mira and Oosek helped him back down into the water, and Oosek ordered some of the saplings to go find him food. More was brought for Mira and Kraven as well.

When the bogey was finally settled, Kraven began their tale. He spoke in Itsrec the best he could, switching to Fransec when he could not. Between them, Kraven and Mira filled the bogey in on what had happened to the dwarves, how Kraven had cancelled the contract, how he came upon the bogeys, how the dryads found Mira and Atlan, and finally, Kraven's unexpected return. After figuring out the mystery of the siren's poison, Kraven had tended Drake, then set off to follow his friends' trail. He'd been surprised to find Atlan missing from the pond, though of course, Cavore's prints had been easy to follow.

When Kraven finished speaking, Atlan set a hand on his chest, a thoughtful expression on his face. His brow furrowed, and though he was still visibly weak, it was clear he was already gathering strength, putting together a plan to face the oncoming threat. "And she didn't give any clues as to who the other bogey might be? What he wants?" he asked, repeating the questions in Fransec. He was referring to the dying bogey to whom Kraven had spoken.

Kraven shook his head. "'Empire forever,'" he said, "But I do not understand."

Atlan nodded, his fingers finding their customary place under his chin. "*Empire pour toujours,*" he translated. "Except, so far as I know, that's impossible. There's nothing that can't be undone or overcome by another wish in a future age, no way to make the empire live forever. *C'est impossible.*" He frowned, then shook his head, moving on. "How long before the yochni blinks?"

He repeated the question in Fransec. Kraven looked to Mira, but she only shrugged. The best estimates anyone could ever make were based on the Guardians' end-of-age disappearance. Mira held up two fingers, passing on Cavore's news about when the shadow creatures had left.

Atlan nodded again, brow furrowing. "Oosek, would your people be willing to help with supplies? Transport or fighting?"

As Atlan translated for Kraven, Oosek frowned, one well-trimmed hand rising to rub his chin. "We are a generous people, willing to give you food and water for your journey.

But we are slow to leave our lands and even slower to fight. I could not promise either of your other requests."

The bogey seemed unsurprised by the answer. For a moment, he did nothing at all. Then he turned to Kraven, translating Oosek's response before asking a question in Fransec. "*Vas-tu aider?*"

He didn't repeat his question in Itsrec, though Kraven could see that Mira recognized the word 'aide.' The bogey had asked if he would help them. Kraven flinched. It was another question he had both expected and dreaded. Partly because he knew it would require confronting the fact of Mira's earlier betrayal and partly because he didn't yet know what his answer should be. The second bogey was terrible, yes. He had murdered his own pack to avoid future betrayal and been strong enough to do it without apparent injury, or at least not enough to leave a trail. Whoever he was, he was cold-blooded and ruthless, someone who enjoyed the pain of others and would likely bring just such qualities to the empire forever.

On the other hand, he had seen similar proclivities in Mira, both when she had betrayed them and before. She had not yet openly rescinded her wish for bogey genocide, and if he continued to help her, he ran the same risk he had run before of being party to her pending bogey slaughter. If he helped only Atlan, he would still be helping an empire of slavers, to say nothing of the potential harm to himself or his dragon if he helped either ally. So far as Kraven was concerned, helping either one would only lead to pain and heartache. Then again, to do nothing, to let the rival bogey champion win....

"Mira hurt you," he said at last. "Me."

"She did," said Atlan.

"And you help her?" he asked.

"I will," said Atlan.

Kraven frowned, then asked a question in Fransec. *"L'aides-tu même si elle ne change pas son souhait?"*

He had asked the bogey if he would still help even if Mira didn't change her wish. This time the bogey looked to the sand. He considered the question, though Kraven could already see the resolution dug into the bogey's face. Atlan licked his lips, grimacing, then straightened. When his yellow gaze met Kraven's blue one, his eyes were no longer dull, but shining. Firm. "Yes."

Kraven's lips twitched, his mouth nearly opening in surprise. He put his bandaged hands in his pockets, then, flinching in pain, took them back out. The bogey was crazy. If he helped Mira, or if she somehow got away from them or betrayed them again....

"Kraven," said Atlan, interrupting his floundering. *"C'est bon. Tu peux me faire confiance."*

"Mais...but...." Kraven's face wrinkled. It was insanity. There were no good answers. He glanced at Mira, but she only looked confused, unsure of what the two were discussing. He looked to his hands, but Ines' burned gloves were still in his pack. They couldn't guide him. Ines wasn't there. What would she have done? What should he do? He'd been wrong to abandon them before, but this...this...Kraven's gaze settled on Atlan. The bogey, as ever, was steady. Calm. *Tu peux me faire confiance.* You can trust in me.

"Okay," said Kraven. "I will help. I will help."

Mira's face lit up like a freshly sparked torch. Kraven moved to stand, but Atlan's entire body went stiff as a stone.

"Stop," he barked. "Wait."

Kraven, confused, did.

The prince pointed. "Your hand," he ordered. *"Ici."*

Kraven glanced at Mira but didn't resist the order. Atlan grabbed Kraven's hand, lowering his snout until it was nearly touching the gauze. He scented once, twice, three times, eyes squeezed shut as if that might somehow block out the surrounding scentscape.

Then his grip tightened. Kraven, yelping in pain, yanked back, and Atlan fell forward, collapsing on the shore. If the bogey could have paled, Kraven was certain he would have gone deathly white. A keening whine slipped from the bogey prince's chest.

"What is it?" asked Mira. "What do you smell?"

The bogey swallowed, fists tightening on the sand. When he spoke, his voice was strangled, weak. "I know who it is. The second champion."

"Who?" asked Mira.

When he spoke next, Atlan's voice was little more than a pained whine. "My cousin. Crucius."

Mira and Kraven shared a look, the word for cousin mercifully the same in both languages.

"Are you close?" asked Mira.

"He's the second-place prince behind me."

"That's not what I meant."

Atlan looked up, tears brimming in his eyes. When he spoke, his voice was faint as a ghost's. "He's my best friend."

TWENTY-THREE

Atlan forced himself up from the shallows, propping himself on his arms. He had not the strength to get up any farther, only years of diplomatic training keeping him from collapsing on the sand to weep and gnash his teeth. Crucius was the second champion. His cousin. His friend. His replacement.

"Are you sure it's Crucius?" asked Mira.

Atlan nodded. There was no mistaking his cousin's scent. Though the blood on Kraven's hands did not belong to the younger prince, the scent of victory, the virile rush of adrenaline and violence overlaying it, and Crucius' sweat were impossible to deny, even with the faded time between the kills and Kraven's arrival and the secondhand nature of the scent.

"It's him," he said.

"Could he be part of the pack that was killed?" asked Mira.

Atlan shook his head again. "They would never turn on the second-place prince like that," he said, though his voice lacked its usual confidence. The acrid taste of bile bit the back of his throat as he thought of all the things Kraven had described, as he imagined Crucius doing such violence. But it was not impossible to imagine, nor even difficult, he realized, and the revelation only deepened his conviction. "He has always had a...penchant for these kinds of things. He is ferocious in battle, ruthless, almost senseless. If anyone could take down a pack, it would be him. And with how close he is with our uncle...."

He drifted off, mind sinking into the mire of such considerations. Mira told Kraven to describe what he remembered of the bogey bodies. The medic had tried not to look at anything too closely while he'd gone through their belongings, but he could still provide general clues regarding fur color and size. It was of no use. None of the dead matched Crucius' description. Atlan had not expected them to.

"Maybe the empire thought I died in the village," he muttered. "If they heard in time, thought I was dead, perhaps they sent a replacement."

But he knew that wasn't true. The village he had been attacked in was far from the bogey capital in the south. The only way Crucius could have caught up in time was if he had been following from the beginning, perhaps even known it was going to happen. Bogeys never sent more than one champion, let alone a pack. The only reason they would have done so was if they'd expected—or intended—for him to fail.

In sum, his people had sold him out.

It was the unavoidable conclusion. Atlan knew the others were smart enough to figure it out, too, though they were kind enough not to say it. Mira asked if there was anything they could do, but Atlan shook his head. Kraven had said Crucius wanted the empire to live forever. Assuming such a thing were even possible, with the empire's current state, such longevity would mean the end of Mira's people, if not everyone. They had to stop him. After that, who got to make their wish...Atlan shook his head. It was not worth considering now. A waste of time they did not have.

Instead, he buried himself in preparations. They all knew the timeline was short, and so, though he had little physical strength, he did what he could in other ways, meeting with Cavore and Oosek to discuss routes and timelines and to barter for supplies. The dryads, thankfully, were a friendly race, eager to help their new friends on their way, and while they were unwilling to escort the party beyond the bounds of their lands, they were more than willing to send them along with fresh provisions and medical supplies.

It was also decided that they would leave Batcha with the dryads. Though the mini hart had healed from his injuries, he would not be able to keep pace with Drake and the added weight, were the dragon to carry him, was more than they could afford. Cavore would bring the mini hart to meet them after the yochni blinked, and whoever was left, if anyone, would take the creature home.

Between Atlan's diplomatic experience and the dryads' friendly nature, it was not long before negotiations were finished. Under normal circumstances, the deal he'd made would have been nearly criminal for its lopsidedness, but, given the dryads' generosity and the fact that they had no use for the same kinds of supplies or food, he didn't think they begrudged the expenses. Oosek set the larger dryads to fishing and foraging, then, perhaps sensing Atlan wished to be free of his usual sapling coterie, mobilized the youths to assist with collection. Kraven, still looking troubled himself, kept a similar distance, focusing instead on preparing and tending Drake. Mira and Cavore had disappeared into the woods not long after the decision to leave Batcha so she could teach the dryad how to care for the beast. Atlan had seen the dryad return alone not long after. The prince slipped into the woods to look for Mira.

He found her in a clearing not far from camp, rubbing the thick, coarse fur along Batcha's neck. The mini hart nuzzled her chest. At first, Atlan took it for a sign of affection, though he soon realized the creature was only trying to move past her to get to his next patch of grass. Mira, more well versed in the emotional ranges of such creatures, only smiled, scratching his ruff and getting out of his way.

"Love you, too," she said.

Atlan smiled. He had not seen such a tender side to the dwarven champion before. He wondered what had changed, though he suspected such a facet had existed all along. It had just taken him time to see it. Clearing his throat, he stepped out of the trees, Mira startling at his approach. The leaves Oosek had bound around Atlan's feet crinkled as he walked. Thankfully, his burns had been minor and Oosek's medicine potent. He still moved heavily from the siren's poison, though he was lucky to be able to move at all. "Are you ready?" he asked.

"Y-yeah," she said. She gave him a tight smile. "I'm good."

"Are you sure?" he said, nodding to her shuffling feet. She stopped their movement, though he could still see the tightness in her limbs, sense the buzz of nervousness in the air. She had more to say. He waited and was rewarded for his patience a moment later.

"I...wanted to apologize," she said. "I shouldn't have betrayed you, in the caves. I still hate your people, what they've done and do. But despite being heir to them, you've always treated me...well, maybe not *well*, but not completely terribly. And you have been useful sometimes. I just...you haven't acted like the king of the slavers, or the almost king, and that's been...good. I should have...I should have tried to help you, instead of telling them all those things."

Atlan crossed his arms, a look of mock severity tracing his features. "I believe the word you are looking for is 'lies,' not 'things.' And that has got to be one of the lousiest apologies I've ever heard. But..." he said, softening and uncrossing his arms. "I have not always acted as princely as I might have, either, and I'm sorry I didn't believe you. A good king listens to his people."

"I'm not one of your people," she said.

He shrugged. "Maybe. Maybe." With a pained groan, he kneeled before her. "Mira, I am sorry for what my people have done. If we survive this, I will do whatever I can to make it better. I'm sorry."

"Me too," she said. She paused a moment. "Atlan, what did Kraven ask you earlier? Before you found out about Crucius?"

Atlan's smile twitched. For a moment, he considered lying, but resisted the temptation. "He asked if I would still help you even if you would still make your wish."

She stared at him, astonishment plain on her features. "And you said yes? W-why?" she finally managed.

Atlan smiled, though his sadness was hard to keep from it. There were half a dozen reasons why he'd given his answer, some harder to explain than others. He paused, the temptation to lie surfacing again, then did his best. "Mira, do you know why the bogeys were wished into creation? The real reason?"

He could see by her expression she had to bite back the first, cruel words which leapt to her mouth, but for once she held her tongue, shaking her head instead.

"We're defenders," he said. "Born of Teva Anosh, mother of dogs. She was pregnant with pups when the end of the age came, heavy with them, in fact, but she loved her master and wanted to go with him. He went with another, the two assuring each other they would share the age, that they wouldn't betray each other. But of course, as such promises always do, it failed in the end. They killed each other on the very doorstep of victory, and there was nothing poor Teva could do. Now, dogs are not known for their...higher functions, we'll say, but somehow Teva, whether from fear, loneliness, or curiosity, managed not only to find her way to the yochni but to stay there until it blinked. She was alone, pregnant, and without her master. She'd failed him, and it was unlikely she was going to get out of the caves again. She had seen the cruelty of men and the ineffectualness of her own capabilities. For her pups, Teva wanted more. She wished for more.

"That's the wish bogeys come from, Mira. To defend the people we care for, to be unblemished, *unsullied* by the same lusts and desires of men. We have their might—more, in fact —all their smarts, and, in theory, we were supposed to have none of their flaws. Their pride, their love of power, avarice. Heart and ferocity of the dog, wits and might of a man. That's what we stand for or were supposed to. Our heritage. Goodness. Strength. It's what made us kings. What *makes* us kings. We were supposed to do better than those who came before, to rule, rightfully, without blemish. Except...traveling with you...I can see now that we haven't. I wanted to change that, to right those wrongs, but if I can't...a king's job is to protect his people, to serve them, and if we can't do that, if I can't...I... I want to help you, Mira. That's all. That's all there's ever been."

"Aren't you scared I'll kill you when we get there? That I'll make my wish?" she asked.

She had asked more or less the same question in the caves before they had scared off the hunters. He had answered her harshly then. He didn't wish to do so now. He sighed, the weight of his decision settling over his shoulders like some terrible cloak. Then, after a last moment's hesitation, he looked her dead in the eye.

"Mira, I'm not going to stop you from making your wish. I'm not even going to get in your way. Even if it kills me."

"W-what? Why?"

"Because it's worth it. And, because I trust you."

"I don't—What are you talking about?"

She was indignant as ever, but Atlan only smiled, the corners of his lips not rising quite as high as they normally might have. "Mira, if I can prove to you that even one bogey can be good, that even one of us can change, do you really think you'll wish the rest of us out of existence? Do you really think you can?"

"I—I don't have a choice," she blustered, though it was clear she was struggling to summon her usual vehemence.

"Maybe. But even if it doesn't change your mind, that doesn't change what I have to do. As future king, it's my job to protect my subjects. That includes the ones that don't have a tail. If I have to die to do it, so be it."

She was stammering now, shock tangling her tongue. "Y-you can't do that."

He got to his feet. "Why not? It's my life. Besides, you've already saved my life once, back in the caves. I'm willing to use that as proof of concept." He grinned then, though it was tense, almost a grimace. "And just think, if you wished me out of existence after all that work, well, wouldn't that just be a waste?"

She looked about to argue, but he was already up and turning to go. For all his courage, he found he could not bear to be in the clearing any longer, to have the guts to not turn back on his word. Forcing himself to walk without trembling, he moved towards the edge of the clearing, waving for her to follow.

"Come on, pokey," he said. "The others are waiting."

He did his best to keep his voice light, though even to him the words seemed strained.

CHAPTER

TWENTY-FOUR

An hour later, Mira sat perched on Drake's back, Atlan behind her and Kraven, as ever, up front, straddling the dragon's shoulders as they plodded through the woods. They had decided to take the Confluence to reach the yochni's mountain. Though they would lose time angling to reach it from the dryad camp, they knew the time they would save by taking the straight, even road the rest of the way would far outweigh the initial cost. And, operating under the assumption that Crucius and his pack had in fact killed all of the other champions, it was now far safer to take the Confluence than it otherwise might have been.

Cavore, carrying Batcha along for a final goodbye, strode to their left, his tall form weaving and swishing through the higher branches with surprising deftness, though as before, there were some branches even he could not avoid breaking. Several saplings snaked in and out of the brush below them like gusts through the fields. Batcha let out a semi-regular stream of uncomfortable grunts and groans, but otherwise suffered the indignity with his now usual resignation. If they survived, Mira wondered if the mini hart would be willing to

249

walk anywhere on his own anymore for all that he'd learned to be carried.

If they survived. Her fingers tightened against her knees.

They reached the edge of the woods. Atlan gave a slight bow to Cavore. "Thank you for your assistance," he said. Despite their earlier conversation, the bogey prince seemed as cool and collected as he ever did. If not for a slight tension to his muscles, a sort of over-compensation in his normally smooth motions, she wouldn't have guessed they'd spoken at all.

The dryad smiled, leaves rustling as he bowed his head. "The pleasure is ours, wintering dog. I wish you well on your journey."

"Thank you," said Atlan. "Your aid will not be forgotten."

Cavore nodded again, but his were a simple people, with little to say at the best of times and even less in moments of parting. He lifted Batcha so Mira could give him a last few scritches, then, with the saplings gathered at his feet, waved goodbye, Batcha giving a final mournful bray as the dryad resettled him in his grip. The trio of champions waved in return, and soon the dryads turned back into the woods, even the most adamant saplings vanishing when Cavore called them along. Within minutes, they couldn't even hear his monstrous footsteps. Kraven urged Drake onto the road.

Ahead, the yochni's mountain hunched on the horizon. It was shorter than the range they'd just passed through, though wide, its sides sinking beneath the trees to either side of the road on long, slow angles. The Kinderstorm, the nearly unending blizzard which kept armies from simply camping around the mountain between ages, had subsided for the end of the age, leaving the path clear but muddy all the way to the entrance to the yochni's cave. Mira's breath caught as she realized this was her first real look at the mountain, the goal she'd been working towards all her life.

The elation she might otherwise have expected was cut short by her knowledge of what lay ahead, however, her accomplishment curtailed by the looming death of at least one of her friends.

Drake turned North to follow the road.

With the sea dragon mostly recovered and time short, they'd decided that they would ride most of the way, keeping to a swift but steady pace to keep the dragon from getting too tired. Though Atlan claimed he wished to walk and be active after his long sleep, Mira, and more importantly Kraven as physician, strictly limited the practice, not letting him walk for more than fifteen minutes at a time.

Instead, they discussed the road ahead, Mira and Kraven spinning around on Drake's back so that they could face the bogey prince as they spoke.

Atlan, having spent the majority of his life as a scholar of the ages, was ready to hand with details. "The cave's entrance is in the foothills. Though it started as a natural cave system, it has since been shaped by both a variety of wishes and species. These changes have created several unique rooms, obstacles, and environments, most notably those created by the Treaty of Four."

Mira, who knew most of the basics already—or at least the important bits about the obstacles she would have to overcome to reach the yochni—would rather have skipped the history lesson, but Kraven, having had no intention of going so far when he'd started off, welcomed the lecture, Atlan all too happy to give it.

"The Treaty itself is both the greatest and only example of lasting teamwork among champions. It is both the wish that instigated the end of the Wicked Ages, which extended from the tenth to the twentieth ages, as well as the wish that created the Guardians, the Kinderstorm, and the Trials. As you'll have noticed, the Guardians and Kinderstorm have already subsided for the age, which leaves us, of course, with the Trials.

"There are four of them, one for each champion within the treaty. Technically, there should have been five, as there was a fifth champion, Ylsa, the constant who brought them all together; however, she was killed along the way, her wish now lost to time. What she would have wished for—"

"Atlan," chided Mira. "Focus, please?"

The bogey's ears slanted forward, and she felt a momentary pang of regret for interrupting. No doubt this was one of the few times he'd been able to share his vast stores of knowledge.

"Sorry," she said.

"Not at all. You're right," he said, though she could tell he was still disappointed. Atlan slung his pack forward, drawing out his map case as he translated. He hooked his pack strap on his foot, then undid the case's latch. "The first Trial is the labyrinth. It is fairly self-explanatory and, thankfully, decently well mapped, though it has taken much time and effort to collate the results of the various champions' cartographic efforts."

Drawing a massive, rolled parchment from the case, Atlan unfurled a map that was large enough to have served as a dwarven blanket. It was beautifully done, with delicate lines of stone and various pits and caverns carefully drawn in ink. A river cut through one large region, with crossings etched and labeled by multiple hands. Several sections had faded with time, though others looked more recent, with neat, crowded print demarcating features with names, locations, and dates. A few areas were entirely blank, though Mira was surprised how few they were given the map's great size. Atlan turned the map to face her and Kraven, then traced a long path with a claw. "This, as best I can tell, is a general layout of the tunnels. There are a few gaps in my knowledge, of course, though thankfully I was able to chart what I believe is a safe front-to-end path."

"Did you make this?" Mira asked, leaning close to examine the details. She followed the path with her own small finger. Atlan shrugged, the edges of the map bouncing with a tiny wave.

"Some. Unfortunately, the arts of calligraphy and drawing are hardly prized amidst the bogey elite. The messier parts are mine, though they're accurate, at least. I hope."

"What if you're wrong?"

The bogey flinched at the suggestion, though his tone managed to maintain its academic veneer. "Then I smell for my cousin. If he is our main impediment, then we can take all the time we need once he is removed from the table."

"Unless the yochni blinks before we get there," said Mira.

The bogey ceded the point with a slight tilt of the head, expression tightening. "Naturally, though I should rather none of us take the age than he."

Mira paused, considering the path that lay ahead, then looked up to the bogey prince. "What's he like?"

"Crucius?"

"Yes."

Atlan tightened, and for a long time, he didn't answer. When he spoke again, his voice was quiet and thoughtful, and he sounded as if he were far away. A hint of admiration, of fondness almost, shone through his tone, though grief was heavy in it, too.

"Crucius...loves his people. Fiercely, like me, though perhaps, I see now, too much. I doubt he would have any qualms about making your people serve ours. Whenever the topic came up, whispers of it, he never seemed to care, though of course, whenever I was around, the topic was always quickly changed or brushed aside. Made to seem less than it was. We were close though, as cubs. He was...fiery. All he ever wanted to do was play and roughhouse, dream of our glorious future. He was strong, scrappy, even for his size. Whenever we asked my father for stories, he would always ask for the rise of the bogeys. Bogey victory, bogey glory. It's all he could ever think about. I guess in hindsight it's no surprise that...well, he's always been close to our uncle, the king. I'm not surprised Uncle Ru chose him."

There was a pain in his voice which spoke of old wounds, though he hid it well. It was strange to hear him speak of family after all this time, though she knew she would only have shouted him down had he tried to broach the subject before. The very idea of familial bonds, or indeed any bonds besides that of the infamous pack, were foreign to her in her conception of bogeys, and she realized with a start that she had never even considered that Atlan might have a father. Or a mother. Like most dwarven children, she'd always spun tales of bogeys climbing out of pits or cracks in the ground, writhing out of eggs in fountains of slime to eat their parents in great, big broods. It was, of course, exaggerated nonsense, the kind of thing to fit the bogeys to her nightmarish expectations, though she only now realized that she'd never bothered to upgrade her understanding. With it, came a spark of revelation, a question she'd never considered.

"Atlan," she said. "What about your father? Isn't he there? Couldn't he—?"

"He's dead," said Atlan. "He died when I was seven."

"I'm sorry," she said, speaking before she could stop herself. She realized only belatedly that she'd just lamented the death of a bogey, though she also knew that it was true. "What about your mother?"

He shook his head. "She died when I was young. I don't remember her." He translated for Kraven when the boy asked, and the medic gave his own condolences, the word '*désolé*,' which Mira had come to understand as 'sorry,' giving meaning where the rest of his words were more opaque. Atlan shook his head. "It was a long time ago. A lot has changed since then."

Kraven nodded, rubbing his chin with his hand. He asked another question, which Atlan translated as regarding Crucius' age.

"*Dix-sept*," he said. "Seventeen."

Mira swallowed. *Seventeen.* He was only a year older than she was. She thought of Kraven's description of the murdered pack, then realized she had been hoping to wish for much the same result. Her way would be faster and less painful, but the scale would be far larger, multiplied by thousands, if not millions. She shuddered.

Atlan rolled up the map. "I'd like to take a break now. I want to stretch my legs."

At the bogey's request, Kraven pulled Drake off to the side of the road. Atlan slid down, then reached his hands up for Mira. Kraven dismounted, and Drake slipped into the woods, finding a muddy puddle to wallow in beneath the trees. The road and surrounding woods had grown puddled and muddy from the melted Kinderstorm snow. Mira and Kraven set their packs down to serve as seats, and Atlan, after stretching, joined them. His pack had lost much of its shape after his fall in the forge. He'd checked his belongings at the dryad camp and his harp and case had been badly damaged, crushed by his own weight. His whip had likewise been lost in the fire, though he seemed to grieve the weapon less. Mira and Kraven distributed rations, and for several minutes, they ate in contemplative silence. Atlan seemed to have lost his taste for speech in the discussion of his family, but there was still more planning to be done and several more Trials to discuss.

"Atlan," said Mira. "You didn't finish. The other trials?"

For a second his eyes stayed blank, his mind lost wherever

it was, but then Kraven added his own plea for speech, and they managed to draw him back to the present.

"Yes, sorry," he said. "The second Trial is called Stamoth's River. Typically, one must either ford the river or use one of several footholds or footpaths to cross, each treacherous and slick. Thankfully for us, we have Drake, so fording it shouldn't be a problem."

Mira, who had heard vague stories of the river, felt her stomach tighten. It had always been the scariest part of the stories for her and her siblings growing up. Other than the bogey champion they'd have to kill, of course. "What if we fall in?"

"Nobody knows," said Atlan. "There are no records of where the river leads once it exits the chamber, nor the fates of any who have fallen in."

"You know I can't swim, right?"

"Then don't fall in," he said.

Mira shot him a sour look, but he didn't notice. Kraven prodded the prince to continue.

"The final two Trials should be the easiest. The first is the Hall of Treasures. It contains hundreds of boxes built into the walls, one for each champion each age. Within each box, there is either a deadly trap or what you most want in this world. Given our stakes, I'm not worried any of us will be too drawn in by that temptation. The final Trial is the Fountain of Gold, which contains material wealth, primarily in the form of gems and precious metals. None of it is booby trapped beyond the inherent dangers of collecting such things, so it primarily serves as a deterrent for any who would rather take their money and run than condemn the entire next age to a reign of their greed. After that, it's just the Chamber of Sorrows and then a winding tunnel to the yochni itself."

"That simple," she said.

"That simple," said Atlan.

Mira studied him for a long moment, but the bogey didn't notice, his face once more pinching with thought.

"Atlan," she said slowly. "You know what I want to wish for and what Crucius wants to wish for, but we don't know about you. What was your wish?"

The bogey's ears twitched, perhaps at the implications of her choice of the word "was," or, more troubling, the fact she had used present tense regarding her own wish. He frowned, ears slanting forward.

"I'm...not sure," he said at last, looking sheepish. His troubled expression broke, and his smile grew. "You know, I've spent years studying the ages, puzzling through the implications of every past wish, the nuances of every choice. But when it came to choosing my own, well, I guess maybe I thought I'd figure it out when I got there. I always assumed it would be something to do with the empire, keeping it going or making sure we didn't fall. Now, well, I think perhaps...." He trailed off, then shook his head. "Never mind. I'm sure you'd just think it silly, probably selfish."

"Atlan," she said firmly. "Please."

He looked down at her, then down the road to the mountain, expression going momentarily wistful.

"Well," he said. "I guess if I could have wished, I would have liked to have been a good king."

She noted his own use of past tense.

"Come on," he said, already getting to his feet. "It's time for us to go."

TWENTY-FIVE

It took them to the following afternoon to reach the foothills of the yochni's mountain. The cave mouth they were looking for lay just above a ridge not far up the slope. A disjointed series of paths long smoothed by the passing of champion feet and Kinderstorm snow wound its way up through the shale, ducking in and out of sight behind various spurs and tilted ledges. The group stopped for a break before ascending, and together they crafted torches, tended wounds, and shared a final meal. They spoke little, each lost to their own thoughts. Atlan, certain this was the last time he would see the sun, split his time between watching the world around them and observing his two companions. It was warm, just touching the threshold of unpleasant, but breezy, the wind tickling the just turning leaves. Mira and Kraven ate with a focused determination which belied the tenseness of their muscles. Under the scent of dying leaves and snowmelt, Atlan could smell his cousin.

He closed his eyes, feeling the air spin over his fur and listening to the chirrup of birds and bugs. Drake whuffed at his master, letting out a contented twitter. Atlan's silks scraped beneath his claws. He took in a deep breath, tasting every last scent the world had to offer, then let it out, opening his eyes, and rising to his feet. Well-supplied by the dryads, they'd eaten much and rested long. They no longer had time to wait.

"Come," he said. "It's time to go."

The paths up were not as contiguous as they first appeared from below. Where Atlan had assumed they were a singular trail leading from one switchback to another, they were rather a series of fragmented mini-paths, short ruts or clefts which indicated where repeated champion foot traffic or weather events had chipped away the stone. In certain stretches, whether by means of several equally traversable paths or by breaks in the rock during the intervening six hundred years since the last age, there was no dominant path at all, their group members simply having to navigate as best they each saw fit.

Drake had the hardest go of it. With feet designed for the smooth stones of rivers and the sands of beaches, he struggled with the sharp and slippery shale. Given the delicate nature of the rock, he could not simply charge and jump from stone to stone like Atlan and the others could either. It cost them perilous time to wait for him and his master—Kraven often trailing behind to help his dragon—but Atlan knew they could not afford to leave the creature behind. Not if they were going up against Crucius.

The extra time was not an entire waste, however, in that it gave Atlan time to think. When he had first discovered the truth about his cousin, his mind had raced, tearing through countless iterations of why his uncle had chosen to replace him, why he had sent Crucius, and what they hoped to gain. After his chat with Mira, however, and their subsequent discussions of the trials ahead, he had found his thoughts growing maudlin, his usually logical mind getting lost in a sentimental mire for the world he now knew that he would lose. Had he made a mistake? Was he wrong to trust Mira? If he could not convince her of his species' goodness, did they really all deserve to die? By the time they had settled in for the night, he had found his thoughts so tangled in the anxiety of his despairing ethical web that he could not focus on the actual tasks that lay before him.

Now, with the mountain under his very paws, he found his usual perspicacity returning, the abiding practicality of his species refocusing his wandering thoughts.

The main problem, of course, was that his cousin's wish did not make sense. The yochni could undo a wish. Any wish. That meant even if Crucius did wish for an eternal empire, there was no saying that it would stay as such. All it would take was some industrious dwarf or elf or human to wish for the bogeys' downfall—or genocide, as Mira seemed reluctantly intent to prove—and everything would change. Crucius, for all his apparent impatience regarding anything related to history—and more importantly King Rufius, who had no doubt consented to, if not masterminded, their plan— knew that.

Likewise, they had known that Atlan's own wish would have pointed to an illustrious bogey future. Had Rufius asked Atlan to confirm what his wish was, he would have said, without lying, the continuance of the empire. Even had the king outright told Atlan he wished to send Crucius instead, Atlan would have told them it was impossible had they bothered to consult him.

Empire forever, he thought. *Empire forever....* There was something familiar about the phrasing, too. No doubt Atlan had heard it as Crucius' battle cry thousands of times when they were cubs. But surely his cousin would not have gone all the way to the yochni only for such a childish whim. Something both he and their uncle knew was unattainable, even with a wish.

No, there was something more sinister afoot. He just had to figure out what.

Atlan pulled himself up onto the final ridge. Late day light illuminated a portion of the inner wall of the broad, deep mouth of the yochni's cave, its angle preventing it from lighting anything deeper within. Atlan stretched down a hand to help Mira up, then extended it again for Kraven as Drake made his slow and clumsy way up from another ledge. They lit their torches.

The cave entrance was low, uncomfortably low for Drake, but Atlan assured them it would open up deeper in. Drake, still moaning over the many cuts and abuses his sapphire feet had suffered, seemed reluctant to put Atlan's words to the test, but after some coaxing from his master, he followed them inside. They began their descent down a shallow, rocky incline. After several long minutes of scrabbling and scraping, they emerged into a larger space. Atlan lifted his torch, illuminating a smooth, dome-like surface above.

Though he had known what was coming, the view still stole his breath.

The dome, ringed on the sides by patches of luminous moss, was almost entirely covered in dozens of centuries-old murals that had been chipped and painted into the stone. Heroes he recognized from reams of scrolls and countless books covered swathes of space, empty patches serving as reminders of all the future wishes that could come. Mighty warriors hefted spears and swords. Crafty dwarves and elves hid in cloaks and shadows. The Treaty of Four had been painted in the very center of the ceiling, the constant Ylsa resting wise but joyous within their ring. The image reminded him of Naveen.

It was everything he'd hoped for and more. This was what he had dreamed of, what he had striven for since he was a cub.

He started forward, scholar's inclination impelling him to study, but a bandaged hand touched his shoulder. Kraven nodded towards an arch on the far side of the room, the feature remarkably nondescript in comparison to the rest of the chamber, and reminded him of their current task. Atlan gave the medic a chagrined smile.

"Sorry," he said. He dropped to a crouch, drawing the oversized map from its case and handing it to the boy. Crucius' scent drifted on the swirling air, tickling his nostrils. It was stronger now for the contained space, though still well out of reach. Atlan stood, shouldering his pack and lifting his torch so the boy could navigate. With Kraven and Mira leading the way, they exited through the arch.

As they walked, Atlan couldn't help but examine the walls around them, his clawed fingers tracing the walls. For years he had studied the ages, scoured scrolls and books for any clues he could find regarding the mysterious yochni and the champions that dared to reach it. Were the walls damp and slick with mold, he'd often wondered as a cub? Dry and echoing? Cramped or spacious? Each new parchment had filled in another gap, helped him build a picture in his mind, but now, being in the cave itself, he found his mental blueprint surging to life, like looking from a charcoal design to a stained-glass window, from a sketch to a finished painting. Every step led to some new discovery, some new clue towards an old story or age. He had known that in traveling to the yochni he would walk where others had trod. Now, he realized he was quite literally following in their footsteps.

He shared a few of his discoveries with the others, pointing out a dwarven axe mark here or a blue paint stripe from a Coastal champion there. The others, however, remained tense, and soon their lack of enthusiasm caught, the charm of the tick marks losing out to their monotony, his excitement fading in the face of their pending peril. Crucius was still ahead.

The thought of him tempered Atlan's enthusiasm still further, and soon his mind returned to the questions that had plagued him since he'd learned of his cousin's journey. Did Crucius know he was still alive, he wondered? Had Spider and his men warned him in time? Atlan didn't think the men would have had either the time or the guts to catch up with his cousin, but if they had, Crucius could be on his guard. Perhaps he had set a trap for them or sabotaged the Trials. He could be around the very next bend, waiting to pounce and kill. Except, of course, he could not be around the *next* bend. Not really. His scent, though steadily strengthening, was not nearly close enough yet.

Atlan stopped, the motion so sudden Drake nearly bumped into him. The other two turned. Mira shared a look with Kraven.

"What is it?" she asked.

Atlan sniffed again, heart squeezing, then stepped to Kraven, gesturing for the boy to give him the map. "Where are we? *Où sommes-nous?*"

Kraven took Atlan's torch, handing the map over in exchange, and pointed out their location. Atlan, stomach sinking by the second, traced their path back towards the entrance. They'd already been walking for nearly an hour, and their route, though well marked, was winding, full of side cuts, switchbacks, and loops. Atlan growled. Of course. He'd been so busy thinking about Crucius, he'd forgotten to actually track him, his cousin's familiar scent nearly fading on instinct. *Idiot*, he thought. *Idiot.*

"Atlan, what is it?" Mira asked again. "What's wrong?

Atlan shook his head, shoving the map back to Kraven with such force he nearly knocked the boy over. "He copied the map."

"*Quoi?*"

Atlan translated, then repeated. "He copied the map."

He pointed to the offending parchment, and Kraven lowered it for Mira to see. After a brief look, they turned to him.

"I can smell him," he said, still cursing himself for his stupidity. "It's getting stronger and we're catching up, but his scent has never wavered, never strayed off or away. The path is too winding for him to have gotten this lucky in guessing, and I haven't smelled anyone else for him to follow. The only way he could have gotten this far this easily is—"

Atlan cut off, entire body going slack.

"Atlan?" Kraven asked.

"No...no...." Atlan's knees started to shake. He paced, heart hammering in his chest. His head pounded. One hand clutched at his sagging mouth.

A tiny hand touched his leg. Mira looked up at him, her green eyes steady despite her worry. "Atlan," she said. "What is it?"

Atlan twitched. Nervous energy rebounded him from her touch, but the contact was enough to steady his mind, to focus him enough for speech. He sucked in a deep breath, then spoke. "I know what his wish is. *Je sais quel est son souhait.*"

Kraven and Mira's eyes grew wide; even Drake stamped a foot.

"What is it?" asked Mira.

Atlan snatched the map back, re-orienting it quickly before striding off down the next tunnel. If he was right, they had to hurry. "Empire forever," he said. "I know what it means. It's the empire. He's moving it here."

"Here?" said Mira. "What? How?"

He was already jogging, Mira running to keep up.

"When we were cubs, my father used to tell us stories

about the ages. Like I said, Crucius only ever cared about the bogeys, but we would talk about the other stories too, what we would wish for and why. Crucius was always straightforward about it, bogey power, bogey expansion, dominance. I always wanted something a little more subtle, but one day, I came up with an idea I thought he'd like. It wasn't long after my father died. It was so long ago, and I was in such a state back then I'd nearly forgotten about it, but that phrase, empire forever…. There was something familiar about it, something I couldn't remember. Now I know why. It was me. He asked me how to do it when we were cubs and, idiot that I am, I told him."

They were coming up on another intersection, this one with four passageways forking off. He consulted the map, but he was hardly paying it any attention now, spinning so wildly he soon lost any sense of direction. He was about to make another round, this time to simply choose a tunnel by scent, when Mira grabbed his sleeve. His sheer momentum nearly slung her free, but she grabbed with her other hand, heels scraping against the stone. Kraven and Drake caught up as well, slowing to a stop at their tunnel's entrance.

"What are you doing?" Atlan demanded. "We have to go."

"Stop," she said. "Relax."

He almost ripped her hands off his sleeve, but Kraven stepped forward, putting out a hand as well.

"Atlan," he said. "Please."

"We know you want to stop him. We all do," said Mira. "But we don't even know what his wish actually is. Or how to do it. You said he was going to move the empire here, but how? What does that mean? What, exactly, did you tell him?"

Atlan stopped, forcing himself to take a breath. Mira was right. He had to slow down. He hadn't even been translating his answers. He stopped to do so, relaying the broad strokes in Fransec before continuing.

"Remember what we talked about with the different Trials and the Treaty? The Guardians and the Storm? They were designed to retain the original egality of the pilgrimages, to stop people from getting in early or using numbers and force to stake their claim. The idea was to protect the mountain, to keep the wrong people from getting in or turn them aside even if they made it. But what if, instead of wishing to keep people out, someone wished to stay inside? What if instead of wishing for an even playing field, they turned the world's best security system into their own personal fence? The empire stretches for hundreds of miles. He'd never be able to fit the whole thing in here, but if he moved our center of operations here, the capital, with only some bogey-specific way in or out...with that kind of wish, barring some kind of internal rebellion, we'd be unassailable. The bogey empire really could last forever."

Mira's eyes went wide, the terrifying light of realization starting to dawn. He translated for Kraven, the boy responding in much the same way.

"Look, I don't know for sure that that's his wish, but if I had to bet on it, that would be it. There's no other wish I can think of that would supersede what I would have wished for the empire myself, and both he and my uncle know I would never agree to something so permanent. If this is Crucius' wish, if he succeeds, all of the Trials meant to keep others out will keep the empire safely in. We have to hurry."

Mira stared at him in horror. Kraven's features had drained of all color. Atlan turned to go, but then Kraven grabbed his arm.

"No," said the boy, pointing to his dragon. "Drake."

Of course. The earlier halls of the labyrinth had been low and difficult for the dragon to traverse, but they had now opened up enough for their group to mount again. Atlan nodded and the group got onto the medic's dragon. Kraven gave the order for water when they were all in position, and Drake charged off. The dragon veered off from their intended path almost immediately, taking them into areas Atlan had been unable to chart. Crucius' scent snuffed out like a candle, but Kraven assured them that the dragon's senses would not lead them astray.

The boy, as in all matters relating to his dragon, was right. Soon Atlan could hear rushing water and smell the cool wet slick of well watered moss. The air grew cool and damp, the stone ceilings starting to drip. He'd assumed they would have another hour of walking to reach the river, the map leading them in a wide arc around the blanks on the map. With Drake racing along through the caves, however, they reached the river in a fraction of the time. Light bloomed at the end of their tunnel, supplementing the meagre light from their torch, and they burst out into the massive cavern through which the fast-flowing river ran.

The cavern was perhaps three stories high. Crystals grew from the ceiling, shimmering faintly with their own internal glow. Moss rimed the crystals in great lichenous patches, stretching out in tendrils wide and delicate to reach towards the floor and exits. There were only four outlets in the entire cavern, two for the river to enter and exit, the one they'd come from, and the one to leave. The latter crouched on the far wall almost directly across from them, dark and quiet.

The walls of the cavern were gray and craggy, the floor and walls around the river dark from wet where the spray could reach. The river itself spread some hundred yards across the length of the cavern, with large stone spurs poking out at intervals to form intermittent rapids. Several lines of water-slick boulders peeked out from its surface in calmer portions to form slippery steppingstone paths. In a few places, hand- and foot-holds had been chipped from the wall above the river's entrance or exit, most now looking so frail or small as to be nearly impassable. Under normal circumstances, they might have spent hours trying to discern a safe crossing, even with Atlan's exhaustive knowledge of previous attempts by former champions.

Thankfully, with Drake, they did not have to concern themselves with normal circumstances. Kraven did not stop the dragon long enough to admire the view, instead urging Drake to the river's edge. From there, he let the dragon choose their route. Drake, understanding little of their urgency save for Kraven's insistence, chose a spot near the river's entrance to the cave. The dragon stepped into the river, the power of the speeding current thrumming all the way up his massive limbs. Atlan sealed his arm tight around Kraven's waist. They had all slid closer together to decrease the number of weights for the dragon to balance. Mira now sat safely sandwiched between Kraven's back and Atlan's stomach. She dug her fingers so deep into Atlan's arms he thought she would tear the silks all the same, but the water never rose higher than his knees—not even touching her toes, which she had brought up close beside her—and soon, though the current threatened to take even Drake on a few occasions, they reached the other side. Atlan sniffed as they dismounted onto damp stone, and his cousin's scent still filled his nose. It had taken Crucius much longer to cross than it had taken them, the wet dog and silk smell of him so fresh now that Atlan half expected to see his damp footprints leading to the door, but the river had not claimed him. Crucius had survived.

Atlan helped Mira down, Kraven dismounting as well. Together, they raced to the dark archway leading to the Hall of Treasures.

The interior of the hall was dark, lit only dimly at their end by the moss and at the other by a hellish glow emanating from the room's far exit. Boxes of varying sizes and type stretched from floor to vaulted ceiling, nearly a thousand of them carved into the stone. Each box had a door on the front, each styled in a different fashion. Some were bound with leather or scales, others painted or carved.

"Who moves the treasure inside?" asked Kraven.

"Nobody knows," said Atlan, his keen eyes scanning the dark. "There have been many who have tried to find out, but whoever fills them always came too close to the champions' arrival for anyone to research in safety before, and now the Kinderstorm is around to keep anyone else from trying. In any case, I wouldn't try to open them. Temptation is a tricky thing."

"Why look at treasure, when the yochni is there?" asked Kraven.

Atlan allowed himself a small smile. "If a mysterious creature put what you most wanted into a box, wouldn't you want to open it, even just to see if they were right? Curiosity can be a dangerous thing." His features darkened. "Greed can be even worse."

Kraven nodded and drifted back closer to the group. Atlan saw his own box, a rich burgundy wood with gold studs and edging, then Mira's, a large one of plain stone. They didn't see Crucius' or Kraven's, though with the boxes stacked so high and the lighting so poor, it was difficult to see many of the names, even with Atlan's night-tailored vision.

In any case, they didn't stop to look. With Crucius ahead, all three of them had something more important to do than peek into their perspective boxes.

Unfortunately, the same could not be said for Drake.

Lifting his brilliant blue head towards a point some fifty feet farther down the wall, the sea dragon let out a shrill whistle and charged.

Their sea dragon had found his box.

CHAPTER
TWENTY-SIX

The box Drake was after was coated in a layer of bright chipped sapphire scales with a thin rim of twining silver-like waves around the edges. Its small silver handle was embedded at the very edges of the dragon's hind-footed height. Atlan reached the dragon first, but to little avail. Kraven's screams for the dragon to stop were likewise ineffectual. Whatever it was that the dragon sensed or smelled, it was too important for him to obey even his master's orders.

Atlan took matters into his own hands. Dodging past the dragon's tail, he leapt for the creature's mouth. Snagging the dragon's bottom jaw with both hands, he pulled down with the full force of his weight, dragging the dragon's head down and away from the handle.

Drake snarled, throwing him against the far wall with a fearsome buck. Atlan yelped in pain as his back smashed into several stone handles, breaking not a few in the process. The dragon turned on him, ready to finish the job, but Kraven leapt between them, raising his hands to stop any further violence. Mira rushed to join the medic, waving her axe, but Drake only turned away. He wanted to get back to his box. The dwarf and the medic split up, Mira running for Atlan while Kraven redoubled his efforts to stop his dragon.

"Are you okay?" asked Mira. "Can you get up?"

Atlan rubbed the back of his head. His back throbbed, but he nodded. "We have to stop him."

"How?" she asked. "He's obviously determined to open it."

"I know," said Atlan, wincing as several pin pricks of pain jabbed his neck and shoulders. "But if it's a trap, a box that can kill a dragon might just as easily kill us all." He moved to stand, still rubbing his neck.

Mira moved to help him, but then her eyes went wide. "Atlan! Stop!"

Too late. Atlan caught the back of his skull on one of the box doors he had broken when he'd landed, swinging the door fully open. Realizing just in time, he dove forward, throwing his hands over his head.

It helped, but not by much. Three jets of boiled skin fang shot out from within the box, the farthest-reaching drops splattering his legs and ankles like acid. Howling in pain, he struggled to gain his feet, stumbling and scrabbling to get as far from the liquid as he could.

In his panic, he bumped into Drake.

A small patch of his tainted fur swiped against the sea dragon's leg, transferring some of the concentrated herbs. The dragon let out a furious hiss as the toxic oils burned into his scales. Drake had warned the bogey not to interfere when he had thrown Atlan the first time. Now, the dragon raised himself to his full hind-footed height, looking as though he had every intention of bringing his full weight down on the defenseless prince.

"No!" cried Kraven. Running between them, the boy flung his arms wide. Drake, unwilling to harm his master, shifted, but he was already on his way down. He couldn't stop his weight, only shift it. He twisted towards the wall, one claw catching on the handle of his box.

It was a lucky snag. It was also enough to open the box's door. And, as the rest of his bulk slammed and scraped its way down the wall, it wasn't the only door to open.

A sound like rolling thunder rumbled from above. The chamber shook, and Atlan looked up to see a mountain of stone falling from above. His legs were still burning, his mind numb, but before he could even pull himself together enough to react, he felt a pair of hands slam into the small of his back. It was Kraven, shoving him out of the way. Mira was in front of both of them. Atlan stumbled, just managing to grab her and pull her safely beneath him as he fell. Then, the tumbling stones arrived.

The avalanche was tremendous, hundreds of rocks and small boulders crashing down upon them. Atlan did his best to prop himself over Mira, shielding his head with his other hand. Smaller stones bounced off of his legs and back. Behind him, he heard Kraven shouting, Drake shrilling and thrashing. At one point the boy screamed.

And then, it was over. Atlan waited several more seconds before moving, terrified some part of him had been crushed or worse, but he felt no pain, and when he moved, all his limbs moved freely. The rocks, though many, had neither been large enough nor hit hard and often enough to do him any lasting damage. He could hear Mira coughing beneath him, and through dust-clogged ears, he could hear Kraven moan.

"Kraven? Kraven," he wheezed, trying not to suck in dust. "Are you okay? *Vas-tu bien?*"

He heard another moan in response, and quickly dragged himself free from the rubble. He could feel heat against his skin, his legs stinging as he pulled them loose. He helped Mira to her feet, then, waving dust from the air, looked back for

Kraven. The avalanche had snuffed out their torch, but the fiery light from the next chamber was still enough to see by.

The boy was buried almost up to his chest in stone, his face and clothes coated in a layer of grime so thick that Atlan could barely discern their original colors. Darker patches and muddy smears indicated where blood peeked through. The boy breathed in rapid, frantic breaths, and Atlan could smell more blood from under the stone. Looking beyond him, Atlan could see Drake, just as thoroughly pinned.

Mira, standing at Atlan's side, looked up at him, face drawn with worry. Atlan, unsure how severe the boy's injuries were, crouched down next to their medic. He asked a variety of diagnostic questions, trying to discern where the boy was injured and whether he was safe to move. Kraven, between pained gasps, managed to give his answers. When Atlan was sure moving the stones would not cause more damage, he began the work of unburying their medic, gesturing for Mira to do likewise.

"He's got a broken leg, a bruised or broken rib, and multiple bumps and scrapes, but from what he can tell, nothing fatal," he said to the dwarf as they shuffled stones. Mira shoveled several of the smaller ones aside, and Atlan lifted a larger one to reveal the medic's broken leg. The bone had not breached the skin, though there was a definite crook to the boy's shin that should not have been there. Mira moved more rubble, and eventually they cleared enough for Atlan to pull Kraven free. Atlan attempted to carry the boy, but Kraven smacked his arm, insisting that he walk—or rather, hop, himself. The medic directed them to the wall, where, with Atlan and Mira's help, he removed his pack and slid down to rest.

"I think I am finished," he said with a grimacing smile when he managed to catch his breath.

"Kraven..." started Mira, but the boy shook his head.

"Non. C'est fini. Drake?"

He rolled his head along the wall to look at his dragon. Atlan trotted back for a quick look, but if the dragon was seriously injured, he could see no sign of it in the creature's penitent countenance. Likewise, though he smelled a few metallic, fishy traces of blood, he did not smell enough to be deeply concerned. Drake, letting out an embarrassed warble, strained against his rocky casing, but made no progress. Atlan pulled a few large stones from the pile, but it was of little use. Freeing the dragon would be the work of hours. Hours they did not have to spare.

Atlan looked back at the others, shaking his head. Neither Kraven nor Drake would be well or free enough to come with him and Mira to the yochni in the time they had left. They were going to have to leave them behind.

"Kraven..." said Mira, sitting on her heels beside the medic and setting a hand on his knee.

"It is okay," he said. "I am...fine."

He winced as he spoke, his leg far from okay, but when he was finished, a smile touched his lips.

"What is it?" asked Atlan, already searching for a new torch. He scented the air, his cousin's scent dangerously close now, though mercifully coming no closer. Whether that meant Crucius was simply lying in wait or had already moved into the final tunnels, Atlan couldn't tell.

"Ines," said the boy, drawing Atlan's attention momentarily back. "I...understand."

"Understand what?" asked Mira.

"Why...she..." The medic paused to catch his breath, face paling under the dust. "I..." he made a pushing motion with his hands, indicating how he had shoved them both out of the way of the falling rock. He smiled. "She would have helped."

Mira set her hand over his, face puckering. The boy turned

his palm over, grabbing her fingers, then squeezed and released. Leaning forward, he drew Johann's knife from his boot, handing it hilt first to Mira.

"Protect Atlan. Stop Crucius," he said.

Mira nodded. "I will."

"Atlan," he said, looking to the bogey prince. "Protect Mira."

"I will," said Atlan.

"Packs?" the boy asked.

Atlan nodded. Save for weapons, there was no need for supplies ahead. Anything else would simply weigh them down. He waited for Mira to remove her own pack, then handed her the torch and did the same. He could feel the odd slump of his damaged case, the avalanche putting an unquestionable end to what little had remained of his precious harp.

"*Pouvons-nous faire quelque chose? As-tu besoin de quoi que ce soit?*" he asked, asking if there was anything they could do or anything the boy needed.

Kraven patted his pack, then leaned back, shaking his head. "*J'ai de l'eau et des médicaments. Je vais bien.*"

Atlan nodded. The boy, he knew, could tend himself, at least for the time being, and if they waited any longer, it wouldn't matter anyway. Leaning down, he patted the boy's shoulder, then straightened to his full height. His legs still stung and burned from the skin fang, but he could walk. Fight. It was time to go. "*Désolé, Kraven.* Sorry."

"*Je sais,*" he said. "I know."

"Bye, Kraven," said Mira. "We'll come back for you."

Atlan wondered if that was a lie, or if she really believed that they would stop his cousin. That both of them would survive. He supposed it hardly mattered. Kraven nodded, then waved them on. Mira rose from her place beside the boy, and together they turned towards the entrance to the Fountain of Gold.

TWENTY-SEVEN

An almost unbearable wall of heat met Atlan and Mira as they stepped into the next chamber. Instantly, beads of sweat swamped out of Atlan's pores, coating his silks and fur. Glancing down at Mira, he saw an equally shiny layer spreading across her skin, the salty scent of it filling the air. As the Fountain of Gold's name suggested, several rivers of molten metal flowed from crevices in the walls. Dull splatters of cooled gold rimmed pools of the glowing hot metal and rainbows of gems crouched in the walls. The room appeared empty aside from the riches within, though there were plenty of columns and piles of gems and coins that Crucius could easily have hidden behind. Atlan knew many a potential champion had met a terrible end after being shoved into the bubbling pools. Mira gave him a nervous look, but after a preliminary sniff, he shook his head. The second-place prince wasn't there.

There were only two other places he could be, then. One was the Chamber of Sorrows. The other was the cave which held the yochni itself. Either way, their pilgrimages would be over soon.

They made their way across the room at speed, Mira

jogging to keep up with his longer stride. Before they reached the door, however, he slowed, coming to a stop some ten feet back from the arch.

"Crucius?" whispered Mira.

Atlan stared into the darkness ahead, the light from the Fountain chamber brightening only perhaps the first five feet. Crucius' scent was so powerful Atlan could almost smell the very contours of his cousin now, the rival bogey almost certainly in the next chamber, but he shook his head. He looked down at her, then gave her a small smile. "I just wanted to say I'm glad I met you."

"Yeah. I guess you're alright," she said. She grinned, but it was a malnourished attempt.

"I'm sorry, for everything," he said.

"Me too."

He waited, sensing there was more she wanted to say, but she didn't speak again, and they were running out of time.

"Well then. That's it," he said, and stepped into the Chamber of Sorrows.

The chamber, save for the small half-circle of illumination near the entrance, was dark. While there were a few smatterings of the luminescent moss on the ceiling, its usual glow dimmed in the light from their torch and the Fountain of Gold, leaving the farthest reaches foggy with shadow. With his night vision, Atlan could make out two narrow, curving ramps at the room's far end. These, he knew, led to the chamber's exit and the narrow tunnels to the yochni beyond. Pillars, stalagmites, and stalactites lined the walls, pinning through and blossoming from the various stone shelves which grew from the walls like the caps of mushrooms. They left plenty of places for Crucius to hide, though as of yet Atlan could see no movement, nor hear the telltale clicking of claws. He drew in a deep and scenting breath.

"Maybe he kept going?" whispered Mira.

Atlan shook his head. A low growl pulsed through his chest, and he pushed her gently behind him. "No. I can smell him. He's here."

Despite his best efforts to speak quietly, his voice carried through the room.

Another voice, harsh and cruel, rang back. "You made it. I'm impressed."

Mira swung the torch towards the sound, perhaps halfway down the wall on their left. She raised the torch, illuminating more of the stone, but there was nothing. Atlan's hand twitched for his whip, but of course, there was nothing there save the empty silk loop where his weapon had been. His claws flexed instead, and his shoulders rippled under his silks.

Crucius' disembodied voice continued. "After those villagers tried to off you, I thought you'd be dead, but when they didn't find your body, well, you're just *so* smart, aren't you? So well-studied. I should have known you'd find a way to survive. Then again, smells like you got help from the locals." They heard a dark laugh. "I always knew you'd be a poor champion, but really, joining up with a dwarf? That's low even for you."

"She's my friend, Crucius. This ends here."

"I'm well aware of that fact, Atlan—"

"High Prince," said Atlan.

"Not anymore."

"I am High Prince until I am dead, and you will bow to your future king. You owe me your respects, coward. Come out of the shadows." Atlan stepped farther into the room. Mira, despite her usual courage, stayed close behind him, so close she could have set his tail on fire. Atlan paid it little mind, simply moving his tail away from the heat. He had to pay attention. He had to watch for his cousin.

With the added insult he'd just given, Atlan was not long

in having to wait. Even with her proximity, Mira had managed to keep the torch high enough to keep most of the stone illuminated. Atlan saw a twitch of shadow, and then Crucius curled out fully from behind his pillar on one of the shelves. He had always been broader than Atlan, though he was shorter, too. Like Atlan, he wore red and black, his gray and brown fur poking out through wide swathes of tattered silk. Several scratches lined up with the stripes, though not as many as Atlan had hoped. Crucius' pale blue eyes shone in the light of the torch, and his teeth spread wide into a savage smile. Dropping to the floor, he unfurled his whip, giving it an experimental crack.

"What happened to your whip, cousin? Lose it along the way? Hang it up?"

"Bow to your prince," Atlan ordered.

"I'll never bow to you. Not now and never again," Crucius snarled.

"This is treason."

"This is approved. What, did you think I came here without Uncle's permission? Did you think he would really send you, the philosopher's son, to be our champion?"

Atlan took half a step back, the words raining against him like physical blows, but he did not retreat for long. He had suspected that Rufius had been involved. This was just confirmation.

"The right is mine," he growled.

Crucius laughed. "All the more's the pity you weren't up to the job!"

Crucius let his whip fly, aiming for Mira. She leapt back, but he caught her knuckles, making her drop the torch. Atlan jumped to get between them, and Crucius let fly again, laying two quick blows across Atlan's shoulders. Pain seared across his skin as two long cuts ripped open across the flesh. Atlan's mouth blazed open, a fierce, animal anger awakening in him.

He charged for Crucius, speech devolving into little more than growls and barks, and soon the pair were on the floor, wrestling in a snarling ball of teeth, claws, silk, and fur.

They fought furiously, bites and scratches exchanged as readily as punches and kicks. Red splatters flung wide across the floor and soon the metallic scent of fresh blood flooded the room.

In between flashes of Crucius' claws and teeth, Atlan looked for Mira. She was still there, hands firm on the haft of her axe. Her eyes were following every motion of the battle, searching for an opening, but the way he and his cousin were fighting, Atlan knew she wouldn't find any. At best she'd get him or herself hurt, at worst get both of them killed. Worse, in having to watch out for her safety, Atlan was making mistakes, circling to keep Crucius between him and Mira when he should engage, or making reckless dives just to pull his cousin near. It was costing him wounds he couldn't afford to take, and soon he was losing blood he didn't have to lose. His cousin pounced, pinning him to the floor. Crucius clawed mercilessly at Atlan's chest and face, nearly blinding him and splitting his nose almost in two. Atlan howled and bit his cousin back, vision washing out with blood.

Mira had to get out now, to make her wish or at least find some way to block Crucius from following. Atlan sank his claws deep into his cousin's arms, striving to hold him in place.

"Go," he snarled. "Go!" He didn't know where she was anymore. If she was smart, she was already gone.

"Aaaagghhh!"

The scream was hot and fierce. It came from behind Crucius, approaching at speed with the rapid patter of tiny feet. Crucius started to turn, but Atlan sunk his claws in deeper, holding the bogey in place. He heard the wet *kurnch* of axe in flesh, and Crucius howled. He ripped one arm free of

Atlan's grasp, swinging it back towards Mira. Bogey power hit dwarven flesh, and she screamed, the noise trailing her as she flew across the room. Crucius' fist slammed into Atlan's sweet spot, making what little vision he had left go momentarily dark, and then he was in the air as well, Crucius flinging him across the room. Atlan landed hard, rolling several feet, but despite the pain in his sweet spot, his burned legs, his bleeding body, he had to get up. He had to stop his cousin. He had to help his friend.

Shaking his head and swiping at his face, he cleared his blood-smeared vision. Crucius held Mira high, one hand sealed around her throat. He was bleeding heavily from the back of one knee; Mira's blood-stained axe had been flung aside. Frantic, Mira drew Kraven's knife, stabbing it deep into Crucius' arm, but he hardly seemed to notice, nor when she scratched and kicked, nails raking over his fur. Crucius laughed. Lifting her higher, he let out a victorious howl.

Atlan scrambled for anything he could do, any way to set her free. Several rocks lay along the base of the wall. Grabbing one, he sent it flying, pegging Crucius in the back of the head. His cousin turned with a snarl.

Atlan growled, gripping another rock. "Let her *go*."

Crucius' eyes narrowed to slits. With a single quick motion, he threw Mira against one of the pillars, her body hitting with such force Atlan worried his cousin had killed her. He did not have time to check. With a jerk, Crucius yanked Kraven's knife from his arm. Atlan lunged for him, but Crucius swept out with the blade, slicing Atlan's fingers before he could get close. Whipping out a foot, Crucius kicked Atlan hard in his battered chest, booting his cousin back. The younger bogey had dropped his whip in the fighting. Now, he stooped to pick it up.

"So, cousin, why were you traveling with a dwarf anyway?" Crucius sneered. He wiped blood from his face with the back of his hand, spitting out a mouthful more. "Before I kill you, I'd like to know."

Atlan didn't bother answering. He lunged again, but Crucius knocked him back, unfurling his whip with a harsh crack. He snapped it against the burnt flesh of Atlan's ankles.

"Certainly not for her help," said Crucius. "You know as well as I do there is no challenge here which we could not overcome ourselves. Perhaps you found out about their true condition. Was that it? A mission of mercy?"

Crucius cracked his whip again, this time striking Atlan's face. Atlan yelped and held up a hand to defend himself, which Crucius jerked out of the way with another well-placed lash.

"I heard you outside, dog. 'Please forgive us. Good luck.' She's a dwarf, you worm, a slave, prey, garbage. She's expendable, just like you. All of that time reading your books, learning your stories. A waste, worthless. Lessons, your music, everything you've ever spent time on, worthless, just like you, just like your father."

"My father was not a wast—" Atlan started.

Crucius whipped him again.

Beyond his cousin, Atlan could see Mira stirring, trying to gain her feet. Mercifully, Crucius didn't seem to notice.

"I'll have you cursing his very existence before I'm finished with you," he snarled. "I should have killed you long before now, years ago, when he died, the miserable worm."

"Don't talk about him that way," Atlan whined, struggling to gain his feet. Crucius whipped him again, but this time Atlan held his ground, pushing himself up to a crouching position. Crucius sneered.

"Why are you even trying? You know you can't stop me, help them. You can't stop any of this, just like your father couldn't. You're weak, just like he was. Poison in the family veins."

Atlan growled but Crucius only laughed, suddenly, as if struck by a joke. He twirled his whip, lips curling into a sinister smile. "Well, now, how fitting my choice of words."

"What are you talking about?" Atlan snarled. Now on his feet, he started to circle, moving opposite to Mira, drawing Crucius' attention away. The dwarf was on her feet now, wobbling towards the exit. Crucius scoffed.

"Well, I guess I can spare you the secret," he said. "It's not as if you'll be living long enough to do anything about it."

"About what?"

"Uncle Ru, of course. What? You didn't really think your father died so easily, did you?" Crucius laughed again. "No, he had your father killed. Poison to get rid of him, just like, when the time came, he sent you on this journey to get rid of you."

Atlan blinked, breath catching. A high whine escaped his chest, and he sagged, only just catching his feet. "That's not true."

"Of course it's true. I have no reason to lie. You think those villagers that tried to kill you would really have gone against a bogey champion without prodding? Payment?"

Atlan's mind was spinning. Mira was almost halfway to the ramps, but the news about his father...was Crucius lying? Bluffing? "But Uncle..."

"Thinks you're worthless. Just like everyone else does." With a snarl, Crucius raised his whip a final time. "Goodbye cousin. At least sometimes it was fun."

"No!" Mira shouted. She was still several yards from the exit.

Crucius' head snapped up. Atlan, not sparing a look, sprang.

He had forgotten about the knife. Searing hot pain flared through his body, everything inside him seizing like some kind of stick had been jammed in his internal gears.

Because, in effect, it had. Crucius had hit the sweet spot.

Atlan sagged, slumping against his cousin. Tears pooled, running with the blood down the side of his face. He brought up a hand, resting it on Crucius' shoulder. His breath hitched, life draining from him as quickly as water from a glass.

"I told you," said Crucius, getting ready to slough him off.

Lifting his sagging head, Atlan whispered into his cousin's ear. "I win."

Then, with a final look to Mira, he stabbed hard, burying his clawed fingers deep inside his cousin's middle. He pulled back with a jerk and fell. His hand flopped out beside him, fur and claws coated with blood.

Crucius turned, clutching at the deep hole where his sweet spot had been. He fell to his knees, then the floor. Atlan's lips curled in a sad smile. As the light slipped from his yellow eyes, the last thing he saw was Mira.

TWENTY-EIGHT

Mira turned and ran.

The arch leading out of the Chamber of Sorrows led into a narrow tunnel, its roof so low it would almost have been too small for a bogey champion to navigate. Mira, for her shorter stature, faced no such difficulty, though with her torch gone it was almost impossible to tell where she was going. She banged her shins and toes on stones and stalagmites as she stumbled through the darkness, terror of Crucius pushing her to reckless speeds. Tears streamed down her face, and she flung her hands before her, scraping her palms and fingers on the stones.

Her mind buzzed with questions she had thought she'd have more time to answer—what her wish would be, if she could save the bogeys, if she could really kill them all.

Atlan had been sure she would spare them if he could only prove that they could be good. Except Atlan was already dead, and he was the only good one she had ever known. Atlan had assured her his father had been a good bogey too, but he was dead as well, poisoned by his own brother.

Mira swiped at her tears with grimy fists, the phantom sound of footfalls tracing her every step. Several times she froze like a rabbit, sure she could hear Crucius' voice, feel his claws reaching for her throbbing back. Her scars burned at the thought, her breath ragged and hot in lungs that seemed all too thin, but he never came, never followed.

After what felt like hours, mind numb with grief and fear, Mira entered a wider portion of tunnel. Light blossomed in a pale blue sunrise around her as luminous moss began dotting the ceiling. Mira stepped into the final chamber and, exhausted, dirty, and wounded, fell before the yochni. Its single eye, taller than she was, stared straight ahead from its perch on its four clawed feet.

Mira's eyes were too dry for tears now, all her sorrows poured out during her journey through the black. Collapsing, she fell on her side, so tired she felt she could die and sleep before the yochni forever.

She had hurt her people, lost her friends. She wanted it all to end.

Mira closed her eyes, her breath coming in short painful shudders which cried where her eyes could not. A single word ran through her mind over and over again. She knew what she wanted to wish.

Peace.

With a feeling that great blinds were being drawn over her, being drawn over time and the world, Mira Goldfist made her wish.

The yochni blinked and all was still.

When Mira woke again, her eyes felt scratched, like she'd dragged them over the coarse stone floor. The yochni was before her, staring straight ahead as it had been when she'd closed her eyes. She hadn't seen it blink. She merely knew that it had. That something in the world had changed.

Struggling to her feet, she muttered a thank you to the

creature and searched against the darkness for the entrance back into the tunnel. She hardly remembered how she had gotten where she was. How long had she been sleeping? Hours? Days?

Grabbing a handful of the glowing moss from the walls for light with another thank you, she stumbled wearily into the dark mouth that would be her entrance back into the world. The yochni did not move, its single, giant eye unshifting. She hadn't expected it to.

As she followed the tunnels back out to the world, exhaustion hung heavily on her, weighing her shoulders down like a woolen blanket. She traveled for what felt like half a day, but the exit to the tunnel never seemed to get any closer, and how long she actually walked was impossible to tell. Hunger gnawed at her stomach like a clawing hand and several times she had to stop to rest, closing her eyes with a calm which told her every time that she might not wake again. If her wish had been granted it didn't matter. She had accomplished her goal.

During one such resting period, she thought she heard the prince. Closing her eyes against her tears, she curled into her knees, cursing her weak and tired mind.

The sound came again, calling her name. Searching her out in the dark. *He's calling me from the dead*, she thought. *This is it. I'm going to die.* She submitted herself to the call, tired, dirty, and starving. She wondered what would finally kill her, her hunger, exhaustion, or the simple fact that she'd given up.

"Mira Goldfist, where are you?" the call came again. It was angrier this time. Cross. She heard stone shift nearby.

"'M here," she muttered softly, drifting off towards final sleep.

"Mira?" it called. "I can hear you. You're close. Say something else!"

"Atlan...I missed you...'m sorry...'m sorry you died." Her voice was nearly lost in the crooks of her arms, her head tilted toward elbows and knees.

Light danced across the side of the tunnel walls, the sign of an oncoming torch. Mira didn't see it, her breath little more than a flutter, but if she would have, she'd have seen Atlan coming, seen him come around the corner like an angel of morning with his black fur all of one piece and shining underneath the layers of dust.

"Mira," he said, catching sight of her. "You little gremlin."

The scent of her filled his nostrils, and he came forward with a relieved smile. She was unconscious, nearly dead, but he picked her up, her weight almost nothing to his renewed strength. Tucking her into his chest and shoulders, he ducked under the lower parts of the ceiling, carrying her back out into the Chamber of Sorrows. Crucius was still there, lying dead, but Atlan had moved him into a more respectful position before he had gone to retrieve the dwarf. He'd sought out Kraven after he had awakened, making sure the boy was okay and confirming that the yochni had blinked—not that, given the fact Atlan had woken up at all, it had been difficult to tell. Now the boy was there, waiting for them both as he leaned against a pillar. His eyes lit when he saw Mira, and though he was not well enough to walk, there was an almost cub-like earnestness to him, a sort of standing at attention to say hello.

"She is okay?"

Atlan nodded, holding her in one arm and coming alongside Kraven to offer his other for support. The medic hopped along, wincing with every step, and they made their slow way back through the Fountain of Gold to where Drake lay, still half-encased in fallen stone. Helping Kraven back down to the floor, Atlan set the comatose Mira beside him.

He returned not long after with Crucius' body and laid his cousin out beside them. Kraven assured him that Mira was alive despite her unconscious state, and Atlan set to work on releasing the dragon.

It took much of the day for Atlan to free him. Without Kraven or Mira to help, it was an arduous process, though of course, the real work was done by Drake in the end, the sea dragon the only one strong enough to move the last of the larger rocks when the time came. When he finally managed to stand, sending a small storm of stones and dust down as he did, the door to his box, previously covered by rubble, swung back open. Letting out a victorious twitter, the dragon stuck his face in the small hole, coming back with a small black velvet bag. Letting out what Atlan would have sworn was an apologetic coo, the dragon dropped it into his master's hands.

The boy opened it, then tipped its contents into his lap. He let out a small gasp, and Atlan leaned over to look. There in the boy's lap was a brand-new pair of black leather gloves, twin shields embroidered on the backs.

Kraven looked up, tears brimming. "Drake," he said. "*Merci. Merci beaucoup.*"

After a quick washing from their canteens, Kraven slipped his hands into the gloves. Atlan helped him to his feet, then nodded from Crucius' body to Drake.

"Do you mind? It is okay?"

"Please," said Kraven, and nodded his assent.

When Crucius' body was safely secured, Drake none too happy to be serving as ferry to the dead, they exited the Hall of Treasures, crossing back over the river and through the maze of tunnels that had led them to the yochni's cave. It took them some hours to make their way through, but as they exited, they were just in time to see the sun setting on its first new day. Cavore was there, almost to the foothills with Batcha skittering along beside him. As the dryad ascended, Atlan helped Kraven down to rest against Drake. Then, he set Mira down beside him.

As he pulled his hands away, her eyelids fluttered, then opened. She'd been unconscious for their entire exit, recovering from her journey through the dark. She lifted her head, gaze landing first on the fierce reds and purples of the setting sun, then on the medic smiling beside her. Finally, she looked to Atlan.

"Atlan?" she asked, voice cracking. "Is that you?'

Atlan beamed, setting a hand on her shoulder.

"Hello Mira," he said. "Welcome back to the world of the living."

EPILOGUE

Seven months into the new age, Atlan, Mira, and Kraven sat around the table in the noble house of Monteyeaux. Kraven was dressed in the blue and white uniform of the Guard, his mark now gleaming on his silver chain. Atlan wore the latest noble fashion in red and black, Mira the fine, practical clothing that was becoming the normal fashion of her people. Kraven's parents and brother sat in frightened silence before the imposing figures of their second son's friends. Outside the window, their new permanent resident and guest of honor Drake guzzled water from his personal fountain and trough, which was now kept eternally full by Monteyeaux servants.

"It is a great honor to have you with us, your highness," Monsieur Monteyeaux said, voice thick with his Fransec accent and the fear which consistently marred his poor attempts at Itsrec.

"The honor is ours," Atlan said. "And how have your two sons been?"

"Wonderful. They are both doing good, your majesty. Err, uh, well," the poor man stammered.

"Good," said Mira. She glowered at Kraven's brother Arnaud, who shrank under her gaze. "About time."

"I think she means it was about time we paid you another visit," said Atlan. "Thank you for welcoming us into your home on such short notice."

"It's quite alright," said Madame Monteyeaux, slightly better than her husband at handling their guests. She nodded to the golden circlet resting on Atlan's brow. "I hear your coronation is now official, your highness."

The former high prince nodded, thin circlet of a crown glittering in the setting sunlight coming through the Monteyeaux's windows.

"The charges against my uncle were finally approved last month."

"And he was executed?" Madame Monteyeaux said lightly, speaking over the lip of her glass.

"On the eve of my twentieth birthday," Atlan said, bowing his head. "Killing any member of the royal family is considered high treason, even for the king."

"And you are not a traitor?" Monsieur Monteyeaux asked, less tactful than his wife.

"Traitors become exempt from such protections as soon as they commit their crime," Atlan said, voice flat. "I wish neither of them had had to die, but such was not the way of things."

The new king's tone brooked no further argument or suspicion, and the table fell to silence.

"You must be very busy," said Kraven. "I assume there must be a great deal of negotiation to be done between you and the dwarves?"

"And everyone else," Atlan agreed, smiling at his student's linguistic progress. "There is much work to be done. That's actually why we're here."

"Oh?" asked Kraven. He had been taking lessons in Itsrec

since his return—his family taking them too once they realized they could not keep up in the socially elevated conversations of their son and his friends.

Atlan had noticed his improvement on their last visit and said as much. "Yes. As I'm sure you know, the relations with the dwarves will be the first to be improved. I am already unlocking funds and resources to improve their standard of living, but much will have to be done to right the previous wrongs they have incurred. I will be acting as chief negotiator for my people and Mira will be serving as one of the dwarves' chief advisors. We will need a third, unbiased party to act as mediator between us. You are, of course, a little young for the job, but we were hoping you might serve as an advisor during the process and when all is said and done, act as arbiter?"

"My husband is a much more skilled arbiter than Kraven," Madame Monteyeaux interrupted. "You should use him instead."

"I see," said Atlan. "How unfortunate it is then that I have not asked him."

The sharp look in his yellow, hawk-like eyes told her he had no intention of doing so.

"Well, Kraven?" Mira asked, helping herself to another serving of beef.

Kraven held back a smile, gloved hands twisting the mark that now hung from his neck. He could not hold it back for long however, and soon his smile broke over his face.

"I'd be delighted," he said. "When do we leave?"

ACKNOWLEDGMENTS

Where does one begin when thanking everyone who helped one publish a book? Surely, there are too many to name, so, as is a rare occasion, I will attempt here to be brief.

First, thanks to God, who has blessed me beyond all I could dream or imagine. Next, my family members, each of whom has done and sacrificed so much time, work, energy, and sheer listening hours for me to make it this far.

Thanks also to the members of Inklings, past and present, who have helped, coached, and traveled with me on this journey. Burritos for you all.

To my friend Kristin, for all her coaching; Bobby for help with swag printing; and all the friends who have believed in and cheered me on throughout this journey.

Thank you to Beth for help with Fransec.

Thank you to my Beta Readers Becca, Kayley, and Mason.

Finally, last but not least, thanks to Tim Storm for developmental editing and Peggy Joque Williams for copyediting and proofreading. I hope this novel can make you proud.

About the Author

Abigail Morrison is a Wisconsin-based genre and young adult author with over a decade of writing experience. She loves genre-fusing stories that feature grace and redemption, ask questions (without necessarily answering them), and point towards possibility. When not writing, she loves dancing, reading, all things nerdy, and throughout all, the indispensable enjoyment of tea.

You can find Abigail's home on the web at: amorrisonbooks.com.

If you enjoyed this book, please considering leaving a rating and review on Amazon, Goodreads, or wherever you buy your books. Other than telling fellow readers about it, this is the single best thing you can do to help an indie author.